PHOTO: GIL HANLY

MW01490431

Stephanie Johnson is the author of five other novels, two collections of short stories, two volumes of poetry and five stage plays. She has been the recipient of several awards and fellowships, including the Deutz Medal for Fiction in the Montana Book Awards (for *The Shag Incident*, 2003), the Bruce Mason Memorial Playwright's Award, the Auckland University Fellowship and the Katherine Mansfield Fellowship. Stephanie is the co-founder and co-creative director of the Auckland Writers and Readers Festival.

MUSIC
from a
DISTANT
ROOM

STEPHANIE
JOHNSON

V

VINTAGE

National Library of New Zealand Cataloguing-in-Publication Data
Johnson, Stephanie, 1961-
Music from a distant room / Stephanie Johnson.
ISBN 1-86941-617-1
I. Title.
NZ823.2—dc 22

A VINTAGE BOOK
published by
Random House New Zealand
18 Poland Road, Glenfield, Auckland, New Zealand
www.randomhouse.co.nz

First published 2004
© 2004 Stephanie Johnson
The moral rights of the author have been asserted
ISBN 1 86941 617 1

Text design: Katy Yiakmis
Cover design: Matthew Trbuhovic, Third Eye Design and Graphics
Cover photo: Image Source
Printed in Australia by Griffin Press

In memory of Judy and Peter,
lovers of the sea and a good yarn

The hand is the visible part of the brain.

— IMMANUEL KANT

In the moonlight we caught a glimpse of Castle Rock, so a fairly accurate course could be laid.

— MULLET BOAT *VARUNA* LOGBOOK, 1925

In an age of personal effort towards independence, few girls will want to remain at home until the wedding march . . . Of all the careers being offered today there is none more congenial, more satisfying than that of a school dental nurse.

— A FRIENDLY CAREER, NATIONAL FILM UNIT, 1953

Words such as 'pain', 'sore' and 'hurt' should be used as little as possible as they have unpleasant associations in a child's mind . . . No matter how great the provocation the child must not be slapped . . . Even a good natured child has the tendency to bluff a nurse who shows a weakness in her approach . . . Spilled or uncovered mercury gives off a vapour which may be detritous to health.

— LECTURE NOTES FOR STUDENT DENTAL NURSES, 1961

I tried so hard to stay out of your way, girl.

Did you notice? I wanted you to be able to make music to the small hours, make love on the sofa if you felt like it. I became adept at sinking through walls, at disappearing.

By anybody's standards, my behaviour was exemplary.

But yesterday, despite our shared grief, I came close to hating you, though I'd never thought I would. There we stood on either side of the coffin, in that shining beige church with its cheap gold cross; its tan vinyl pews and execrable electronic organ playing bad Christianised pop as counterpoint to the sing-song tones of Pastor Everett. I kept my eyes down and deafened my ears and thought only of Carl and what he would make of us: you, skinny in your head-to-foot black, black shades on your dark face, a black band around your wild hair; me, dry-eyed in my colours: red skirt, yellow jacket, diamante clasp in my hennaed French roll. When he was little, you see, until he was four or five, Carl could perceive bright colours and I had worn them for him then: home from work I'd come and change straight away, out of my white.

We stood, you and I, on either side of my boy, and every time you lifted your lowered head in my direction — those blind twin mirror-shades blurring burnt orange and purple — drawing breath for your next wail, your next roof-lifting, sobbing heave, I wished you would quieten, take control of yourself. Even after I came around to your side and stood with my arm around you, and Sina, Skew and Liu joined us in a heavy-armed group hug, you persisted, the mobile side of your face in spasms of grief, the long scar on the other cheek keeping that side static.

Yesterday, while you wailed and heaved and your narrow shoulders shook, I was grateful for my pacific soul, for my old, deep acceptance of the inevitability of his early death.

It is boorish, I know, to start my story with a funeral; it makes too many emotional demands on the listener and I would not have done so if this were not meant for your ears only. Who else would take an interest? A stranger coming into the room would anticipate a grim account of the loss of a son and a lover, a man who died before they had so much as shaken his hand.

Neither do either of us have, just now, any wish to relive yesterday or any of the events of the past fortnight, so we will leave it there with just that one earlier moment: you and I invited to leave our seats by the young pimply pastor in suit and tie — in that clinical brown auditorium of sad faces, brown and white: musicians, listeners, the sighted, the sightless, all the people Carl had touched — and doing as he told us, rising to our feet. You stumbled a little at the wide, shallow step and I offered you my arm, pressing it into your side and lying your hand along it to let you know it was there. At the polished wooden oblong box we separated, one on his left, one on his right, before the altar of an ugly concrete church on a suburban hill.

There we are. Do you see us? Pinpoints on a map.

Now we'll begin to retrace our steps.

Listen to me, Tamara. When I came in this evening from my stall at the mall, when I came up the rickety wooden fire-escape that leads to our front door, I looked up and saw Carl. Not as he was only two weeks ago, a heavy-set man of forty-two, but at about eleven, the way he used to wait for me then in the Glenlyn house: one ear pressed against the glass to listen for the vibrations of my homecoming — the wheels up the drive, the creak and graunch of the garage swing-door, the tremble in the floor beneath his feet as the motor purred and died. It was just his shadow, the profile of it, a dark boyish shape between the golden blind and the glass, an instant — but long enough for a great surge of joy to run through me. I hurried inside, euphoric, comforted. I picked up my cat and we danced.

Let me comfort you. Let me show you how a life may change.

CHAPTER ONE

The children were afraid of her. She knew this and it broke her heart a little: it chipped a corner of it, though not enough to overwhelm the pride she felt in her white uniform, the red cardigan, the crisp gauze veil that stood away from her shoulders; not enough to temper her quick, professional strides in her street shoes each morning across the asphalt and up the concrete path to the wooden clinic; not enough to stop her pausing by the step to admire the garden of cineraria tall behind a pattern of pansies that she had made herself, coming into school on the weekends to do it; not enough to dim the pleasure she felt in laying out fresh picture books for her patients to enjoy in the tiny, shiny brown waiting-room, or in renewing the exhorting posters on the walls; not enough to permit any slackening in her clinical standards: her hygiene, the maintenance of her equipment.

Neither was she haunted by the fear of the children, by

their tears and stricken faces, though she felt for them. Eyes and noses were tenderly wiped with the white chin cloth at the end of appointments, crude dolls were fashioned out of cotton-wool rolls with pen marks for eyes, arms and legs cut away from the body with her sharp scissors, and balls of glistening mercury were tweezered out of the Drop Bottle to slip about in tiny, empty pink bur boxes. Sad and difficult kids would leave clutching one or other of these trophies in one hand, in the other a piece of paper inscribed with a name that was not their own, and a number.

From the clinic door she would watch the child make its way down the steep concrete path above the football field, across the basketball court and assembly area to the main body of the school. Each classroom opened onto the court and the instructed child would go along the line of windows to one of the brown doors set in the white ship-lapped wall, knock and be admitted. Little girls were the most reliable: they set off with the mission in mind, legs pumping under their woollen kilts in winter, or cotton frocks in summer, straight down the hill to the classroom. Boys were sometimes distracted by the view from the clinic step over the narrow valley to the hills beyond, where the machines scraped and roared and banged, laying in the new subdivision. In 1959, only a year ago, when Nola had first been sent out into the field, Glenlyn Primary School was at the northern edge of the city, newly built. It was part of the development opened up after the bridge was put across the Waitemata Harbour. There had been a busy stream that ran at one side of the football field; the road at the gate was unsealed. Cattle got in to eat the tops of the infant trees planted outside the staffroom and there was still one Maori family who arrived at school on a hammock-backed horse. Already, after only a year, the stream had become a creek, sluggish and dull, the neighbouring farms had been sold and carved up, the road sealed and the Maori family had moved away.

On this late summer morning in 1960 the name she'd copied from the Examination and History Chart onto the clinic slip read 'Brett Tyler, Room 1'. He wasn't long in coming: a ten-year-old boy with all his second teeth, including precociously erupted twelve-year-old molars. Here he was now, a skinny grey-clad figure tearing up the path, welcoming any chance of escape from his lessons, even if it was for a trip to the Murder House.

The outer door opened, there was the faintest brush of knuckles across the varnished surface of the inner door and he was inside, standing at the bench below the clinic window, pointing through it at the earth-moving machines working away on the next hill.

'That's my father,' he said. 'See, Nurse Lane?'

She followed the line of his bitten finger through the glass, across the blue air above the white, flaking goalposts, above the trees lining the gully, to a yellow grader on the flattened peak worked by a man in a black singlet. Another two hills rolled away behind it to the north: the next like the first, scraped bare of trees and topsoil; the third still in paddocks with the scattered remains of the farmer's shade trees. A line of ragged macrocarpa formed a receding hairline at its peak.

'Your dad?' said Nola, absently. While she held the glass slab under the cold tap to chill it, she watched the clouds of brown dust puffing in a fine smoke around the grader's Caterpillar wheels. The man's big head was pushed forward from his shoulders and his left hand shunted the gears as he turned the machine to make another pass along the emerging sweep of road. The shoulder closest to them caught the sun, a tiny microscopic flash, a sheen of reflective sweat.

Surreptitiously Brett had edged one buttock onto her chrome chair. All the children loved it, with its red circular seat and castor wheels. Nola scarcely used it, though occasionally she practised hooking out a toe and drawing the stool in close while maintaining an even pressure with the bur, in the professional, seamless way Dental Officers had at the Training School.

Brett whirled away from her.

'I'm going to see him after this. Just run up there through there.' He was pointing again, this time down to the other side of the football field. 'Through them stink trees. If you squash up the seeds with spit you can chuck it at the girls.'

Nola went on with her work, drying the slab and rubbing it with methylated spirit. She shouldn't have let him in so soon; she should have sent him out to wait for her like the other kids had to, but once he'd ripped a page out of one of the Bertie Germ booklets.

'Were you gentle cleaning your teeth last night?' she asked him. 'You didn't eat anything hard?'

Yesterday he'd sat in the chair for a full hour, which was against the rules — but who was to see? Hers was a single-practice clinic and the boy's teeth were appalling. She'd prepared a third cavity just before the three o'clock bell and had had no time to line and fill it.

The bench shuddered. Brett had taken hold of it and was now propelling himself backwards, rotating like a planet in its orbit. Arm outstretched, she went after him, but he had evaded her — and collided with the Allan table.

Gently, though.

'You were lucky,' she said. 'Hop up into the chair.' She

measured out the zinc onto the slab, divided it into small portions, dripped in the phosphoric acid and mixed it with the spatula. Brett had fallen quiet as soon as he'd sat up, and when she glanced up from her work she saw that he had clasped his hands over his chest.

'He's got a pear for a head,' he announced of the Be A Healthy Kiwi poster she'd pinned on the wall to distract and entertain her patients. 'He's got rhubarb legs and a green plum coming out of his bum.'

'That's enough, Brett.' She came towards him, bringing the mixed cavity-lining. 'And you mustn't go and see your dad after this. Wait till after school.'

'Not allowed. Mum told me not to. Didn't say nothing about in the day. I've got to.'

'Have a rinse-out.' She drew the Allan table towards her and selected an instrument: the cement plugger. Brett spat out the pink water and bumped his head back, hard against the head-rest. The chair shook.

'Quietly, Brett,' she said. 'Let's get started.'

With a whiff of sweet biscuit — or was it Vegemite? — Brett cranked his mouth open and Nola bent to him.

Stopped.

And straightened again. Laid bare by his heavy, fair fringe slipping away, a large blue shiner gleamed on his freckly brow. Its surface was speckled red. Brett was watching her carefully.

'That's why I have to go and see Dad, see. 'Cause Kev did it.'

'Who's Kev?'

'Mum's boyfriend.'

'What did you do? Anything?' She hadn't meant 'to deserve it', not really — she just wanted the full picture, but the crowded little buck-toothed mouth beneath her pressed its lips together and turned its angry, flushed cheek away. On the bone below his right eye a faint bruise was just coming to the surface. A second blow, then.

'Did you tell Mr Wylie?'

'Nup. No one. Just Dad. I'm going to tell Dad.'

She finished as soon as she could, hurrying through the mixing of the amalgam, squeezing the excess mercury in the cloth and plugging it into his teeth. The wind had swung around to the north-west, bringing with it the rumble and grind of the work going on on the hill, her own engine a high whine above it. Brett's eyes formed a blue, unfocused stare at a point somewhere beyond the edges of her veil. Was she hurting him? Was the drill consistent in its whirling? She listened carefully to its seamless spin; the marvellous new electric motor encased in beige metal — she shouldn't be putting him through it. Not when the lad had a shiner like a miner's lamp.

'Wait a minute,' she said, while the boy was climbing down. In the nurses' room she took off her white practice shoes and slipped on her brown lace-ups.

'Come on, then. We'll go and see your father.'

'I know the way' said Brett, taking her hand as they went down the steps.

'Perhaps we should go in my car,' she said, a moment later. If Mr Wylie, or any one of the other five teachers, were to look out of a window and see the dental nurse slip-stepping down the steep, dusty bank before hurrying across the football field just behind the goal line, they would think it highly irregular — and more irregular still that she was accompanied by Brett

Tyler, who was known for skiving off in the middle of the day. She was glad when the boy gave the lead down a track overgrown with wandering Jew, onion weed and nasturtiums, into a grove of trees. They leapt the creek, choking in its grey detergent-smelling scum, and turned hard left, away from the noise of the machines.

'It's all right. We have to go this way to get to the bottom of the track,' Brett called over his shoulder. He was running ahead of her on a narrow dirt strip beside the creek, which bordered the football field inside its last remaining fringe of manuka. A few houses down, the mangroves started, fanning out in an irregular V towards the Waitemata Harbour. Here and there a shaft of bright sunlight pierced the trees, making spots of white heat in the milky water. A small cloud of gnats — or were they mosquitoes? — hovered in one, illuminated.

She heard the boy's footsteps thud away to the right; the quick, dappled figure had disappeared. Hurrying along, the smooth soles of her street shoes skidding a little, she drew level with the point of his tangent and saw him, his grey back against the dull green as he climbed hand over hand among onion weed and cutty-grass up the first steep part of the hill. He was heading for a sheep track above their heads, almost at the tree line. Grabbing at weeds, her white stockings smeared now with mud, Nola followed him.

Light broke upon them at the same moment the noise did, louder as they went in single file along the track, which was more of a deep groove, each successive step having to be placed exactly in front of the one before. At either side of the narrow deep path, green tussocky grass made a tough, scratchy ruff, which Nola could feel lacerating her stockings as she pushed along in Brett's wake. A daggy sheep, alone of all its vanished flock, lifted her head to watch them go by.

At the edge of the subdivision vibrations shook the earth under their feet. 'There's Dad!' said the boy and he took off, sprinting towards the yellow machines. There were two trucks, a roller and a grader; the grader being the furthermost, with the roller following slowly behind. When the boy vanished behind the high machine Nola broke into a run: had the driver seen him? He darted past it, only half as tall as one of the massive, slowly spinning concrete cylindrical wheels.

Past the trucks parked at the mound of metal chip she sprinted — and caught the eye of one of the truckies in his cab, a Maori bloke with grey hair, who grinned at her. She supposed she did look ridiculous, sprinting through the dirt, veil flapping, her white hem catching at her legs.

As soon as the father saw his son he lifted his hand in acknowledgement and pointed to a small turning bay up ahead, gluggy with yellow clay. Immediately Brett stopped running and so a few seconds later had to suffer the nurse's arm at his back, and allow her to draw him across the unformed road in-between the grader and the lumbering roller. A black plume of diesel smoke followed them, drifting over Brett's head but catching the dental nurse in the face as they turned to watch the grader slow and halt. She coughed and waved a dispersing hand.

Hopping from one foot to another while he waited, Brett climbed the two high yellow steps to the driver, who laughed, swung him onto his hip and jumped down with him. He was a big man, who wore his black singlet very well, Nola considered, although above the wad of his rolled-down overalls blimped a small paunch. He was older than she was — much older, at least thirty — and so hard-baked brown she wondered if his skin in cross-section would show the cells of the epidermis thickened and impervious, like soft leather. Brett walked beside him now, holding his hand.

'Trouble?' he asked, as he came towards her. One word. His mouth hardly moved. He wasn't going to bother with introductions, but then men hardly ever did, in her experience.

Now that she was there Nola had no idea what to say. Behind them the roller shuddered to a standstill and the driver began to roll a cigarette. Brett's father was looking at her expectantly. He had clear, sharp blue eyes, like his son.

'He been misbehaving?'

'No, no — he wanted to show you something and I didn't want him to get into trouble so I —'

'Look!' Brett pushed his fringe back and lifted his face to his father, who laid his heavy, blackened hand on top of the boy's head.

'It was Kevin,' Brett said quickly. 'I didn't do anything. He just walloped me. You said if he ever did it again you'd bloody wallop him back, Dad, you said you'd —' But his father had turned away as suddenly as if he had been struck himself, his jaw swinging and his shoulders following. He was walking away, back towards his machine.

'Dad?' Brett's voice swelled with indignation.

'I'll come round tonight,' the father said, and the son spun to glare at Nola. Go away now, his little face said, less triumphant, all pinched with worry — and he ran after his father, who was heaving himself into the cab.

Nola looked away. Directly opposite, across the narrow valley where the school lay, the dental clinic windows glinted in the morning sun. From here it was a Wendy house: a neat, white cottage on a sun-baked hill, with its sweet garden and red roof. As a child she'd loved the little building at her own school and the white lady inside it. She'd loved how everything shone, and how it smelt so clean your nostrils squeaked. Nola never had cavities, or hardly any — one or two shallow ones painlessly filled. It was a trait she'd noticed in her fellow students at the Training School: most had good, straight, strong teeth. Girls with rabid decay never made dental nursing a career choice.

She snuck a glance at the father and son. The man had come down from his cab again and was talking earnestly, his palms resting on Brett's shoulders. Covertly, he glanced in her direction and away again. He gave his son a gentle push in her direction and turned back to his grader.

When he reached a distance of a few feet away from her Brett swerved, his pale face set determinedly back in the direction they'd come from. Nola fell into step beside him, saying nothing, the machines roaring behind them as they walked away.

'What did he say?' she asked when they were back on the sheep track.

But Brett wasn't talking. A large flock of seagulls skimmed in from the sea, only half a mile away, and settled on the football field below them.

'What did he say?' she asked again, when they were down among the stink trees.

'He was embarrassed,' the child offered, finally. 'He said I should of come on my own and just copped it if old Wylie caught me.' He leapt across the creek. 'He would've given me the strap, old Wylie. But you won't let him, will you?'

'I'll talk to him,' she said, stepping after him. On the other side she took out her packet of cigarettes, which she'd tucked down into her deep uniform pocket in the Nurse's Room when she changed shoes.

'Wait a minute, Brett.' She'd only have a couple of puffs. The goalposts glinted at them through the spindly grey trunks. The boy watched her.

'Kev smokes those,' he said, after a moment. 'Peter Stuyvesant, The Sportsman's Cigarette.'

'I don't smoke much,' said Nola, even though some nights, alone with the radio and the cat, she could smoke a whole packet. But that was only when her mother was out in town with her old friends from Grafton Theatre, or down the RSA with her other friends.

'Are you married, Miss?' he asked her. Nola blew smoke and shook her head.

'I live with my mum,' she told him.

'She got a boyfriend?'

What stories she could tell him. But she wouldn't. Besides, none of the injuries done her by Peg's gentleman friends could compare with his. They were more to do with coldness: a steely eye turned in her direction; a demand directed at her mother that she be removed to another room, or to the Tudor picture theatre on a Saturday afternoon. They were more to do with her birthday being forgotten by the few who stayed around for as long as it took to learn it before Don came on the scene — two or three years, maybe. Most of them she didn't mind, though neither did she mourn or miss them when they parted company with her mother. As Peg said, it was a blessed relief when she got the change of life and lost interest in men altogether. It was around then that she decided Don would do.

'She's a widow,' she said instead.

'Oh,' said Brett, shoving his hands into the pockets of his too-small grey shorts. 'A widow.'

'I'll go back that way,' he said, pointing off up the creek

towards the school. 'Then I can come out of the trees by the cloakroom.'

She nodded. It seemed like a good idea; it was the kind of thing she had done to keep out of trouble all her life: keep to the edges, out of sight. Though not at school. She'd loved school.

'Hooray, then,' said the boy and he took off, light-footed. Nola hurried back to the clinic and exchanged her grass-smeared, laddered stockings for another innocent pair.

During lunch hour she thought she might talk to Mr Wylie in the staffroom about their escapade, but in the end had to stay in the clinic catching up on work. She soaked her handpiece in an immersion of oil and ran it backwards and forwards, she wiped over the bracket tabletop and spittoon, she attended to the Drop Bottle of mercury which was blocked, blowing through its narrow aperture with a chip syringe. She readied the chair for her next patient. By three o'clock routine had closed over her head, lulling and productive, and the day seemed almost like any other. On her way to her car she went in to see the headmaster, but he'd left early.

It was only a distance of four or five large, modern blocks, a journey she could have taken each day on foot. But they were still laying the scoria for the paths in places — and white sucked up every particle of kicked-up dirt. So here she was, only five minutes after she left the school gate, climbing Seddon Rise in the 1958 Ford Prefect she and Peg'd bought with money from the sale of the old place in town. Carefully, swaying slightly, the little brown top-heavy car took the rising corner into Universal Crescent, veered left and up a steep concrete drive, through the open garage doors into the brick basement.

An internal door led up into the kitchen, all done out in salmon pink and donkey brown, where Peg sat reading the paper and drinking Corbans cream sherry.

'Evening, Nurse Lane' said Peg, as she always did.

The radiogram was playing: Benny Goodman, or some overblown forties dance music of the sort Peg liked. On the new electric stove three pots set up a ferocious rattling of aluminium lids. Nola poured a sherry too and lit up.

'Give us a clue,' she said as she always did, as soon as her mother turned to the crossword page.

During the day Peg must have walked down to Val's Salon, down at the main road intersection in between the new hardware shop and the half-built Four Square. Her hair had been 'brightened', as she put it, and Val had done her eyebrows in a new way: pointed, like twin gables. Peg maintained they'd gone grey when she was twenty, a freak of nature, and ever since then she'd had to shave them and paint them on. When Nola was little the story was that they'd got a disease and dropped off, and Nola'd always thought she might come across them somewhere — under the radiogram, or on the stairs — and be able to return them to her. She was sure her mother would be pleased to see them.

'You look like you've had a fright, Mum,' she said, giggling over her third little glass of sweet gold stuff.

'Do you think so?' Peg asked. 'What's wrong with them?'

'Too pointy.'

Her mother lifted her face to the light and patted her hair. 'What do you think of the colour, then, Miss Critical?'

'Suits you very well.'

Nola watched her mother's head dip towards the

crossword again. The tap dripped and the fridge hummed.

'What else have you done today?' She worried about her mother, that she was lonely since they'd made the shift out to the new house in the new suburb. In town she'd had her friends from the Grafton Theatre and a steady stream of people coming to their flat to have their hands read. So far, business was slow in Glenlyn.

'I met a lady in the salon who wants her palm read,' said Peg. 'She's coming up after tea.'

This last statement was made with a glance towards the ringing pots. 'It's ready now, you know, if you'd like to dish up.'

Dollops of mince with discs of carrot floating, a gleaming round of mashed potato, a frill of boiled cabbage. For Nola's afters there was Edmonds custard, bright yellow with a skin on it, and tinned peaches. Peg had hardly eaten a few tiny forkfuls before she was up and scraping the leftovers out onto the newspaper-lined bench.

'When she comes, this lady,' said Nola, 'take a note of her teeth.'

'You're not still on about that,' snorted Peg, her back to the table, running water.

'Well, it's true. You can learn a lot about a person from their teeth.' Nola scooped up the last of her custard. 'I'm adding to it all the time.'

'In your notebook?'

'Yes.'

'You mostly only see baby teeth.'

'Yes, I know. But teeth are something I notice about people. I always notice them.'

'You shouldn't go around looking at men's mouths,' began Peg. 'It gives them ideas. Better to meet their eyes —'

'And of course you're right,' Nola went on. 'Baby teeth are all more or less the same. The true personality emerges in the adult. For instance, I've observed that women with protruding canines make good mothers.'

'For goodness sake!'

Maybe Peg was offended by this, thought Nola. Her eye-teeth didn't protrude at all, because she had dentures all neatly arranged in two lines, upper and lower. Her own teeth had deserted her head in a Full Clearance, and that had happened before she was married, about the same time she lost her eyebrows. Nola had never even seen a photograph of them: in the one picture Peg had, a studio portrait for her twenty-first birthday, her lips were pressed close together.

'It's true,' she said again. 'Of all the children at the school, the happiest and most serene come from mothers with protruding eyeteeth.'

There was a knock at the front door and Peg went down the hall to answer it. From the kitchen Nola listened to her mother greet the customer and take her through to the lounge, which was sparsely furnished with two shabby armchairs from their old place. They were still saving for a couch. The only picture on the beige walls — other than the school staff photograph on top of the radiogram, with Nola standing tall with the men at the back, veil gleaming — was a luminously naked blue velvet lady, which Don had given Peg for Christmas a few months before he died.

Nola finished the dishes and ran a bath. The bathroom — with its green linoleum and lemon-coloured fittings — was the best part of their new life, she considered, luxuriating. She could lie almost full length. Reaching out, she wiped her hands on a towel and took up her tooth-reading notebook. Peg might scoff, but Nola had been proved right more than once.

Square, wide incisors suggest a generous, rational and optimistic personality, she read, and below that: *If the central incisors cross or overlap, while the other teeth are relatively straight, the personality is most likely to be fun-loving, though given to practical joking and therefore giving offence.'* She was still working on that one. On the next page she'd noted: *People with a wide gap between their central incisors are destined to great wealth.* This was not original, she knew, it was an old wives' tale, but she'd developed it a little by adding: *They are also capable of great selfishness.*

The next page was headed *Molars*, but she hadn't written anything there, other than a short observation about tooth-grinding and a possible link with over-sensitive natures. She put the notebook back on the stool and submerged herself entirely, with just her nose sticking out, and let the day wash off her.

What of that little boy Brett? Should she tell Mr Wylie what he had told her? A few of her patients had her worrying half the night. The worst thing to do was to start imagining what was happening to them in the dark, possibly at this very moment . . . she emerged, shook the child from her head.

On her way down the hall she listened for a moment outside the lounge door: the murmur of voices, Peg's and the customer's; a faint smell of cigarette smoke; and yes — there — the chink of the sherry bottle on the lip of a glass. She smiled. Peg had turned a reading into a little party, just as she liked to.

She thought she'd read something light, one of Peg's 'Auntie Mame' books, but after only a page sleep came heavy and soft with the light still on. Brett came tearing up the hill towards her as she stood on the clinic porch, his hair flying from his brow to reveal his purple shiner, a whole line of children following, and once she'd led them into the clinic she found they'd variously suffered broken limbs and cuts and welts, and although when she woke she supposed the dream should have been a nightmare, she hadn't experienced it as one. On the contrary, her dream self was calm, deft, sanguine as she mended, set, bandaged and plastered — until at length she'd looked around at all the little faces and seen them looking up at her, soothed and pacified.

Perhaps if the dream had gone on it might have soured, but Peg woke her from it, calling out in the dark, 'Nola dear, I can hear the milkman.'

And she'd got up, pulled on her pink-and-white brunch coat with the puffed sleeves, and gone down the brown veneered internal staircase, through the garage and down the drive, clinking the metal token against the glass.

Outside, it was just dawn. There was the smell of damp earth, and also of the blood and bone Peg had tipped around her chrysanthemums and pansies, which almost overwhelmed the scent of the roses nodding around the letterbox. The little milk truck had its headlights on and was at the corner, pausing outside a drive, so Nola waited for it with the bottle in her hand. As usual the milkman had his girl with him: a swollen, sullen pubescent who couldn't keep up. Her boss — perhaps her father — would wait impatiently for her, edging his truck forward at the last moment to make her run to catch it.

Today, as Nola handed her the bottle, the girl loomed in close and met her eyes.

'You the dental nurse from the school?' she asked.

'That's right,' said Nola and smiled at her. Maybe the girl had never been a patient: she was about fourteen and would be at the high school. Maybe she recognised her from the Miss Craven A picture that was in the *Star*.

'Brett pointed you out one day at the hardware shop.'

'Oh.'

'You got him in trouble. My stepbrother. Brett.' She had a determined jaw, small chalky teeth in an underbite.

The man in the cab jumped out, leaving the motor running, and carried a jingling crate to the other side of the road. The house opposite was a mirror image, another lazy L bungalow turned the other way. Hands separated the venetian blinds and a child's tousled head was momentarily diagonally framed. Almost immediately the front door flew open and a boy came out at the run, flying across the grassless, clay-lumpy front to collect the milk.

'So that's Kev?' Nola asked the girl, who nodded. The milkman was coming back now, around to the back of the truck with the empty crate. The girl's wet mouth began to whisper quickly, about how Brett had come home last night with strap marks on the backs of his legs and how Kev had got out of him why they were there . . .

A car, a beaten-up old Vauxhall, pulled up behind the milk truck and a big man leaped out: the grader operator, Brett's father, who looked much larger hemmed in by houses and fences than he had on the open ground of the next new subdivision.

'Oh no . . . Bernie,' breathed the girl.

He wasted no time; he laid into Kev straight away.

For a moment Nola stood at a clinical remove: so this is what it looks like, she thought, men fighting. Fights at the movies bore no resemblance, she supposed because somebody had planned them out. This fight was graceless and ugly. The first blow hit Kev on the back of the head — he was distracted, watching his daughter make her lumbering escape around the corner and down the Rise — and startled a fart out of him. The smack of a second fist — Kev's on the boy's father's cheeks — sounded like a steak slapped to the bench. Snot and blood streamed from his nose. They were weirdly silent, as were the over-the-road children, watching. Boots and fists did all the talking and nobody came out of the neighbouring houses to stop them, which was no surprise as the house next door was unfinished and unoccupied and the couple on the other side were as square-jawed as bulldogs and pathologically unfriendly. Even so, Nola found herself running up and down outside their blind windows, the multiple lids of the venetians turned down for the night.

'Help,' she hooted. 'Help!' She was a strangled chook, a chook with its head off running up and down the path.

The men had rolled onto the ground, tightly clenched to each other, their legs half under the tray of the truck. They seemed pathetic, boyish — and she felt strong suddenly, wide across the shoulders, her tennis arms invincible. Fleetingly, their boys' faces played across the faces of the men: how sad and tragic — they really were hurting each other. She felt a terrible pity for them; she tried to wrench them apart at the shoulder.

'Don't be so bloody ridiculous,' she said.

Kev grunted and ground his fist into Mr Tyler's stomach; his arm was caught between them. Mr Tyler had a handful of Kev's curly, greasy hair and was yanking his head backwards. This close she could see that he was a good deal older than the milkman and that even though Kev was wirier and smaller, Mr Tyler was coming off worse. Kev's face had some hard living in it, though: perhaps they were more evenly matched than she thought. They rolled away from her and she saw that Bernie had torn the back out of Kev's white overalls. They rolled again, this time completely underneath the truck.

A head collided with the axle — or the chassis, or whatever that bit was called — and bending she could see they'd wedged themselves between the kerbstone and the wheels.

'Stop it right now!' Nola shouted. 'Damn you!' And she took off around to the other side of the milk truck, where she rained blows on whoever it was on top.

'Damn you, you beggars!'

No doubt Peg, coming down the driveway with her do-protecting pink hairnet drawn over her head, would think that was pretty strong language for the recently crowned Miss Craven A, let alone the school dental-nurse, but see here: Kev's small, neat ear was torn and bleeding. The truck, left idling for too long, was spluttering and stalling. Nola tried first gripping Kev's hair, then the scruff of his neck, her other hand curled around his belt. Peg called out sharp.

'You! Get up off him or I'll call the cops!'

The man on top brought one knee up into the other man's balls and sprang away, knocking Nola backwards onto the path. In slow, fluid motion she fell to her rump, to her side, to her shoulder — like she'd got carried away and done once or twice on the tennis court — away from his indiscriminate kicks as he made his way between her and the other man, around the side of his truck to the cab.

'Get up away from there!' Peg was saying, as Nola struggled to her feet, giving thanks that she wore pyjamas under her brunch coat and therefore hadn't given them all a poppy show.

The truck was spluttering back to life, the key scraping in the ignition, squawking and turning it over. Clouds of black smoke blew out over a pair of prostrate legs in a pair of grey trousers, sticking out from under the tray of the truck.

'Are you all right? Get up,' said Peg again, and somehow the man did, rolling out, heaving up and standing, swaying, his eyes rolling back in his head. Nola took one side and her mother the other and they led him onto the footpath, up the white concrete drive luminous in the early dawn, while behind them the truck jerked away, bounding around the bend in the crescent.

Mr Tyler groaned with every step.

They sat him down at a kitchen table.

'My goodness,' said Peg, 'whoever he is, he's taken a battering.'

The man gave a tremendous lurch and began to slip slowly to the floor. He was too big to try to push back: Nola took his head, cushioning it, kneeling with him as he slid. His big nose was broken, though it was obvious from the way it spread across his face that it had been broken before. Blood seeped from the skin beside his ear; the dark hair around it was cut in an old-fashioned style, a severe short-back-and-sides like a soldier. Sunburn flared on his wide brow, on his cheekbones around the abrasions and bruises. Through his slightly open mouth she could see a glimpse of his teeth. He still had his own, and they were very white, and strong.

'Go and get a pillow for him,' said Peg, watching Nola looking into the man's face on her lap.

'I know what to do, Mum. Be quiet,' she snapped. The man was breathing heavily, almost snoring. 'See that breathing?'

she told her mother. 'That's part of it. Stentorian breathing. He's got concussion.'

'For goodness' sake, let him sleep it off a bit and come and have your breakfast. He probably hasn't been home all night.' Peg put the kettle on and went to fetch a cushion herself from the settee in the lounge. When she returned to the kitchen Nola hadn't moved.

'He doesn't smell of alcohol, Mum. He isn't drunk if that's what you think. He's like this because he's got concussion.'

'Humph,' said Peg.

'I'm all shaky.' Nola held up one of her hands. 'See?'

'You look pretty steady to me.' Sympathy Peg doled out arbitrarily and in small doses. She didn't seem to have any concern at all for this poor Mr Tyler. 'Have a cup of tea and a ciggie and you'll feel better.'

Nola shook her head. Sighing, doling tea-leaves with one hand, Peg lit a cigarette with the other.

'His son came up to the clinic yesterday,' Nola began, and told her about the bruise on Brett's head, and was up to the part where they had gone across the football field and up the creek bank when the front-door knocker went, hard. They had a visitor; someone had come up the terrace steps beside the zigzag wrought-iron railing and across the porch. Had they left the front door open? She went out the kitchen door into the hall, where the shiny, pale wallpaper and the varnish on the dark piano flickered with blue light from the cop car outside.

'Turn the hall light on and close this door,' Peg said quickly. 'Don't tell them he's here.'

The policeman was young, only about her age, and Nola could tell that not only did he think she was a bit of all right, but he believed everything she told him. Both men had taken off, she said, and no, she had no idea where to. After he left she detoured into her bedroom and hauled on her uniform and red cardigan.

Back in the kitchen the sight of the man on the floor suddenly frightened her. Maybe she should have told the cop he was here; maybe they should ring an ambulance. At the bench she stood beside her mother and looked at an advertisement for television sets upside down. The small print assured buyers that the sets were fitted with two sheets of glass over the screen to protect the viewer from radiation. Was that really a concern? Had they done experiments? She should try to think of something else for a while and let Peg figure out what to do . . . She knelt beside him again and saw the edge of his wallet in his back pocket — cheap beige leatherette, cracking at the corners, and empty of any address or money. He only had two bob on him. She slipped it back into his wallet and patted his shoulder.

'Wake up!' She bent to his ear, spoke loudly. 'Come on, wake up —'

'Leave the poor cove alone.' Her mother was making toast, squeaking open the rust-speckled silver wings and slipping in the slices.

'No, you're supposed to rouse them every twenty minutes.'

One of the man's eyes was fluttering, opening; the other was swollen shut. He groaned and Nola stroked his forehead, took his hand and patted insistently.

'Mr —? Mr Tyler?'

She turned his hand over and looked at his palm.

'Will you look at that?' said Peg softly, leaning over to see. 'An arrowhead, clear as can be.'

'What does that mean?' asked Nola.

'Sign of the soldier,' replied her mother. 'Don't often see it.' She put her glasses on, knelt beside them. 'All ties in: that horizontal line of head says he's a realist, and look — he's in for a journey on the sea. An ill-fated one —' and Peg would have gone on, but Mr Tyler moved suddenly, his hand closing on Nola's wrist, squeezing it softly. Peg stood and took a step away as the man's mouth opened, as if he wanted to say something, and Nola saw that his left front incisor was gold. A sweet thrill passed up her arm, across her shoulder and down her breasts to her stomach. His palm was warm and dry; he smelt spicy, warm and clean; she had the surprising idea of lying down beside him and breathing him in . . .

She gathered herself away from him, gesturing for him to get up. He got as far as the chair and lowered himself gingerly into it.

'I think Nola should drive you to the hospital. Where do you live?' Peg was wielding the butter knife.

'On my mullet boat. I move around.'

'Where's the boat now?' Peg put a piece of toast down in front of him.

'Don't give him anything to eat, Mum!' said Nola. 'You'll make him ill.'

'Down Waikowhai,' the man said, as if she hadn't spoken.

'Right over on the Manukau?' asked Peg.

'That's right. Bloody miles away,' he said. 'Only just come from there.'

'You were on your way to work?' asked Nola, but Peg was talking over the top of her.

'Can you get yourself back to it?'

He pushed the toast away.

Maybe his injuries were all superficial, blood and broken

skin, thought Nola, except for his shoulder. He cradled it, under the armpit.

'Can you make it down the stairs to my car?' Nola took charge, picked up her keys. 'I'll take you to the hospital. I'll drive you into town.'

The man gave an infinitesimal nod and stood again. Peg wiped her hands on her apron and would have come to help him, but he put out one hand to stop her, pushing past towards the internal staircase where the narrow wooden handrails bent and squawked under his weight as he heaved himself down. As she went down the dark well behind him, Nola wondered how he would fold himself into the Prefect.

'No hospital,' he said, as soon as she got the car going, which took several attempts. 'Just take me back to Waikowhai, if you don't mind.'

'I'll be late to work. How about . . .' Nola began, and stopped while she concentrated on backing the car out of the garage, 'how about I take you to a doctor? There's one not far away. His kids go to my school.'

Mr Tyler didn't reply, his big head in sullen profile, so she took him to be agreeable and drove down the street, past the wildly parked Vauxhall and on to the doctor's house, three blocks towards the water.

The houses were bigger here: they took up more of their quarter-acre sections, though still of the lazy L or block-shaped bungalow type, with double, brick garage-basements and weatherboard upper storeys, their dull tiled roofs. But the gardens were neater, more established, two years older. Nola took the car up the drive, beside a lawn sprouting with strange shadowy shapes: tall wading birds.

'Look — some herons have come in land. Perhaps the

doctor has a pond,' she said conversationally, to give him something to take his mind off the pain, as she opened the car door to walk up to the house. The porch light flicked on a minute after her knock and she saw they were concrete flamingos, painted pink.

How stupid he would think she was. Her face burned as she returned to the car.

'Come inside,' she told him. 'He said he'll have a look at you.'

He hobbled up the path and down the carpeted hall to a bathroom, very modern and with the doctor's foamy shaving water still sitting in the basin. A bunch of sleepy blond children in winceyette clotted together silently in the doorway, slippered feet on reflective linoleum, watching. The older two looked at Nola with astonishment: the school dental-nurse in their bathroom with a bashed-up man.

'Fell off my bike,' Mr Tyler told them.

'I can only use what I've got here,' their young father said, before putting gentian violet on Mr Tyler's cuts, bathing his split lip, applying a plaster or two and binding up one shin. The arm he put in a sling he made out of a nappy.

'Needs an X-ray. Your shoulder.'

But Mr Tyler smiled and shook his head. 'No you don't, nothing like that,' he said. 'I'll be right as rain now.'

On the front porch with his good arm he offered his two bob, but the doctor pushed his hand away. He left the money on top of the letterbox anyway, a casual flick of the hand, metal rattling on metal — but the young man had gone inside and closed the door.

'I see the herons are still here.' He grinned at her before limping to the Prefect and forcing himself stiffly inside.

In an inadvertent diagonal she reversed towards the

letterbox. While she straightened up, working the wide, stiff steering wheel, he said, 'Take me down to Waikowhai. I'll see if Patu's there.'

'Who's Patu?'

'He can row me out.'

As the sun came up they drove in near silence, except for his directions. Bumps and corners had him wince and rise up on his seat and Nola couldn't help but picture the clenching of his powerful buttocks. It wasn't sexual at all; it was more that her mind sometimes automatically formed cross-sections of bodies and body parts. It was something it did without warning: show her the span of bones in a hand; the moving parts of the hinge of a jaw; the enamel, dentine and pulp heart of a tooth; the loll of a liver in a gut. She pictured now the red, muscular fibres of gluteus maximus, the dimples forming at the hips and the smooth skin of his rump, which must be whiter than the rest of him.

Over the Harbour Bridge they drove, through the city and along Dominion Road.

'Why do you have the boat so far away from where you work?' she asked.

'Where it was when I bought her last year,' he answered. 'Got a mate with a truck. We're going to move her over to the Waitemata before the winter comes.'

'Why?'

'Because it's safer. Calmer. Manukau's a bitch. Cops all the southerly gales.'

She snuck a look at him. Perhaps he was angry, perhaps the pain from the fight was making him bad-tempered. He sounded as if he were only just reining himself in.

The closer they got to Waikowhai, the fewer the houses

and street lights, the more bumps and corners and the more Mr Tyler's breathing jagged when his shoulder gypped him. Nola slowed the car to walking pace — and stalled twice.

'It's all right,' he said each time she lifted her foot from the accelerator and struggled to double-declutch. 'The quicker the better.'

Hillsborough Road was fuzzy grey in the early light. The houses looked soft, as if they were made of felt, like geometric shapes to be pressed to a board to make a child's picture. There was a small crescent moon just setting, sharp and bright as the sickle on a tooth explorer.

'Left here,' he said, suddenly.

'Where are we?' she asked.

'Just keep going.'

But she had stopped, her steady headlights casting up the end of the seal, a stand of gangly pines and a dirt road dropping away steeply beyond. Mounds of rubbish — scrap iron, old bicycle wheels, a rusted boiler, wood, paper, a glint of glass — heaved on either side of the rough, declining road.

'This is a tip,' she observed.

'Keep going!' He sounded snaky.

Bother you, Nola thought, and she felt wounded, a little irritated herself. Wasn't she doing him a great favour, coming all this way to take him home? He hadn't said they'd have to drive down a virtual cliff-face.

'Down here.' He lifted an arm to point, almost swore, and lowered it again.

She let the car crawl on down the hill and into the first hairpin bend. A wirewove bed base stood on its end against a scrappy tree; a couple of sun-bleached, torn gumboots, one enormous, one a child's, stood oddly paired side by side at the edge of the road; there was a hillock of inner tubes; of pig iron and builder's waste; tin cans; a ghostly pile of shoes. It was eerie, she thought. And it was smelly and completely silent.

Should she be afraid? she wondered suddenly. She knew nothing about this man, after all. Except that he was little Brett's father and that he had abandoned the child to a brute who beat him. Her breath caught in her throat.

'You can go faster than that,' said Mr Tyler, and either his jaw had seized up or he was clenching it, molar to molar. She applied a little extra pressure to the accelerator and pushed the clutch in at the same time. The car flung forward, into the side of the road, one wheel spinning in a shallow ditch, and he called out 'Bloody hell!' and the next word, as he was flung forward but saved himself was 'Fuck!'

It was perhaps only the second or third time Nola had heard it aloud in her whole life, and she burned with shame for him as much as she did with disgust and fear, and then embarrassment for her driving as she backed out, stalling five times at least and bunny-hopping on down the steep hill to the sea. She could feel him looking at her — maybe he was even smiling — and did her best to ignore him.

'Sorry,' he said, at the end of the road, when finally she graunched the car out of first gear and turned it off. 'Bad language. Sorry, Nurse.'

The rubbish was thinner down here, much of it taken out by the tide or blown away. The beach faced due south, across the wide, muddy reaches of the Manukau Harbour. This morning it was still and clear; the high tide shifted grey and placid in the early light.

'Put your headlights back on,' he said, hobbling off, and she followed him along a narrow curve of shells and pebbles around a rocky point, until three boats came into view about forty feet out. One of them showed a smeary light, dimly, through a strip of glass in its low cabin.

'Hey! Patu!' yelled Mr Tyler.

What a voice, thought Nola. It came from somewhere in his boots and echoed off the cliffs.

'Hey! Hello! Patu, you bastard!'

He was at the water's edge, but not so far in as to dampen the toes of his work boots, incongruous under the cheap suit pants, now torn. Had he worn the boots on purpose, Nola wondered, the better to batter Kev's shins? A tiny tremor ran through her, guilty, pleasurable.

A silver-haired figure came out onto the quarterdeck of the ketch with the light.

'Patu!' Mr Tyler yelled again. 'It's me, Bernie.' The old man was at the stern, peering towards the land. Lurching against his bruises, half running, Bernie took off back along the stony shore to where the dark lump of the Prefect cast its round golden beams on the grey sea.

Sitting on the bonnet, taking off his boots and rolling up his trouser-legs, Mr Tyler kept his headlights on Nola. That's what it felt like: as if she were all lit up: as if in the soft, exposing light of the dawn she gleamed like the bones in an X-ray. He was looking at her, and seeing all there was to see of her, as she came towards him across the uneven ground. He didn't take his eyes off her once from then on, not until the dinghy was close in and the old man called his name.

'So, Tamara from across the Tasman — for although you are American, Sydney is where Carl found you — that is the story of how it was when I first met Bernie.'

'Why don't you tell it straight?' she asks. 'Why's it she not I?'

'Because that girl doesn't exist any more. I'm no more her than you are.'

'But you're rhyming it up. Filling in the gaps. Things you couldn't know.'

'I've been back there so many times, Tam. I know. I've had time to work it all out.'

She nods, not convinced, and goes back to her stacking, kneeling opposite me on the living-room floor. It's nearly three weeks after the funeral and we are sorting Carl's cassettes, CDs and records, which are in piles around us, each striped with a strip of Braille glued on to identify it. Every time Carl made a purchase, or received a gift of music, he would make it a tag with his Braille machine and then catalogue it. We sort them together: Latin, electronic, mystic Islamic, gospel choirs, symphonies, fugues, concerti and quartets, Gregorian chant, blues, Moors and Tuvans, Bic and Bo, Anika and the Finns and Greg Johnson and a few others of his countrymen — all kinds of music from every corner of the world. The bulk of it is jazz: from Duke Ellington to the blind and brilliant Art Tatum, Thelonius Monk to John Coltrane, Erroll Garner, Woody Herman, Dave Brubeck, Nat King Cole to Chick Corea, Keith Jarrett and Courtney Pine. There are over a thousand of them, obscure and celebrated, and the idea is for us to divide the collection in two: half for Tamara, half for me. Her half we'll pack into a strong box and send by sea, to follow her home to America.

'So — what do you think happened next?' I ask her.

Her long legs folded under her on the carpet, her back against the sagging sofa, Tamara looks coy, then just as quickly lascivious. My cat Cheiro has lain his long body along her thigh, his eyes half closed to her stroking, purring, blissful.

'You got him down in the white lilies and did the do.'

'No, of course not — not that night.'

'When then?'

'Not for two weeks. But he did kiss me, on the mouth, just as Patu lifted his oars to coast the last few feet onto the beach, and I liked it very much. He said, "Thanks, Nola" and gave me a gentle kiss — he had a split lip, after all. It was just the lightest brush.'

'Sexy . . . '

'Yes, it was.'

You must remember your first kiss with Carl, though I'd never ask.

'God. I just thought!' Tamara says with some of her old vigour, and I love her for it. I love her for making an effort, for being interested. 'Maybe you'd never been kissed before!' She runs her hands through her stiff hair, making it stick out on either side of her head.

'Yes, I had.'

'Who?'

'A couple of the younger actors Peg knew from the Grafton Theatre. One of them I was keen on.'

'You let this actor kiss you is all? Nothing else?' She's picked up a Chet Baker CD. Tamara lost her sight as a teenager in a street fight and was never taught to read Braille — she recognises her favourites by the feel of the cases a scratch here, a chipped corner there, a rough patch where the price sticker was — and sometimes a sniff for an identifying smell.

'Shall we have this dear old druggie?' she asks. 'I'll put him on.'

'Since you must know: if I can recollect, I think I let one of them squeeze my bra cups, his warm hand on stiff lace . . .'

'Has to be bark on bark,' Tamara says knowledgeably, 'otherwise it's nothing much.'

'I thought it felt like rather a lot.'

Chet's smooth, smoky voice slips from the speakers, slippery, modal as his trumpet, half in love with death.

It's dusk, that particular hour Peg used to call blind man's holiday, when it's too dark to see properly but too early to turn the lights on. From the angle of her shoulders, her tilted face, her hands fallen to her lap, Tamara's gone into what Carl called a slump. Her broad lower lip protrudes, her heavy eyelids quiver. They come upon her suddenly, these collapses of spirit, profound and frequent. I can do nothing but wait with her until they pass, and they are deeper and longer, now Carl has gone.

Chet is possibly making this one worse.

The last of the sun streams low and warm through our old high west-facing window, the view bisected by the flung arc of the Khyber Pass flyover, the rumble and roar of traffic a constant accompaniment to our lives. Until a few years ago I used to worry that this building would be demolished to make way for an office block, or modern apartments, but the two-storey wooden houses are now more likely to be sold to company directors, or doctors, or lawyers: wealthy families who return them to their former splendour. Between the twin forces of gentrification and development, the Grafton of my girlhood scarcely exists any more.

One of the beams envelops her. She could be praying, kneeling the way she is with her high-browed face in solemn repose, like an African saint.

'Get your sax out, Tamara. Do you good,' I suggest. She hasn't played, these last few weeks.

No? I reach out, touch her on the shoulder, stroke her coarse, undressed hair and she flinches — not being able to see me coming. But then she's shifting sideways, leaning into me, her long neck curving around my shoulder, her arms tight around me, and she cries dry and hot from her subsided eyes, without tears, like Carl did.

I will not cry. I keep my mind busy, ticking over with the plans: today is Monday. At the end of the week, after nearly ten years away, Tamara leaves for Chicago. She could never persuade Carl to visit America with her because he had a schizoid attitude to the place: a passionate, all-consuming love of its great melting pot of music, which mostly triumphed over the other extreme — his loathing for its foreign policy, its exploitation of the poorest nations, its warmongering, its fouling of the world's atmosphere and oceans. Falling in love with Tamara only seemed to polarise him more, though maybe it helped that she was black. They could stick the boot into white America together, laugh themselves stupid over the President's mangled sound-bite speeches, rage against his murderous activities in the East.

Please stop crying. Oh, how I'd love to say that to her. But I don't say anything, just wrap my arms around her, and over her bony shoulder rest my eyes on the closed cases of his keyboards, on the sarcophagus of his black amp and against the far wall, his beloved old piano, battered and scuffed.

Suddenly he's there, at the stool, his strong white hands on the keys, his face thrown back in that vulnerable, exposed way he had. When he first started playing like that, when he was nine or ten, my heart would ache for him. His whole soul seemed to come into his face, the map of himself, intimate, laid bare — but as he grew older it seemed to disturb me less. I can see Tamara up there too, and the shapes of the other musicians they'd played with: the violinist, Liu, a true New Zealand Creole of Asian, Polynesian and Pakeha; Sina, the big, bluesy Samoan girl with the powerful voice and tumultuous love life; and Skew, their skinny old Pakeha dopehead of a hippie drummer.

Then, before they've even properly arrived, the band fades away and it's only my son and his girl here at home, just the two of them. They've drifted over to their instruments, they're picking up and sitting down, it's any time of the day or night and they're in their own private heaven.

I knew she loved him when I first heard them playing together.

A few words, mumbled into the crook of my neck. 'What was that?'

'Said — I didn't think I'd be like this, so sad. Thought I was kinda inured to death. You don't grow up in the Robert Taylor Homes like I did and not see it. I saw lots of death till I lost my eyes.'

'Stay here, then.' There, I've said it. I've been wanting to since she decided to leave. 'Stay here with me.'

'Nope.' She pulls away, sits up again, scrubs at her face. 'I'm going home. Least for a while.'

'You might come back?'

'Doubt I'll have the cash.'

I rub her back gently, feeling the lumps of her spine under my hand. She's thin, too thin.

'You want something to eat?'

'No,' she says, as she usually does, an automatic reply, and before I can press her on it she goes on straight away. 'Where'd Carl get the music in him? Bernie?'

'Yes, of course. He gave him his music, passed it down in his genes.'

'You ever hear him?'

'Once or twice.'

'Tell me the story. How it was for you and him, both the players of the song.'

'I can do that,' I assure her. 'I can sit inside both our skins; I've remembered our times together so often.'

CHAPTER TWO

The first night she rowed out to *Ngaire* with him was after a party with his friends in a villa in Mount Albert, and she was tiddly on Pimms. It was a while later, maybe a month after they'd met: it'd taken Bernie that long to recover from his bruises and sprains. A few days after the fight on the crescent, he'd limped up from the bus stop to fetch his car without even coming in to say hello. Nola thought he could have left a note to thank her and it was that — Bernie's definite lack of manners — that motivated her to write a note to him on her pink stationery, care of the road-building company. It was a brief note and very polite, enquiring after his health. A couple of weeks later he'd appeared at the door and asked her out.

Bernie's mates were working men like him, and their girlfriends, who were factory workers or clerks, had nasal vowels and sharp voices and seemed to talk only of hairstyles and make-up and cooking. One of them, a married one with an expensive hairstyle and a shiny new gold ring, was the hostess. June took them all into the kitchen to see her marvellous new appliance: an electric frying pan. It had a thermostat and could cook whole meals. Nola could scarcely contain her boredom, which was sharpened by envy — not that she would admit it. One day she would have her own electric frying pan and shiny pop-up toaster, though she wouldn't show them off to people because that was crass, and weren't these gadgets just a part of modern life? Anybody could have them who saved up enough to buy them. She had more important things going on in her head.

There was a group of blokes who could variously play the guitar, piano — that was Bernie — and one of them was a dab hand at the trumpet. He looked like a paler version of Louis Armstrong, his brown cheeks puffed out shiny and round. They did Elvis and the Everly Brothers and lots she didn't recognise and she found herself dancing alone, at the end of Bernie's piano, while he played and sang. Her feet twisting and stepping on the swirling pattern of the hostess's maroon carpet, circular skirt flying, she moved among the couples but never out of his view. Now and then Bernie would look across and smile at her. She should have guessed he could sing, she thought, that night when he bellowed across the water. Between songs she sipped on her Pimms, which she carried in a small flask in her evening bag.

Now she leaned into the flank of the wooden dinghy, trailed her fingers in the water and wondered what it would be like on board the mullet boat. Possibly it would have that closed-in boat stink of damp and engine oil, wet socks and in-evitably fish. Away over to the east were the low sheds and lights of Onehunga Port, and beyond that the shadow of Mangere Bridge with its string of sparkles over the dark water.

'Won't your mother worry?' asked Bernie.

'I rang her from your mate's place,' she told him. She lay her jacket over her knees for modesty while she unhooked her stockings from her suspender belt and rolled them off. 'And told her what?' asked Bernie.

'That I might go out to your boat.'

Bernie laughed and lifted the oars; the dinghy skimmed closer to the mullet boat. It was low tide — not far to row once she and Bernie had carried the dinghy between them down the beach. She'd walked in the sand on her stocking feet and snagged the nylon. Now she rolled them up and tucked them into her bag.

'Hadn't even invited you then.'

'Thought you might.'

Bernie smiled. 'Peg doesn't mind?'

'She told me to be careful, like she always does.'

Bernie's face clouded. He dug the oars in, took the dinghy the last two sweeps to the stern of the yacht.

'She didn't mean —' Nola began, but trailed off, embarrassed. What a stupid thing to say. Her cheeks burned.

As soon as the leading rope was made fast she stepped past him, carrying her handbag and shoes, up and over: one foot onto the bench beside Bernie, the other high to the stern of the mullet boat. Under her bare soles the dinghy seat still retained some of the warmth of the day; the stern was smooth with new paint, cool and shiny in the moonlight.

Bernie was quick behind her.

'You know boats, then?' he said, pushing past.

'Not really. Don had a boat. A mullety. Like this one, sort of. They're all quite different, aren't they? His one had a higher cabin — he had it changed to make it more comfortable, you know, so you don't have to scoot around on your backside when you're below. Before that he used to say going away on it was like spending a week under the dining-room table. I never saw it when it was like that. He'd altered it by the time Mum met him. But they're odd boats, really, aren't they? Heavy and difficult to sail. Lots of them get wrecked. Go nose down.' Was she gabbling? She closed her mouth.

Bernie said nothing, just stood beside her in the soft dark, breathing. What was he thinking?

'We went out on it sometimes,' she finished, lamely.

'Don, eh?' said Bernie, getting down on his knees to move into the shallow hull. 'What'd he do for a crust, this Don?'

She followed him, crouching, into the dark.

'This and that. Ran a pub for a while. Tried it out as a bookie after that. Had his own business and interests in some others. Fingers in lots of pies.'

There was the scrape of a match: its orange flame met the wick of a candle wedged into the block in the centre of the cabin. A scent of clean carbon and a hint of sulphur mixed with the air, which didn't smell at all, except of the sea, and also of Bernie, which was to be expected, since he lived here. She liked it very much. The cabin was spartan, neat, divided at the front by the narrow, varnished block with its winches and ropes. A bundle of bedding was tossed forward into the hold beyond the base of the mast. Two long oars lay along the sides, against the base of two low bunks.

She shuffled around on her bum and leaned up against one of the bunks, which had an old grey army blanket neatly folded on top. In the flickery light of the candle she could make out a lumpy shape on the bunk opposite . . .

It was a child. Wrapped in two blankets, Brett's tousled

head rested on a duffel bag, from the end of which dangled the sleeve of a brown knitted jersey. A narrow squab cushioned him from the hard wood; one bare foot hung loose, muddy and black-toenailed.

'It's all right,' said Bernie, watching her. 'He won't wake up.'

'Has he been here all night?' she whispered. 'On his own?'

She glared at him and saw how silly he looked, how it was impossible for Bernie to sit upright in the cabin: his back was curved, his head tucked down.

'Often is on the weekend. I pick him up after work on Fridays sometimes.'

'And you leave him on his own at night?'

'If the weather's good. What else can I do? He likes it here.'

Nola looked at the sleeping child. He was disturbed by their voices, twisting around in his tight blankets. Bernie had safety-pinned him in at the red-stitched edges. His eyes opened, bleary, blue, and widened slightly at the sight of her. But it was as if his sleepy brain couldn't cope with the idea of the dental nurse in his dad's boat, so he closed them again and rolled to face the cabin wall.

'Beer?' offered Bernie. 'I could make a cup of tea on the primus.'

This last was more a statement of fact than an offer, Nola considered. He could, but he'd rather not.

'Beer,' she said quickly.

'We'll take it outside,' said Bernie, bending into the space under the bunk beside her. He produced a long brown bottle of DB wrapped in newspaper, picked up the lamp and carried it outside.

'Who was Don, then?' he asked, digging a coin from one

of his pockets, leaning into the stern and using it to flick the top off the beer. It flipped away, off the side of the boat, a flash of silver and a tiny splash.

'My stepfather, sort of. Mum's last boyfriend. He died a year ago.' Nola perched up on the side of the boat, opposite him.

'She's had lots of boyfriends, then?' Bernie passed her the bottle.

'Haven't you got a cup?'

'Not within reach,' said Bernie, stretching his arms out and clasping his hands behind his head. She sipped at the beer: it was warm, grainy on her tongue. A light wind tipped up the waves around them; the boat shifted a little, woke up, like the child had in his blankets. Way behind Bernie, Mangere Mountain squatted, a giant frog.

'You'll be thinking I'm broke,' said Bernie, 'and you'd be right.'

'I wasn't thinking that at all.'

'He had a few bob then, this Don? Had the boat altered, you said — didn't do the work himself. Paid someone to do it, eh?'

She supposed Don was rich, though she said nothing. It was none of Bernie's business. He held out his hand for the bottle and she sat down on the side of the boat.

'Was he like a father to you?' He was joining her. She could feel the warmth of his thigh against hers.

Nola shrugged her cardigan around her shoulders. She didn't want to tell him about the beauty competitions: how she'd worn the crown and sash for Miss Craven A, the summer she was eighteen Miss Mount Maunganui, and a year later Miss Blossom Festival, all of which had been Don's idea. Not that she didn't enjoy them, after a while, but in the beginning she'd had to work at it; it wasn't in her nature to enjoy being looked at, not like it was for Don and Peg. She'd made a deal with Peg now: Miss Auckland 1961, next May, would be her swansong. 'You may as well give it your best shot one last time,' Don had said a week before he died, suddenly, in his own bed of a heart attack. 'You may as well. You're a good-looking girl.'

'It was Don's death-wish,' Peg liked to say dramatically, whenever she sensed mutiny.

'Don was married,' Nola told Bernie. 'He had his own kids. He never lived with us.' She had been glad he was married. It meant she and Peg had long periods without seeing him —without having to listen to him drone on — sometimes for weeks if he went away on business to Australia or the States.

'So Peg worked?'

'She was a secretary for Samuel Parker's.'

'The plumbers' suppliers?'

'Yes, that's right.'

There was a long pause then.

'Where's your real father?'

'Died.'

'Sorry,' he said, so quietly she only heard the sibilant 's'.

'It's all right.'

'So Peg worked even when you were small?'

Was she making him so uncomfortable he had to keep on with this dull talk? She reached out and touched him lightly on the shoulder, gave him an encouraging smile. What was he really thinking about?

'So you've had a lot of freedom?' he said, very quickly then, in a monotone.

'No, Peg was . . .' Ah, she thought, so this is it. 'She kept an eye on me.'

'You've done all right, kid. Don't go making the same mistake I did. Getting married and all that rubbish.'

'I do want to get married one day.' Nola heard her voice ring out, innocent as a schoolgirl.

Bernie laughed and lifted the bottle to his lips, his gold tooth flashing in the moonlight. Probably lost the real one in a fight. She felt a little tremor run through her, warm in her belly and making her legs feel restless.

'Not for ages, though. I want to travel. I want to see the world. Do you?'

She reached for the bottle and he leaned forward with it, but he kept hold and waited for her to kiss him, which she did, and he her, just as she wanted him to. His mouth was firm and warm — he tasted a little of beer, but more of exertion and contentment, a sweet musky scent. Maybe that was what aftershave tried unsuccessfully to mimic, she thought, never quite achieving the right chemical balance. She supposed it had to do with hormones, or genes, or maybe even peace of mind, and while he kissed her she imagined beakers full of distillations of a smell as delicious as Bernie's, whereas men like dreary old pontificating Don had to pour on cologne by the gallon . . .

Bernie's hand slipped up her thigh, his tongue was in her mouth and she saw it in a flash of a cross-section: his tongue, her teeth, her own tongue entwining . . . She suppressed it and felt instead how the soft spikes at the back of his head prickled her hand, and under his kneading palm one breast felt as if it would burst into flame: the nipple ached, hard into the stiff cotton of her bra. He held her now at her waist with his good arm, moving the rest of his body towards her, his flat hand against the warm skin of her back.

'Dad?' The boy was at the cabin door. She felt Bernie die away from her — a brief flare of resentment, then he turned to face the child.

Brett had lit the stump of a candle and was carrying it, the other hand clutching his blanket, which he'd unpinned. He must have been awake for some time, moving about in the cabin, and they hadn't heard him. Had he heard them? Nola felt ill suddenly. He might have been sitting there for a minute or two. What if he told some of his mates at school, what if it got back and all around the school . . .

'What's the matter, fella?'

'Can't sleep.'

'Why not?'

'Too hard on the bunk. I want to go home.'

Bernie sighed and took the candle from him, blowing it out before he hooked an arm around the child, pulling him in close.

'No, you don't,' he said. 'I'll tuck you back in.'

But the boy shook his head, into Bernie's side. 'Want to go home,' he said again, more sullenly. He yawned, wide enough to show his fillings. He looked better than he had the last time she'd seen him at school — more flesh on his bones.

'What about our fishing tomorrow morning?' Bernie asked.

The boy shook his head again, more violently than he had the last time, and Nola stood up, made a show of brushing down her skirt.

'You could take us both home,' she suggested. 'It's time I went.'

'Get your stuff,' said Bernie then, and the boy went below deck. 'Misses his mother. Comes on him all of a sudden and I can't fight it.'

He took her hand and squeezed it and Nola felt his sadness blow open and close around her like a membrane. It was visceral. Her stomach dropped.

Brett's pillow and brown leather school satchel preceded him out again. Bernie untied the dinghy and rowed them in to shore.

It was three quarters of an hour back to Glenlyn — all the way across town and then the Harbour Bridge — and Bernie's face was set all the way: that angled jaw; the corners of his straight mouth slightly turned down. At his ex-wife's place a party was raging. The curtainless windows of the house were lit up, Johnny Devlin booming out of the hi-fi. Cars were parked all over the long grass, a kid's tricycle was turned upside down on the terrace and for a moment the boy seemed to lose his nerve. He paused at the end of the concrete drive, his tousled hair spiking up in silhouette, his duffel bag over his shoulder with the ragged jersey sleeve still protruding. Bernie wound down his window.

'Go in the back door and just get into bed.'

The boy took a couple of steps and stopped again.

'Go on,' said Bernie, an edge to his voice. 'I'll still come and get you first thing in the morning, eh?'

The promise gave Brett the impetus he needed and he took off then, fast, around the shadowy side of the house where the steel ribs of the Hills Hoist clothesline protruded, gloomy washing flapping, and vanished into the darkness.

Up the empty hill they drove, the houses still and quiet.

'Is that where you lived?' she asked him, 'in that place?'

'For a couple of years.'

'Why did you leave?'

'Wife went off her rocker with loneliness, I reckon. Blamed me for it. Then Kev came along.'

Perhaps he was bitter underneath it all, Nola thought. There had been adults she'd met during her childhood who had overflowed with bitterness: close, mean, hard-working men and women. She had learnt to recognise them by a taste that came into her mouth before they even opened theirs: sharp and metallic, a faint and nasty sherbet. Aunty Vi, Peg's sister, was one of them, and one or two of Peg's gentlemen friends who hadn't lasted long.

'Was it your fault?' Nola asked. 'Did you love her?'

'I dunno.'

'Why did you marry her then?'

'Ask a lot of questions, don't you?'

'You must have loved her when you married her.'

'She was karitanied. Up the spout. With Brett.'

She was blushing again. 'Sometimes men ignore their wives.'

There was that schoolgirl voice again, high and holy like a church bell.

He sighed. 'You don't know the full story.'

'Really? I'd never have guessed, but then I stop men fighting outside my place every day of the week.'

Outside the house in Universal Drive Bernie turned the engine off. Nola took one last drag on her cigarette, wound down the window and threw out the butt. It struck the metal letterbox and emitted a little shower of sparks.

'I knew Kev on the inside, banged up for burglary. He

came to find me when he got out a couple of years ago, got to know Kay. That's my wife. Day he came I wasn't home, but she was — bored out of her mind and looking for entertainment. He used to visit her during the day while I was at work.'

'You've been in jail?' That was how he'd got his nose broken. Maybe he'd stolen something. Maybe he'd done something much worse. She didn't have to see him again, not if she didn't want to.

'I was a prison warden. Mount Eden. He was doing time and he hated my guts. He's a weasel.'

'Why did he hate you?'

'They all hate the screws. And mostly we hated them.'

'How long did you do that for?' Nola asked after a moment. He'd taken the key from the ignition and was flicking and tapping it on the wheel, metal on metal.

'Eight years.'

'Why'd you leave?'

'Long story.'

'Another one. Not that the first one really told me anything.'

He was silent in response to that — it probably wasn't the way to get him to open up. She tried again. Her own father had spent a lot of time in jail, not that Nola could remember any of it: he died when she was three.

'My father was locked up during the war. He was a conchie.'

That was a mistake. The side of his body closest to her seemed to stiffen and pull away. It was like Peg said: men in uniform were all the same and prison wardens wore a uniform too; they were probably like a pretend army.

Bernie sighed, put the key back in the ignition.

'Off you go,' he said. 'I'll come and see you one night after work, if that's all right with Peg.'

He saw her hurt face in the street light as she turned away and pretended he hadn't. The lever on the passenger side was faulty — her hand pumped at it, the workings inside the door clicked and caught. He leaned across her and wrenched it back, pushing the door open. She went off without a word.

Bernie watched her go inside, then struck a match and looked at the time. After midnight. Suddenly he was feeling dog-tired. The prospect of driving all the way back to Waikowhai was un-endurable; the thought of the row out against an incoming tide made his bones ache.

At the bottom of the rise he turned left and passed through the intersection, where a petrol station was under construction. Two bowsers stood side by side like two short, fat men looking across the road to the last green fields for miles, which lay on a hillside above the new Four Square, the hardware shop and a beauty parlour. He'd park down by the school somewhere, sleep scrunched in the back seat and head up for Brett early.

Just after a new cutting in the pink clay of the hillside there was an old rough service road that led down a valley. He kept watch for it, almost missed it, spun into the tight corner with the metal chip flying, and took the car down as far as the place where the trees met overhead.

There was a morepork calling for its mate, or maybe a bite to eat. He wound down the window, leaned back and listened, his thoughts drifting. He had to find somewhere to live on land, he had to come ashore for the winter, that was final. Then he'd be able to have the kid to stay every weekend and get him away from Kev. He shouldn't have bought the bloody boat, bloody mad idea. But it'd given him something to hold on to after the marriage fell apart, after he left the prison service. He loved everything about it. He wished he was on the boat now, his radio on quiet, a beer in his hand, the candle flickering around the boards of the cabin, the gentle rock of the waves.

At the last second, when he was nearly asleep, he dragged himself up and with his last pulse of energy laid himself across the back seat — judging it just right, he told himself: he'd sleep instantly. But his eyes opened, blearily, and if he tried to close them it felt as though they were dredged with sand.

She was beautiful, that Nola Lane. You could say that about a lot of girls and still be able to find a flaw, but not her. She could have made a career out of it. He wondered for a moment why she hadn't. Because she had both: beauty and brains. You had to be pretty smart to be a dental nurse, he supposed. It must be scientific. He didn't even have his Leaving Certificate.

The old resentment welled briefly, the one that went with the memory of his father telling him it was a waste of time to stay at school, that he'd be better off out of there and working . . .

The problem was, he thought a moment later, she was so young — and sweet-natured, and too keen. And how did he know she didn't come on to all the blokes, like she had with him. She was hardly slow in coming forth. Maybe she took after her conchie father and got mad ideas. She was certainly nothing like her mother, who was a tough old bird, tough as they come. That Don must've been a sucker.

In the early hours of the morning a wind came up and whistled around the Vauxhall. The trees bent and shoved one another in the fitful moonlight until just before dawn, when the clouds moved in to cover the sky and he couldn't see them any more. It was too dark even to see his hand in front of his face. He got out of the car to have a pee and slipped into a ditch, which was dry but full of cutty-grass. Lucky he hadn't already got the old fella out, he thought to himself, clambering back up, bladder bursting. Could've done himself some real damage.

At first light he backed the car to the top of the road and turned into the cutting.

All was quiet at Prospect Road. He parked at the mouth of the driveway, beside the letterbox. The visitors from last night were gone, the ranchsliders onto the deck stood open and a stained green curtain fluttered out, billowing in the wind. A row of brown beer bottles stood in a row on a windowsill, the yellow ball of the kitchen light glowing in the ceiling behind them. Watery sun picked up the dull gleam of broken glass on the driveway. Asleep in the house would be — he listed them off — his own boy, Kay, Kev and two of Kev's girls. There were two daughters who lived with him there, in Bernie's house, and two others, younger, who'd stayed on with their mother.

He waited until seven o'clock before he started up the drive and crossed the long grass, paspallum heads whipping at his trouser-legs. Up the three concrete steps he went, across the terrace to the door, which was cheap, light, hollow veneer — and unlocked.

Under his hand it opened easily. A shadow flitted across the hallway in front of him, barefoot on the hardboard floor. It was the older girl, who accompanied Kev on his Arthur Lydiard-style milk runs. She had been there that morning, he remembered, but she'd taken off. He hoped she'd keep her mouth shut now, hoped he hadn't put the wind up her coming in the door like that.

The girl had gone left to right, into the first door — the sitting room. She was watching him from the tan vinyl couch, bulky and sad in her flowered baby-doll pyjamas. Bernie nodded at her.

'Brett asleep?' he whispered.

She shrugged and looked up into the far corner of the ceiling, above his head. He continued on, treading slowly and carefully, to the room at the end of the hall. The kitchen light lit his way; there were no obstructions. Perhaps the party hadn't ended so late that Kay was too off her trolley to tidy up.

The girl was following him; he could hear her rubbery, arrhythmic tread. He stepped into Brett's room, quickly now. What the hell was he doing? He shouldn't be here; this was a bad idea.

The girl had stopped in the doorway, her face pushed forward, a pugnacious set to her shoulders.

'Go away,' she said loudly. 'You shouldn't be inside our house.'

Brett rolled over, pulling his pillow down over his head, the lumpy, kapok little mate that accompanied him on his nights with his father. There was the sound of something shifting in the next room, a bed — or was it a pair of feet hitting the floor?

'Brett.' He bent to his son, shook his shoulder. 'Wake up and I'll take you down to the boat — I'm on my way now.'

'You shouldn't've come right into our house you didn't even knock at the door you just came right in —' The girl again, rapid, monotone, high-pitched.

'I'm going now,' he told her. While he spoke he bent down and lifted the boy into his arms, straightening with him over his shoulder. Immediately the boy struggled and stiffened his body, slipping down to stand on the floor.

Kev. He was there, behind the girl, now pushing her to one side. In the grey light of the net-curtained window he looked half asleep, his weatherbeaten skin crumpling around his bleary eyes. Back-lit by the open kitchen door, his wiry hair stuck up in two tufts like the ears of a bewildered and none-too-bright animal. There was no way to get past him.

'Sorry, mate,' Bernie tried. 'Didn't want to disturb you.'

'Get out of here.' Kev didn't move.

'Leaving now — be right out of your way.' With his left arm Bernie scooped Brett around behind him, so that they could pass in single file through the narrow gap between the chest of drawers and bed. When Kev didn't shift from the doorway he kept coming, collecting his shoulder on the way through. Balling it as he raised it, Kev brought his right hand around and connected it with Bernie's closest ear. The girl was screaming and Bernie was aware, as he planted his fists into the small of Kev's back — a double punch to the kidneys — of Brett leaping into the doorway and slithering past them, liquid, quick, and vanishing away out through the kitchen and the back door. The men thumped each other back and forth on the opposing walls, denting the particle-board, Bernie holding Kev steady now, pinioning his arms and swinging him around up the hall towards the front door. At the brink of the living room Kev gave a great lunge against him, heaving him off balance, forcing him backwards: he caught his heel in the body-carpet, which had lifted at the door and nearly fell — but saved himself. And kept his grip on Kev, who he knew would try that trick he'd tried on Seddon Crescent: he'd hook one ankle around his and pull his leg out from under him. Kev liked to run, from the new subdivision down to the Harbour Bridge approach at Sulphur Bay and back again, hill work and speed work, up hill and down dale. He'd surprised Bernie with his strength — maybe Lydiard was on to something.

Someone else, taller — Kay — had come into the room. The couch loomed in the soupy light, was eclipsed by the green curtain, revealed again. He flung Kev into it, spun, and ran for the sliders. Which end were they open at? His fingers plunged through the billowing fabric and struck glass — he flung it back, knew Kev was coming at him again from behind and stepped out across the terrace, hurdling the wrought-iron railing, catching his still bruised shin and heading for his car, where he could see Brett sitting up waiting for him in the passenger seat.

The kid had locked the doors, which showed foresight but also created a delay. On the other side of the smeary glass he was fumbling and pulling at the chrome knobs, shooting anxious glances at his father. Kev's footsteps were thundering behind him; he caught up and grabbed him by the back of the collar. Bernie tried to shake him off, but it was no good. The smaller, wirier man was full of righteous indignation, expelling the invader, swearing at him, snatching at his clothes, sending one punch then another to the back of Bernie's head. Something snapped in Bernie's chest: a fine nexus of self-control. He recognised the sensation — that happened first, then there was the one that always followed — here it came, the ground bucking under his feet, flinging him around to face his assailant. There was a distant roaring in his ears, as if someone had parked a cage-load of lions out on the road, and he swung into Kev, a heavy, fast roundhouse, catching him in the side of the jaw. There was the crack of bone on bone, a tearing in

Bernie's afflicted shoulder, and he paused long enough to see Kev fall to the long grass, face down among the clods of clay and dandelions and paspallum.

He turned back to the car, limping again, cradling his shoulder, and drove away.

Tamara is setting the table for our dinner while I stir the pots. There are only two, but the lids rattle fiercely enough, as satisfyingly as Peg's did.

Condensation has formed on the windows above the bench, fogging my view over the darkening, narrow Grafton street. The steeply pitched gables of the houses opposite have blurred edges, wavery in the rain. It's like a child's drawing, like a drunken memory, less real and defined than my impression of Bernie finally making it inside the car, cupping his hand once around the back of his son's head in a rough gesture of affection that the child could have seen as punishment, before he threw the car into reverse and swung the wheel.

Every step of the way. During the long years of Carl's early childhood there was plenty of time to identify them all — each step that led me to him — and most of them were taken by his father.

'Didn't anybody ring the nabs?' Tamara asks.

'Yes, of course,' I answer. 'That's what the ex-wife was doing. She was inside, on the phone.'

'And the fat Little Eva?'

Interesting that Karen's fleshiness is how stick-insect Tamara defines her, not the baby-doll pyjamas or her bellowing in the dark bedroom.

'She was still bellowing from the terrace.'

Tamara is quiet for a moment, thinking.

'Still worried you're rhyming it up,' she says eventually. 'You can't know what went down inside every conk.'

'No, of course not.'

'Why do you pretend to, then?'

'To do them all justice. I might not have everything right, but close enough. And in the end it'll mean the same thing — it's only a story about something that happened over forty years ago. No matter how I tell it, it'll have the same ending.'

'Carl,' says Tamara, softly.

'Yes,' I say carefully. 'I'll give you his beginning, and then you can tell me his ending. In exchange.'

Tamara's face clouds, her brows draw together. One eyelid flickers. Roughly, she draws a chair out from the table and thumps herself down into it, rigid and silent.

'Let's eat.' I bring the food over.

There are three chairs around the table, all mismatched. Peg's old mahogany carver, with its cracked leather seat, was Carl's chair. Nobody has sat in it since he died. Tamara's is red and chrome, a short-legged version of the stool in my old clinic. Mine is scarred wood with a tatty cushion, rescued from a streetside pile of discarded furniture. I have never wanted things matching — not cutlery, furnishings or even clothes — which is just as well. Fortune-tellers and musicians don't make a lot of money.

'Here's yours.' I put a serving of pasta in front of her. She feels for her fork and spoon and the edge of the bowl. It's shell pasta and tomato sauce — the first because lengths of spaghetti are difficult for her to manage, the second because Tamara is vegetarian. She eats fast and hungrily for a few moments, then slows down almost to a standstill, as is her pattern. If she ate in a more measured way she might put on a bit of weight; I'm sure she swallows a lot of air eating like that. At least her body has softened with the business of eating: she's managed to force her mind away from what I said a few minutes ago. She's thinking about something else, not the night that Carl died.

'Who's Arthur Lydiard?' she asks now, with her mouth full.

'He invented jogging.'

'Invented it? For the whole fuckin' world?'

'That's right. He travelled about, spreading the word —'

'You New Zealanders!' she splutters, spraying red sauce. 'You folks think you invented fuckin' everything. You invented hardly anything. Crazy. Rutherford Syndrome, Carl used to call it.'

'Are we still like that? I think we used to be. Not so much now.'

'Your generation, then.' She takes another tiny mouthful, chews. 'You creakers.'

'Well . . .' I pour some wine — into a stemmed glass for me and a shot glass for her, shot glasses being less likely to meet with accident, as Carl discovered early in his drinking life.

'Actually he did. He made jogging world famous. And nobody remembers now. There are lots of people who should be remembered and aren't. Like Judi Ford.'

'Who?' She sniffs the air. 'Mayonnaise.'

'You see?' I push the bowl towards her, lay her hand on it.

'Not the salad,' says Tamara, who makes a point of never eating anything that hasn't been dead for long enough to get into a tin or a packet, 'just the mayo.' She finds the jar herself, her fingers crabbing across the table and finding on the way a spoon.

'Miss America 1969,' I go on, not watching her. 'Instead

of giving the judges of the Talent Section a sweet tune on her violin or playing the piano or dancing, she did tricks on her trampoline. She smoked and spoke her mind. She was my heroine — I wished I'd been brave enough to do that.'

'She did all those things at the same time?' she asks, licking mayonnaise from her lips. 'Now, that would be something.'

I sip my wine, watch her eating mayonnaise like soup.

'Don't eat too much of that, honey, it'll make you sick.'

Tamara ignores me.

'Anyway,' I conclude, 'she's forgotten.'

Tamara does her expressive who-cares shrug, which is more extreme than it would be on a sighted person. Her right shoulder almost touches her ear.

'Why you remember all that boot-snitch? What's the point?'

'Because I was a beauty contestant myself. Once or twice.'

Tamara isn't interested in this. A sighted young woman might remark now on how frightening it is to witness evidence that beauty may fade and disappear; she might well lean over the table to discern under the bags and lines the youthful cheekbones that could have brought me brief fame and fortune. Instead, Tamara pushes the mayo away, eats another single shell.

'So. Getting back to Bernie. You haven't even let him do the do, so far.'

'No.'

'So why not? You could've, in your little clinic, in your little tooth-booth on the hill. Didn't you say it had a bed?'

'I would never have done any such thing,' I tell her. 'You dreadful girl.'

'I would've.' She pincers up a slice of cheese between two fingers.

'No doubt,' I reply, and she sniggers. Carl used to say she had the dirtiest laugh in the business. It was a grubby little beast, he said: it was a tough, dusty little bird rolling in the dust, physically manifest, a living creature.

Tamara eats her slice of thickly buttered white bread, her upper lip glossed with fat. Before she met my son (if she is to be believed) she put herself about, never worrying about AIDS or herpes or any of the myriad other diseases, and her blindness certainly didn't stop her. At the most inappropriate moments she would pipe up with details of past lovers' prowess, or otherwise, and Carl mostly seemed to join her in spirit and find it as amusing or as interesting as she did, especially if the details were about the Australian who'd taken her to Sydney: the man she was with when my son met her and wooed her away. Neither of them saw anything unseemly in the analyses of the man's technique, or lack of it.

'Different men used to say how crazy zanzy I was,' Tamara said once, soon after I met her for the first time, 'considering I never saw a flesh film. They said I blew fire.'

I would wonder sometimes if she was telling the truth. Her hands are conical, long, and the Liar's Fork opens at her palm edge like crocodile jaws — although the sensualist's Girdle of Venus swings deep and unbroken between her first and fourth fingers: the sign of the erotic artist.

'Nah,' she says. 'Maybe you wouldn't've turned it up then, old girl, when you were young. Later on you got out more.'

I wasn't a patch on Peg, I could tell her. Even when I came close I was far more discreet. My mother was a wild twenties girl; my mother who never lost her love of people or instinct for a party. In her sixties she still lit up the room.

I miss her terribly, but not as much as I miss my son,

whose shape still fills his chair at the end of the table, whose clothes still hang in the wardrobe in the other room, whose girlfriend sits across the table from me, all urge to make conversation evaporated with the last of the steam from the pasta.

The shot glass is upended into Tamara's wide, saxophonist's mouth, the last drops shaken free.

'So when did you, then? When did you become lovers?' She rattles the glass on the table for more wine.

'It didn't happen straight away,' I tell her, pouring out. 'There was a time lag of about a day and a half before the police came looking for him. I can only think now, looking back, that communication between Bernie and his ex-wife was so sparse that she had no idea where he lived. Brett must never have told her exactly where *Ngaire* was moored. And the police might've had difficulty finding him — even with only a quarter of today's population people could be hard to locate. There weren't the records kept. Brett wasn't at school on Monday, so Bernie must've had an inkling of what he'd actually done.'

'So what did he do?' Tamara is digging into the pockets of her baggy pants, pulling out a little metal pipe and a tin.

'He took off. Stole a truck, made the journey across the high-sided strip of the Harbour Bridge, past the sheds and rubble at the foot of the St Mary's Bay cliffs, through the city, along Great South Road to the easternmost point of the other harbour.'

'The other harbour . . .' repeats Tamara, packing her pipe. 'Think I would've known what this city was built on, even if nobody had ever pitched it to me. Which they didn't, not for ages. How it kind of roosts on this little narrow perch of land with the big moists on either side, how the air mostly doesn't smell like land air. And there's always gulls crying. Weather changes every ten minutes — may as well be on a boat, at sea.'

'May as well,' I agree, watching her set the tiny bowl of the pipe aglow, and the great heave of her skinny chest as she sucks in the smoke.

'Go on then,' she says, exhaling, 'spin it on.'

CHAPTER THREE

The keys to the truck hung in the hut the company had dumped at the top of the job, back when they started it in the spring of last year. They weren't in a cupboard, just hanging on a cup hook — but the hut door was locked. Bernie took off his shirt, wrapped it around his fist and smashed the little window. It was just big enough for Brett to get through, to clamber onto the desk thick with the foreman's dusty papers and slide onto the floor, sending a tin mug clattering. Peering into the gloom after him, Bernie saw the thin shape of the boy's hand reach for the dull glint of metal high on the wall.

'Next one along,' he hissed, in a whisper harsh enough to sound his vocal cords in a broken squeak. Where the watchman? Lazy bastard hadn't shown up yet — lucky for them.

The boy was up on the desk again.

'Careful. Get back a bit.' He smashed the last of the glass

from around the inside of the wooden frame and the boy climbed through.

She took a bit of starting, the one-ton truck with the winch and flat tray on the back, but he got her going eventually, thumping the square black pedal with a horse's kick, forcing clouds of blue diesel smoke into the still morning air. Across the valley, above the school, the windows of Nola's clinic caught the light — for a moment he thought he saw her standing over the chair, but it was the shape of her machinery, the new drill Brett reckoned didn't hurt as much. From this distance it could have been a bowed head.

At the top of the subdivision they passed the beginning of the service road into the bush, where he'd spent the night and hidden the car, on the other side of the clay cutting in an old dry creek-bed.

'What are you doing?' the boy kept asking. He was frightened now — and wouldn't've been, Bernie thought, if he'd answered his questions instead of snarling at him to shut up.

They'd been on their way over to the boat, halfway down Onewa Road before he'd swung the car around back towards Glenlyn to get the truck. He'd covered the car with bracken and fern, cutting his already lacerated hand on the fibrous stems.

'Where are we going?' the boy kept asking. 'What are you doing, Dad?'

He'd grabbed his arm, harder than was necessary, told him to hurry up, dragging him up out of the bush back onto the dirt road. There he'd picked him up, wrenched shoulder screaming, and hurried across country to the dip in the hill, where the hut was, where they'd got hold of the keys.

Now the truck climbed the lift of the Harbour Bridge, banging and clattering.

'Why won't you tell me what we're doing?' The boy wasn't looking at him. He'd leant his head back, looking ahead from under lowered lids.

Bernie looked back to the road, and what he'd seen reflected in his side mirror as he'd driven away from his ex-wife's superimposed itself over the grey rise: the lumbering daughter in her pink pyjamas hurrying across the lumpy lawn to her father, who lay face down, unmoving, and who Bernie knew had been the reason his front wheels had lifted as he'd backed the car out, swinging its nose around to clear the white letterbox on its rusting pole.

'We're taking the truck to Otahu. Find somewhere to leave it.'

'Why?'

Because I think I killed the bastard, Bernie thought, but didn't say.

He stayed on Great South Road until the hulking sheds of the Westfield Freezing Works came up on his right. Through the half-open truck window came the smell of blood and shit, the brown, bad-sausage stink of animals herded together, the smell that clung to his father's shirt. He used to bring that stink home with him from his place on the line at the Works and it would stick to him even after he'd lain in the narrow clawfoot bath in the wash-house. The prison had smelt something like that — it'd taken him a while to make the connection, when he'd first scented it at Mount Eden. Fear and rage.

This was familiar territory: Bernie had grown up not far from here, on Portage Road. Mount Richmond's grey water-tower rose up now on his left, a concrete structure on the low, green volcanic mound he'd played on as a boy. It had been good as a fort in games that were mostly inspired by stories his father told him. Later he'd heard stories about men who came home from the war and kept silent, but not his father. He was a talker. Didn't this morning's idea for the fern-covered car come from one of his yarns about a camouflaged tank somewhere swampy on the Malay Peninsula? The name of the place was gone, but not the tone of his father's voice as he yarned on, slightly boastful, slightly regretful.

Regretful, Bernie saw now — not for what he'd done but for the time passed. After he came home from the war he was a knife-hand at the Works for over thirty years.

'Used to play in there when I was a kid.' He gestured with his left hand towards the domain and Brett turned obligingly to look as the truck swung right, at the corner of the Works. I'm the opposite to the old man, Bernie thought: I hardly talk to my son at all. He waited, mostly, for the child to talk to him, which he did on the rare occasion: usually on the boat, when they were fishing. The concentrated fiddle with hooks and bait, knives and reels and rods, the busy strong little fingers seemed to start him up talking — on and on he'd go then, about Kevin and Kay and Karen and Jackie, and the dental nurse. She'd entered the picture a year ago when she started at the school and straight away turned her attention to his little black choppers, one of them right in the front. Brett must have been one of her main customers for quite a while.

At the bottom of Portage Road were the railway lines, and beyond them the mangroves slumped in the mud. This was the flattened, eastern extreme of the Manukau Harbour, the Mangere Inlet. The wide, shallow water had a yellowish tinge, as if it had seeped up through the silt rather than come in from the ocean, through the faraway heads. He swung the truck right again, into an access road that ran between the works and the railway.

As the crow flew his boat was maybe a mile and a half away across the harbour — but he wasn't Jesus, was he? He couldn't walk it.

The truck moved away, crossing the lines, which knocked her around a bit. High on the skyline on his right thrust the stone prick on One Tree Hill. There was bad weather coming in from the north-west: the pink gave way to grey, to deeper shades and black, clouds so dense they lent their shape to the southernmost of the Waitaks, making them appear nearer and bigger.

He parked as close as he dared to the edge of the solid ground, edging the truck back and forth, lurching and graunching, until it was in the right place, allowing for the tide. It would stick out a mile to anyone looking for it, he realised. The cab and tray boards were bright yellow.

'Hop it. Out,' he said to Brett, who already had his hand on the lever, the door opening, ready to jump down. Bernie went after him, standing with his hands on his hips and gazing over the flat expanse to Mangere Bridge. This was where the plan fell down, if it was a plan. It was the void in an idea that had only had a beginning and an end. He didn't feel hurried or panicked, but neither did any answers suggest themselves. He felt heavy, his brain turned to clag. The boy was pointing.

'There's a car, on the Mangere Bridge. See the glint?'

There was no way the boy could make it the whole way around the northern edge of the inlet, even if it were possible. After the freezing works the coastline dipped into a rancid bay, before spreading itself west again around Pikes Point and the Waikaraka Cemetery. It was rough going: swamp and rock, heavy mud . . .

A boat. If they went the other way, left instead of right,

back along the railway line, past the chemical works to Favona Road, they could get hold of one of the dinghies pulled up on the dry.

Brett watched his father, who was no longer looking in the direction he'd pointed, but away to their left. Then, so suddenly he made him jump, Bernie grabbed up his hand and strode away in that direction.

'We'll find a place for you to wait for me,' he told him. 'I'm going to borrow a boat and row us across.'

The nearer they got to the chemical works, the huge dull roofs spreading in the late summer sun, the ranker grew the air. The meat smell was behind them now. This smell reminded Brett of the dental clinic, of rubber and turps. He felt it form a rough-edged ball in his throat. His father was jogging now, towing him past the factory, clambering down off the dusty wasteland that surrounded it to the mud of a small, dirty cove.

'Do you think she's on the turn?' his father muttered to himself, and the boy thought 'Who?', realising, a little while later when they regained solid ground on the other side, that he was talking about the tide.

'Up there —' his father was gesturing. 'Go out to the end of the point and wait for me.'

'Why?' It came out dangerously like a whine. His father's eyes narrowed.

'Because I've got to get across the next creek. I'll come back, don't worry.'

There were tall thistles that scratched at his bare legs below his drill shorts, which were pretty dirty, he noticed now, as his father headed off in his funny new limpy way. Nobody must come here, thought Brett, that's why there's no track. There was a broken beer bottle that looked as though it had been thrown here from far above, out of an aeroplane maybe. It was sort of exploded. He picked up the biggest glinting brown shard and slipped it into his pocket: he might need it later, he thought, to help fight whoever it was who was chasing Dad.

When he got to the end of the land, past the thistles, he could see an island with nibbled edges like a biscuit, like a big Round Wine. Brett could see himself out there on it, brave and alone, pitching his pup tent between the two stubby, wind-bent trees. Maybe he could swim out there. It wasn't far. Only then his father might not find him, and he would have to live there for the rest of his life, off seagull eggs and maybe periwinkles or cats-eyes or the crabs that made the little holes in the mud. Experimentally, he splodged out a little way, the mud seeping up as high as his ankles. The wind was making silvery ripples on the water's skin; tiny waves fanned towards him. He watched intently: did they come a little closer each time? Taking the piece of glass from his pocket, he squatted down and drew some lines in the mud. If he had a watch he could time how long it took for each line to become submerged. He counted instead — one Mississippi, two Mississippi, three — Dad was right. The tide was coming in.

An oar splash had him raise his head. His father was rowing towards him.

Tamara wants me to help her with her hair, setting it in cornrows and tying it up on the top of her head.

I'm so good at this now — I've done it so many times — and I relish the feel of it under my hands: crisp, strong African hair, still exotic for me. I never even met an African until my second career took off — reading passengers' palms on cruise ships. On the *Mariana* one of the stewards was from Ghana. We crewed together for years, Joe and I. And there were a few Afro-American passengers — usually famous or well-to-do. Once, Paul Robeson, towards the end of his life.

'Carl liked to play with my hair,' Tamara breathes, leaning back. 'He used to twist it into all kinds of shapes.'

'I remember.'

I remember Tamara straight-backed on the kitchen stool, shoulders squared, while Carl's hands twisted, pulled and shaped; his intent, working face above set away from it, often drawn up towards the lightbulb if it was night-time. I have him so clearly for a moment: the square tilt of his chin; his full, expressive mouth; the glistening light on his broad, fair brow. You would think from the unerring way he set his face into the glare that he still had some sense of it, but he didn't. Carl lived entirely in the dark. When he first started tipping his face to the light, when he was about four and his sight was almost gone, I would reprimand him: he would twist his body around so far, his shoulders following his head, that he almost looked deformed.

'Keep still,' I tell her, 'or I'll go crooked.'

'I wasn't allowed to touch it till he'd finished,' Tamara goes on. 'Then I'd feel it all over, crazy coo-yon hair.'

'I'm just doing exactly what you told me,' I say. 'Exactly. Like the one I described to you from the magazine.'

'Not Bulla braids.'

'Not them, no. A change.'

I'm not a natural at this, and neither am I as gung-ho as my boy was. I'm too slow and careful.

'Tip your head to one side,' I ask her, gently inclining her over her left shoulder. I begin to divide the rows that will rise diagonally from above her right ear, across the crown of her skull and down the other side to arrive woven into the back, in a kind of exploded chignon of attenuated, tasselled plaits. It will take me about three hours and half kill me, but Tamara needs her hair done and is refusing to go to any of the African salons on Karangahape Road. She's worried she'll hit a wave of grief broadside and lose it, sobbing for Carl in front of the cool sheen of mirror. She'll know the mirror by the way the air cools just before it, chilled by the cruel glass that would reflect her contorted, weeping, blind face to anyone who cared to look and cop it many times over, reflected into infinity.

'Uh-huh.' She's quiet for a while then, making only little fluttery grunts of pleasure in her throat: she's enjoying her pampering and touching. The scarred side of her face twists suddenly into a grimace and I think for a moment that I've hurt her — but it isn't pain, it's pleasure too, an intense expression of it.

'So, old girl?' she says.

It's a prompt. She wants me to go on with my story about the injured man and the brave, bewildered boy in the battered dinghy on Mangere Inlet, rowing the long distance on that late summer Sunday to Waikowhai. It's become as much my story as if I were really there, so often I've imagined it, fleshing it out from the bones Brett gave me later. To avoid the fierce currents in the channel his father had pulled close to the coast, switching from the south side to the north when they reached the bridge. If ever Bernie lifted the oars to rest, the boat would begin to drift with the tide and they'd lose ground swiftly. I imagine the superhuman effort it cost him to pull against his wrenched shoulder, to brace his bruised feet in the bottom of the boat against the push of the tide — and that slightly younger, less defeated face, the hard, persevering set of his mouth.

At Onehunga Wharf he left the boy on the steps, holding onto the dinghy, while he went up to the office to make a phone call. It was another risk he took: later, much later, one of the watchmen identified him as being the man who had limped past him, his right hand cushioning his left shoulder against the jar of his stride.

The braiding, the winding of it all together.

What could Peg have been thinking of to condone my relationship with him? As it has done for years, this question comes to me suddenly, with a rush of wounded indignation, a protective arm extending in a flash around my trusting, naïve, twenty-year-old self. Couldn't Peg see how dark his heart was, how harsh the light that bathed his world? Since I lost them both, I have decided that either she didn't bother to look at him that closely (or she would have seen it, surely) or she was carrying her resolve not to judge her fellow man too far, into the realms of risking her daughter. She did risk her daughter. She risked me. Peg, who'd been married to a conchie during the war and suffered the judgement of every bigot around, who made her living reading palms in a coffee bar through the fifties, had made a resolution of iron never to negatively judge another living soul. And neither did she. Even after everything happened and we were back on land, she extended to the now absent Bernie the same warmth and generosity that she extended to any stranger. Strangers were treated to her apparent lively curiosity and party spirit more readily than the people closest to her: it was just a kind of disinterested good humour.

'After we've done your hair, shall we go for a drive?'

'Where?'

'Down to the water.'

'Will the car start?'

'With luck.'

'You'll be hours yet, anyway.' One narrow hand lifts from her lap to feel how far I've got. Open on the coffee table is the magazine with the picture I'm copying.

'Tip forward a bit.' I need gravity to help me.

The girl in the picture is a beauty: high cheekbones, a proud nose and heavily lidded eyes, Hollywood's idea of a Zulu princess. My Tamara, with her sightless, sunken and lop-sided gaze, her slightly protruding lower lip and acne-pocked complexion, would be a challenge for the camera and a candidate for Photoshop. I wonder if she knows what she looks like, if anyone was ever hard-hearted enough to explain? It's not that she's ugly — she isn't at all — but Lord, she's plain. That American word 'homely' — a word that for some mysterious reason has not travelled, that hasn't been co-opted by the rest of the America-worshipping world — perhaps 'homely' is the word she might have overheard to describe her.

Her face, reflected up to me by the mirror I've leaned against the phone books, is smiling now, a muscular rictus displaying her long and uncared-for teeth. When I met her for the first time I read her mouth and saw her propensity for melancholy writ large. Time and time again I've seen it: the long incisor and the depressive personality. Until she met me she hardly cleaned them at all; I nag her about the toothbrush and tell her she's lucky she's not a middle-aged New Zealander. If she'd been born and raised here, her teeth would be weakened by great plugs of twenty-year-old amalgam — her young adult teeth would have been hollowed, aggressively drilled. Nobody seems to thank us nurses for it, though we were doing our best with our inadequate training. We were acting in good faith; we believed we were doing good: the poor would have teeth as strong and white as the rich did — how often I've had to remind people of these plaintive truths.

My hands ache.

'Next time, you go to the salon,' I tell her.

'Costs two hundred dollars,' she responds.

'You'll be home in America by the time it needs doing again.'

Tamara makes no reply to this. Perhaps she doesn't want to go home, perhaps she thinks she has to, that she has no choice.

Such strong hair, I think, beginning another plait. I'm working now on the strands that escape from the knot on top of her head, the excess of the cornrows. So far, so good — it looks almost professional. After running his hands carefully over her head, Carl would have been impressed.

It's true, she has no choice: she does have to go back to the States — she has no visa. Soon, the immigration people will be after her. Her disability renders her an undesirable resident, an alien — even though she has never yet been in receipt of a benefit, and Carl never made her a New Zealander by marrying her. Perhaps he should have married her . . . if he could have thought ahead to what would happen, maybe he would have.

But Carl's way of dying left no time for forethought.

'Does it cost two hundred dollars in Chicago? To have your hair plaited?'

'Braided. Dunno. Around that. Haven't been home for a long while. Nearly ten years. How would I know?' She's sounding ratty.

'Let's have some music,' she says. 'I want that old Miles Davis.'

Pulling away from me, she makes unerringly for her target. Her fingers coast over the cases in the CD tower: she recognises *Kind of Blue* by the chip out of the corner. I never thought I would tire of Miles, but I'm beginning to. We've had him every day since Carl died.

The CD clicks in and the first long, plangent, heart-twisting tones fill the room. Her face soulful and sad, Tamara returns to where she was before, sitting on the floor between my knees, me on the sofa behind her. I take up her hair again, working the last of the rows at the front, tipping her face up to me.

I'm glad she chose music, and not the story, because I have to think carefully about the next part. There are a number of ways I could tell it, a variety of events I could emphasise. It is a little like how I deal with clients who come to have their hands read when their lives are already in a state of flux, who already suspect my reading won't be all good. Hand-readers these days do not bother much with the Liver Line, but Peg always did and so do I: many secrets are revealed there. On the ships I found that cruising attracted older people who very often suffered terribly from the change in diet and an always available supply of alcohol. I enjoyed being able to reassure them the line was distinct and long — even if it was not, particularly.

'Did Carl tell you about Brett?'

'This and that. Not much. Said his father didn't like to talk about him,' Tamara tells me, and I know the way is clear. 'Go on,' she says, 'slay me.'

CHAPTER FOUR

On Monday afternoon Miss Kipps brought her the note. It was raining — a steady, gentle downpour with no wind — and a soft, steely grey light made all the reds and silvers of the clinic glow: the nurse's red cardigan, the shiny clinic phone, all the metal hand-tools and drill bits. The child in the seat seemed lulled by the rain; a stolid Dalmatian girl whose dreaming brown eyes betrayed either a high pain threshold or thick enamel. Nola hunched over her mouth, picking and sticking into the tiny moonscape of the back right six-year-old molar, not altogether sure if there was decay or just a rough edge on one of the cusps. Whichever, the more she picked and poked, the more the point of the explorer stuck.

It happened all the time in a single-operator clinic, Nola thought desperately, especially to nurses like herself who had come straight from Training School to being on their own at the edge of town or in the country. She was better at excavating and filling, carrying out the actual treatment, than at the diagnosis. Word for word she remembered the ominous instruction from the textbook: *The mere jamming of an explorer tip is not indicative of caries*, and, further on: *A child readily senses indecision or lack of assurance and the usual result is less co-operation or a liberal display of protest.*

The girl needed to swallow.

'Sit up and rinse out, Eva,' said Nola. She'd have one more pick about, then make a decision to fill it or not.

The rain hissed on the roof and the hot asphalt outside. From the mown football field at the bottom of the bank came the scent of grassheads and pollen, which slid warm and spicy through the open window to mix with the sharp, cold smell of methylated spirit. The wall clock ticked and all sound from the main building was muffled by the rain. It was quiet even over at the subdivision, because the men had moved over to the other side of the hill, where a fire had been lit. Moist clouds of smoke rolled, furred like lint or felt, over the line of macrocarpa, and evaporated.

Like dandelion spores, thought Nola, watching, while the child in the chair made gurgling noises and spat pink foam.

'Ow,' said the girl suddenly, clutching her jaw, the side the nurse had been poking.

A patient who simulates pain must be detected early and reprimand should be immediate and emphatic, tolled the textbook in Nola's mind. Some days it was as if her brain fell open on certain pages and she could picture the actual typescript. Other days she went more on instinct — because she did have a feeling for them, she considered: for children and for teeth. She was certainly far better suited than Peg could ever have been.

'One more look,' she told the little girl. 'If there's a

filling you can come back tomorrow.'

The outer door of the clinic opened and closed; snappy high heels made short, quick steps across the waiting-room floor and there was a fierce knock at about child height. Only one person heralded her arrival like that: Miss Kipps, the school secretary. The new switchboard, recently acquired, could easily transfer messages from office to clinic, but Miss Kipps welcomed any chance to stride up the hill on her sinewy little ex-dancer's legs, a bright spot of colour in one of her several home-made Chanel-style suits.

Here she was with her umbrella, all five foot two of her, a golden beehive-do giving her at least four of those inches. She handed Nola a piece of paper.

Had to move the Ngaire *earlier than expected. See you 4 o'clock.*

'The woman who left it said she was a friend of a friend, and that you'd know who it was,' said Miss Kipps. 'Wouldn't leave her name. Said the man who left the message had rung her on Sunday and asked her to ring it through to the school this morning.' Behind her glasses, Miss Kipps' eyes were a milky, wall-blind blue — they reminded her of Mao, Peg's Siamese.

The thick, dark eye-liner Miss Kipps still favoured meandered a little over the fragile skin of the lids. She peered at Nola.

'Was that all?' Nola turned the coarse paper over.

'Said something about Wai something, but I couldn't spell it so I didn't write it down.' Miss Kipps had her own way of doing things.

'Waikowhai?'

'Perhaps. Hello dear,' she said to Eva, who smiled tremulously. A large round tear was trembling at the corner of her eye. Nola returned to her position and took up her handpiece before the child decided to play to the audience. Some of them had a liking for that.

'Thank you, Miss Kipps,' she said, taking hold of Eva's jaw and drawing it down.

'Do you know this man, then, dear?'

'Yes. I think so. Thank you, Miss Kipps.'

'Rinse out again, Eva.' The child's mouth had filled with thick saliva, viscous strings between the upper and lower molars, a curd on her tongue. It was fascinating, how saliva differed from patient to patient, in colour and consistency. She'd noted that children with thicker saliva were more prone to cavities, while those whose mouths were continuously rinsed with a more liquid, less viscous saliva were less so. She reminded herself once again to put this observation on paper, in a letter perhaps, and send it to a dentist or someone in the Ministry of Health. Or to someone who could do experiments, collect data. It was a more scientific study than tooth-reading. It could be taken seriously.

Replacing the handpiece, she bent again to the child's mouth, this time to pack it along the side with cotton-wool rolls.

Still Miss Kipps stood, smiling sweetly at the child in the chair.

'He wouldn't be Brett's father, would he?' she said suddenly.

A quick explore with the pick to see exactly where she was up to before she picked up the drill . . .

'Didn't the lady tell you who he was?' asked Nola.

'No . . . but Brett's not at school today, possibly because his stepfather's in hospital in a coma.'

The drill whirred for a few seconds, then Nola turned it

off. You could never have just stopped like that with the old treadle — it would not even have been up to speed by then.

There must have been a fight at the party.

'I must get on, Miss Kipps.' The drill whirled again.

'You know Mr McNut in Room 3 lives on their corner. He saw the ambulance go by about seven. Chap next door said there'd been a fight on the front lawn early in the morning.'

The cavity was almost fully prepared. The amalgam, freshly mixed, glinted in its glass dish.

'Whoever it was had Brett with him, in the car. Apparently.'

'Let's hope he's all right then,' said Nola, meaning Brett.

'Well, no, he's in a coma, as I say.' The school secretary was being deliberately obtuse. 'That's what Mr McNut said.'

'Right. Thank you.'

'What he said was, he wanted you to go down to that place, whatever it is, Wakwai, this afternoon. The woman left that message.'

She'd blushed, Nola knew she had. She could feel it stinging at its edges on her neck and throat. Miss Kipps noticed too, because she nodded suddenly with a little bird-like movement, taking the blush as proof of some kind — proof that she was right, that Nola had got herself tangled up with Mr Tyler, whom Miss Kipps had met once and deemed to be rather coarse. She'd ring the young woman's mother later and warn her about it, she decided.

Without looking up to watch her go, Nola heard the dry little clip of her pointed toes across the floor to the open clinic door, which she opened and then closed behind her.

Prone on the bunk in the mullety cabin, Bernie saw the alarm in his boy's face, knew without saying anything that the kid understood he was dead beat, that he had to close his eyes, that he couldn't get up, even though it was after eight and he'd usually been up for a couple of hours by now.

'Patu!' The thin voice had come from somewhere above him a few minutes later, 'Patu!' The kid was calling across the water.

Shouldn't do that, Bernie thought, and fell asleep immediately.

When he woke again, Patu was in the cockpit, stirring a battered old pot on the primus. Bernie could smell baked beans. Perched beside the camp stove, Brett's eyes were fixed hungrily on the scraping, circling spoon. Bernie tried to lift himself up, but his shoulder felt loose and fiery and stopped him. He groaned, without meaning to.

'You all right, mate?' Patu asked.

Sensing the shift in his concentration, Brett took the spoon off the old man and used it to start shovelling beans into his mouth.

'Careful, you'll burn yourself,' said Bernie, his view of the boy now eclipsed by Patu, coming towards him.

'Sit up. We'll have a look.'

'What do you know?' Bernie didn't want to move.

'Was a zambuk for Waikato for years, mate. Blokes did their shoulders in plenty of times.'

'Won't be able to fix this with a squirt of water.' But he sat up anyway, slowly, and leaned forward. Surprisingly Patu's hands were gentle: he felt them squeeze around the sore shoulder and the good one.

'Same shoulder you hurt before,' he observed.

'Same bastard as did it to me.'

'Kev?'

'Him.'

'It's only a sprain.'

The energetic pot-scraping from the galley paused for a moment.

'Listen, Patu. I need you to row ashore about four and bring someone out. You do that?'

Patu nodded. 'What's going on, mate? What've you been up to?'

'You finish those beans up top, Brett.'

There was a pause, as if the boy was considering disobeying him, but then he slid down from the cabinet, taking the pot with him. His father's lowered voice followed him up onto the deck and he listened carefully to every muffled word.

'The cops'll be looking for me on the Manukau,' he was saying. 'They won't think to come looking on the other side.' Then he described how he'd gone into the house early to get Brett, how he'd fought Kev. Patu seemed to know who Kev was, or at least he didn't enquire or say anything to interrupt the story, which went on now to the pinching of the truck and where they'd left it, and the rowing of the dinghy.

Through the story, which lasted until the beans were gone and all the sauce scooped up on a finger, there was the sound of ripping cloth. Sitting on the low roof, Brett dipped his head between his knees to look through the narrow light. It was bandages Patu was making, out of his dad's shirt, which was ripped up anyway. He'd got his dad to kneel on the floor and he was wrapping the bandages around his shoulder and back. It was as good a job as the doctor had done after the first fight, the doctor Nurse Lane had taken him to, Brett thought.

He straightened up before the men spotted him. The boat was rocking about a bit on its mooring, and it made him feel a bit sick hunched over like that; it made him feel as though the gobbled beans might be on their way up again. He picked up the pot and went to the stern to lean over and wash it out in the tide.

'We'll have to get the motor going,' said Patu, 'and take the mast down.' He came out then, passing Brett without a glance, and stepped over the stern into his dinghy.

'Where're you going, Patu?'

'Back later. You help your dad.'

But Bernie didn't want him to do anything much except sit tight until Patu came back. Brett straightened up the galley, put the pot and spoon away in the locker under the afterdeck without even having to be asked, then he went to sit beside Bernie, his head on his lap. The harbour slapped gently on the bottom of the boat; his lower ear felt hot from his dad's thigh, which seemed to be burning up on the other side of the thin cloth of his trousers, and now and then the whistle of his cool breath reached his upper cheek. He took his dad's heavy hand and laid it on his skinny chest: there was a sudden ache there, a sense that things were going to go horribly wrong, and the weight of his dad's rough, cracked palm helped, after a long while, to disperse it. He felt it seep away down the veins of his arms while he cuddled in close.

When Bernie was eighteen or nineteen his father had shown him a wartime photograph of a New Zealand nurse arriving at a field hospital in Malaya, pristine in white, bolt upright in the back of a longboat on a wide, muddy river, the jungle around her smoky, ill-defined. He thought of it now, as Patu's dinghy drew near to the mullety with Nola in the stern. He wondered why his old man had the photograph: it was something cut from a newspaper, grainy and distant. Maybe he had known the nurse, maybe he'd been sweet on her. It hadn't been possible to tell if the nurse was old or young, bravely countenanced or terrified.

Neither was it possible to tell what was going on in Nola's head as Patu rowed her out, the Prefect parked on the patch of blue metal chip above the beach. She looked up at Bernie at long last, and their eyes locked and he wished, suddenly, that he could have preserved this vision of her arriving to save him, to have it as a photograph to tuck away. He would want to capture the way the thick hair caught up at the nape of her neck shone in the late orange sun, the way her white uniform flared, the angles of the skirt tucked demurely around her knees.

He took her below, sat her beside him on a squab on the floor and told her the story: how he'd walloped Kev and driven over him; how he hadn't meant to. At first, Nola said nothing. When he tried to put his arms around her she shrugged him off.

'I didn't mean to hit him,' he repeated. 'I only went into the house to get Brett.'

She said nothing, dug into her pocket for her cigarettes, looking away from him with — what was it? Distaste? He was pretty unsavoury: a two-day beard, grime on his cheek, his hands battered and filthy. She took a hanky from her bag, licked the corner of it.

Under her dabbing hand she saw a new abrasion, across the soft flesh on the underside of his forearm — he was more in the wars than anyone she'd ever known.

Approaching from the point came the thud of a diesel engine: it sounded like a launch, or a small trawler perhaps.

Bernie stiffened, twisted around against his shoulder, grimacing, to see if he could catch sight of the approaching boat. The cops could figure this out so easily, he thought — they could have been here hours ago. Thank God he'd never told Kay where he was living. He'd hardly bloody talked to her since the day he left. He'd asked Brett, very casually, if he'd told her, and the kid reckoned he hadn't, only that the boat was parked a long way away.

'Moored,' Bernie had told him.

There was the danger they'd ask some of the blokes at work. He'd told some of them, at smoko, about the mullety, about how he'd be able to see more of his son now he was working in this neck of the woods.

The boat was still too far away to see. What if it was the cops?

'So what do you want me to do? Why did you send me that message?' She was dabbing at him again. He took the hanky off her, a limp scrap of cloth in his big hands.

'I rang you at your place and there was no answer. That's why I left the message with June.'

'What's she going to think?' asked Nola.

'Nothing. Why should she?'

Miss Kipps put two and two together, thought Nola, but not telling him.

'Need you to help. You said you knew how to sail. Your stepfather had a yacht, you said.'

'Sail where? Out through the heads? It's too dangerous. You need a big crew for a mullet boat. You don't know anything about sailing: you've hardly moved the boat since you bought it; you said that yourself. You can't do this, Bernie. You have to go to the police.'

She set her jaw at him, very nursie-ish, Bernie thought, that stern blue light in her eye.

He shook his head. 'Can't risk it. Can't risk going inside. They'd get to me, the cons that remember me.'

'You won't go inside.'

He took her hand, the one closest to him. 'I will go inside, if they get me.'

'But you didn't kill him.' She'd have to tell him what she knew and hope he didn't react badly. There was always something unpredictable about him. She took a deep breath.

'He's in a coma. It's all around the school. It was an accident.'

He digested this for a moment, quietly. She couldn't even hear him breathing.

'Could still do me for assault. Breaking and entering,' he said suddenly, quickly, and reached for her, putting his arms around her and holding her close. She could hear his heart thudding under his flannel shirt, and when she lifted her hands to his back she felt the bandages circling his shoulder.

I want you with me, he thought. I need you to be here. But he couldn't bring himself to say it.

'You're hurt.'

'Not much.' He kissed the top of her head, breathed her in.

'Where are you going?'

'Over the other side. To the Tamaki Estuary.'

'What? How?'

'Portage Road.'

'What?' She sounded bewildered.

The mullety lifted and fell suddenly, on the wake of the passing boat, which was a launch. They watched it chug by behind them through little oval portholes, its white cabin and green stripe along the Plimsoll line. In the cockpit there were two people, a man and a woman, and they weren't even looking in their direction. She watched him watch them pass, nervous.

'You decide,' he said then. 'Come or not. I can row you back in, if you want.'

When he was sad you could see his age, thought Nola: you could see he was in his mid-thirties. The skin around his jaw went soft and pliable. She wanted to knead the top of his neck and feel how soft and giving he was there, on the underside of his jaw, before shifting her hands around to the back of his neck and the tops of his shoulders, where he was hard and ungiving; where, with her hands flat on his warm flesh, she could picture the muscle red and fibrous, the tendon wound around like a white root; where, under her caressing hand, she could sense the danger in him.

She tore her eyes away from him, past him up into the hold. The long sweeps were gone, she noticed; slid away from their places along the ribs of the hull.

Now he was crossing his arms, looking off forward too and muttering, a low line of words she couldn't pick up.

'I've been good to you. I've hardly touched you.'

'That has nothing to do with this. Besides, I wanted you to touch me.'

'Wanted? Not any more?'

'Want, I mean.' She felt hot, fluttery, her face burning.

He turned, gathered her in and kissed her on her throat, knowing his prickly face would be hard and rough at her neck, his mouth at her cheeks now, her lips. She was trembling and he knew she did want him and that there was something she offered him that he'd never had in the narrow world he'd lived in with Kay of booze and barneys, and brutal sex when they were both drunk enough for it. This young woman, with her gracious spirit and her decent warm-heartedness, could save him. He heard again, though she wasn't talking, her slightly imperious, self-conscious voice.

Maybe he loved her.

The cabin darkened suddenly — Patu, bending almost double, a wrench in his hand.

'We should be getting the engine going. When did you last use it?'

'Months ago. The beginning of the summer.' He kissed her once more, a rough bite half on her mouth, half on her chin, and moved away.

'You decide. It's up to you.'

He'd left her alone in the cabin, where everything suddenly seemed significant, portentous, heartbreaking: the dented pot hanging on its hook; the fishing rod with the rusted reel; a grimy, damp towel beside her. There was a cushion at one end of the bunk with a head-shaped depression in it, and a torn strip of shirt on the floor.

Through the door she could see Patu and Bernie bent over the diesel engine, its covers off. Perhaps she should've gone home and changed — there would have been time. Time also to think about what she was about to do, and maybe not do it. As it was, she'd driven like a mad banshee all the way from Glenlyn to Blockhouse Bay, hunched over her steering wheel so tensely that her neck still ached.

Outside Bernie was reaching his good arm down into the innards of the engine. The skin on it shifted over the muscles; his face was intent, lifted towards her in the gloom of the cabin, but she didn't think he was looking at her: his gaze was un-focused, a strangely intimate look, concentrated on whatever piece of greasy metal his fingers were grappling with. Sometimes children in the clinic had the same abstracted expression while she bent over them.

A lithe, smaller figure obscured him from her for an instant, darting over to the port side of the yacht, and a face peered in at her through one of the greasy, narrow portholes.

'Brett?'

Upside down, the face grinned at her. She beckoned to him and he disappeared again, coming in by the door and flinging himself onto her lap.

'I'm glad you're here,' he said, a leg on either side of her, linking his fingers behind her neck and leaning backwards. 'I was hiding. I saw your car come down the hill.'

There was a black smear across one of his cheeks to match his father's; his breath smelt of tomato.

'I've been here ever since Dad nicked the truck. We're going to put the mullety on the back of it and drive it across to the Tamaki Estuary and sail away and live on an island. There's an island over there, much closer, I saw it, but it's too small for all of us. There wouldn't be enough to eat. We'll have to find an island on the other side.'

'What truck?'

'One of the trucks from work. It's over there.' He gestured towards the west.

'At Onehunga Port?'

The boy shook his head just as the engine choked and shuddered to life in violent vibrations that shook the timbers of the boat, making it creak and wallow from side to side. The men were moving quickly, a set of footsteps thumping away overhead to the bow to pull up the pick. Brett's face split open in a wide grin. He sprang up, taking her hand, and dragged her out onto the deck, where Patu was settling the cover down over the engine. The old man looked up and smiled for the first time since he'd collected her from the beach.

'You okay, girl?' he asked. 'You coming on this trip with us?'

'Are you?'

'Have to. I'll see you right, anyway. Can't argue with the boss.'

She nodded.

'I think I will come.'

But I wouldn't if Brett wasn't here, she wanted to add suddenly, even though that probably wasn't true. Patu nodded too, the late afternoon sun gleaming and shifting on his scalp, brown under his thinning hair. Then, as if he'd noticed her looking at his head, he scowled and pulled a knitted beanie out of his pocket and jammed it on. She'd offended his vanity.

She'd seen some clothes in the cabin the night Bernie'd rummaged around for the beer, she remembered. She found them again, in a Dominion Breweries crate. There was a pair of men's corduroys, and an old shirt. The most private place she could find to change was tucked into the corner beside the doorway and she knelt there, whipping off her uniform, slipping into the oversized shirt before tackling the trousers, rolling them up, cinching in the waist with her white uniform belt. The uniform itself she rolled up and put back in the crate. As she pushed it back under the bench with her foot there was a glint of metal: her blue badge with its 'Ut Prosim' and little coat-of-arms medallion, a crown supreme and the proud words 'State Dental Nurse'. It was a disapproving eye with all the weight of the world behind it; a world that seemed suddenly very distant.

When she came out into the light they were passing below

Hillsborough. She glanced up at the cliffs and it appeared for a moment that all the shiny new houses under their tiled roofs were peopled by everyone she'd ever known, silently and critically observing through their picture windows her departure on this foolish voyage. It was foolish.

There was Bernie up by the mast, lifting down the boom. He'd already removed the spars and gaff and laid them alongside. She climbed up beside him.

'Are you taking the mast off?'

'That's right. We've got to get under the bridge, under the centre span. It's the widest.'

'Then what?'

'We'll wait in the inlet until the tide lifts. She's got a shallow draught — we'll be able to get her up on the mud.'

'To the truck.'

'Yes.'

Nola shook her head. 'This is daft.'

'It'll work.'

'But where will we go, over there? Where do you think you'll be safe?'

'Great Barrier.' He was easing the sidestay.

'Leave that,' said Nola, 'Just ease the forestay and pull it down.'

'Why?'

'That's what you do. I did it with Don. You can leave the sidestay connected.'

Bernie laughed and tousled her hair. 'Knew you'd come in handy.'

She was blushing like a silly girl, Nola thought, though the light was fading and maybe he wouldn't notice. They worked together, lifting out the mast and laying it down.

When they reached the bridge Patu shut the engine off. The last of the sun sent spindly fingers up over the faraway Manukau Heads and the darkness under the span was deep and sudden. A car whisked by overhead: they could hear the wheels on the tarmac, the low rumble of engines. Patu and Bernie pushed the boat through, keeping the hull away from the sides. The men weren't talking to one another; even Brett had grown silent, sitting apprehensively in the cockpit, hugging his knees. In one hand he held a slab of white bread, from which he took bites now and then, chewing and undulating his neck to swallow determinedly — like a goose or a duck, thought Nola, watching him. His mouth must be dry. She found the water tank in the locker as they came out into the light and got him a cupful.

'We'll use the sweeps,' came Bernie's voice.

Out from under the bridge they glided, in the last of the Purakau Channel. The long oars were taken up, Patu and Bernie taking one each on either of the side decks, stroking the boat through the water towards Pikes Point.

'It's pulled too tight on one side.'

Tamara is pushing her fingers up under one cornrow and pulling a truly terrible face. I glance at her once and then away, stretching my aching hair-doer's fingers on the steering wheel and looking out over the Tamaki Estuary. Through the open car window comes the salty, clean air, with a hint of grass pollen from the paddocks on the other side. It surprises me that it is still rural over there, and not covered in shabby low-density housing to mirror the suburb on this side. The pumping station with its tall cylindrical towers is the only structure, further upriver.

The slipway here, at the end of Avenue Road, is a replacement of the one we finally got the mullet boat onto and down. Only a few broken timbers remain, sticking out of the mud like rotten teeth.

We sailed away, Patu, Bernie, Brett and I, upriver on a rising tide. In the truck on Portage Road Patu had suddenly started telling us how for centuries his people had used this narrow part of the isthmus to drag their canoes across, and how there had been talk for years — since white men came — of digging a canal from one side to the other. Brett had piped up.

'You could do that, Dad,' he said. 'You've got diggers at your work. We'll do it when we get back. I'll help you.'

'Let's get out of the car,' I say to Tamara, who is beginning to ruin all my hard work with her pulling and scratching.

We go arm in arm to the top of what remains of the old slipway, at the end of a patch of lumpy grass beside the boat club. It's splintered and blackened, encrusted with barnacles. I can hear a blackbird singing from a nearby garden, and there is a huge flock of oystercatchers paddling on their red legs in the shallow brown water. The afternoon is calm, placid, a rare patch of serenity in the tumult of an Auckland spring. Even Tamara has finally stopped fidgeting and is lifting her face to the new sun. Carl used to say that rain was the blind man's sun — the more wind and noise in it the better. He would go out and stand at the top of the fire escape, on our porch under its patch of pig-iron roof, to get the full benefit of a late summer, monsoon-like roar, or a scented evening fine dusting, or a downpour just before dawn. He sought out loud roofs the way a sunbather seeks out a flat rock or a deckchair.

'Did the boat get damaged?' she asks. 'All that dragging it around — only made of wood, wasn't it? Like a tree-suit.'

'What's a tree-suit?' I'm smiling — it sounds funny.

'Coffin,' she says, carelessly, and I shiver suddenly, catch my breath. She doesn't realise what she's said.

'We sat it on a pile of tyres,' I tell her. 'There were lots of old tyres lying around the freezing works. It took hours. The winch broke; they had to fix it. The truck got stuck in the mud and we had to find some planks to wedge under the wheels. It was dawn by the time we were finally afloat again on this side. The boy was crying with exhaustion — I took him below and rolled him up in his blanket.'

'Did you fire up the engine or sail?'

'Sailed. Just slipped quietly through, without much canvas up until we got to Musick Point. Patu tried to get the engine going, but it was temperamental and there was a fuel leak. He decided it was dangerous . . . It was hard work sailing with only three of us. We didn't sleep for another twelve hours.'

Tamara has turned towards me and put her hands on my shoulders. She's three or four inches taller than me: five eight or nine. This close I can see the pores in her skin, the flickering movement of her eyes beneath her lids, the pale striations on her lips. Playfully, she squeezes my upper arms with her strong hands, almost hard enough to hurt.

'You must have been an Amazon,' she says. 'Now you're just a little old biddie.' This is a typically Tamara kind of remark; she doesn't mean it to wound. It's just an observation — won by touch, her demonstrative instincts. She pumps my stringy biceps one more time, then lets go.

'Carl was very strong,' she says. 'He was big all over. He was a big, sweet old ice-cream. I used to lick him all over.'

Tamara, I want to say, please stop right there. I am his mother. I don't want to know. That's your own private memory. The memory I want you to share with me, the one you have so far locked away, is of his last moments, his final hour. What happened? How can I go on with my own life, after you leave at the end of the week, unless you tell me that?

But she doesn't say anything more, just slips her arm around my waist and goes back to tilting her face to the sun, a wicked smile curling her lips. It's not just the complete, enclosing semicircle Girdle of Venus that stirs this girl, but also her Line of Heart, thick and heavy. Perhaps — and it's the first time I've let myself think it — perhaps she'll learn to love someone else.

The river spreads out before us, curling north-east at the next bend towards the sea. Boats are moored further down on either side, far more than the number we negotiated our way through forty years ago.

I was an Amazon, tall for my time, though I'm easily dwarfed now. In those days, if I do say so myself, I shone with health and magnitude, one of the generation of the fittest, tallest and leggiest young women since the war or maybe ever. On the platforms of Miss Craven A and Miss Mount Maunganui my fellow contestants and I strutted: strong-boned, well fed; creamy young beauties of the Lucky Generation. We were all over five foot five, with a newly invented vitality we scarcely knew how to control.

Throughout that long sail, even when I ached with exhaustion, I ached more for Bernie. As we worked that mullet boat through the Gulf, a strong westerly helping us on by the mid-afternoon, we brushed up against each other every chance we got. Desire inured me to the pain of my rope-burned palm, it was analgesia to my numbed blue feet, to a bruise coming up on the side of my arm where the boom had caught me early on, as we went about at the mouth of the estuary. The coast slipped by, the green hummocks of the islands, the morning air so clear and cold it brought them closer than they were — Motuihe silent and mostly treeless, manuka-clad Rangitoto holding hands with Motutapu.

'What are you thinking, old girl?' Tamara says suddenly. 'I can hear your old brain whirring.'

'Can you indeed?'

'Uh-huh.'

'I was remembering.'

'You were remembering without me?'

'Only for a second.'

'I want you to tell me as you remember, otherwise you'll be changing it all around. I want it raw, not cooked with sauce.'

'That's impossible,' I tell her. 'I remember it often, that voyage and its destination.'

How keenly I've remembered it during so many periods of my life, so longingly that some of it has become memories of memories, with aspects of the story weighed more heavily than they should be, depending on what mattered to me more at the time I dwelt on it. I've remembered it from my point of view and I've remembered it from Bernie's. I've looked out of his eyes; imagined myself into his head, into Brett's, into Patu's. For instance, I think I have added in my recollection of the islands passing, of how we turned up the Motukorea Channel between Rangitoto and Motuihe. I don't think I watched them slip by, that day. There was the hard sailing and there was Bernie, and my attention was caught, burning and blind, somewhere between the two . . .

'You're doing it again,' accuses Tamara as my heart pounds with it all, the story wheeling around me now like a vast slippery cloak. 'Come back to the car now and we'll have our coffee out of the thermos. Way too airish out here,' she says, daughterly and bossy.

Could she be my daughter, I wonder, if she doesn't return to America? When I was between ships and ashore reading hands, my reputation would spread by word of mouth. Whole swags of kinswomen would come to see me, one after another. I could link them not only by the similar shapes of faces, fingers and palms, or identical lines, but also by shared turns of phrase, mirrored postures, the quality of their voices. Women who were not blood relatives could be more similar than those who were: old, close friends; or daughters-in-law from long marriages bringing their husband's mothers to have a glimpse of what was in store. There was usually a common impetus for their visit to me: a death, a difficult child, an addiction, a loss, a diagnosis from a doctor.

In the car I pour Tamara a coffee and wrap her left hand around it.

'Let me in now,' she says. 'I'm coming aboard.'

CHAPTER FIVE

Nobody came with them when Nola and Bernie rowed in to shore. Patu and Brett were left to sleep on the low bunks. Bernie had insisted they sail to this inhospitable northern end of the Barrier, past the Pig Islands and Kaikoura Island, to a cove just past the mouth of Katherine Bay, before Miners Head. They were less likely to be found there, he said: it would give him time to figure out what to do next.

Earlier that evening they had eaten, hunched in the cabin listening to the last of the rain on the low-beamed roof. It was beans again (Brett's third meal of them in one day) and Nola's mind for a moment began on a cross-section of his bean-filled stomach — the heaving, orange mass dulled by green digestive juices — but pulled away from it in time before it spoilt her appetite. Her stomach was so empty, it felt almost bruised. Opposite her, so that he could sit with a straight back, Bernie sat on a part of the floor that was still wet, since they'd shipped a wave over the tuck hours before, in the Gulf. He was partly hidden by the block, with its candle stubs fused to the edges of the varnished sides in small lumpy mounds. Nola watched for flashes of him, saw the clear light of his blue eyes, an upturned corner to his mouth, and wondered what he was planning.

It was calm enough for Nola to row them in. She had taken up the oars anyway, without even asking him. For a moment Bernie watched her, with her brown hair tumbling in the light breeze, her reddened nose and chapped lips, the dun colours of his old clothes hued in with the dark, greywacke cliffs above them, her arms pulling in and straightening against the weight of the water — but it was too much for him and he'd looked away. She was too beautiful, too young, too good for him. What did he have that she could possibly want? The sun had re-emerged, fitful and hot, the full weight of the long, dry February behind it.

The dinghy pulled up on a thin strip of shingle in the narrow cove, they made their way up a little gully that ran between two scrub-fuzzed, cliff-faced hills. They were like solidified sand dunes, Nola thought, her bare feet grappling for the smoothest part of the track. It was as if some giant soldering iron had been held to the flanks of pebbly dunes and turned them to glass. It was torture. She didn't think Bernie had even noticed that she had no shoes.

'Do you know where you're going?' she called out after him, just for something to say to pull him back. He was yards ahead, a duffel bag over his shoulder stuffed with a blanket, a small flask of Scotch, a water bottle, a few slabs of bread clumsily wrapped in greaseproof for their breakfast.

He stopped, but didn't turn back to face her. 'When I was a boy I came over for a holiday. My father grew up here.

The place is abandoned now. One summer Dad brought me here to see it.' She could only just hear him; his words blew away from her and her breath rasped in her ears.

Up a bit further, thought Bernie, then left, up behind the brow of the hill. It was only about half a mile. He shifted the duffel bag on his shoulder to a more comfortable position, where its string didn't cut into his makeshift bandages, which he could feel coming adrift under his shirt. They went on in silence up the slope, the scrub growing thicker, the kanaka taller, now and again two of them high enough to cross over their heads. What sort of life had his grandparents lived here? he wondered. There must have been family stories about them, but he couldn't remember any. He wished now he'd listened. Were they religious nuts, maybe? There was something about bees, honey and kauri gum. Hard lives, whichever way you looked at it. The ground grew drier and the light dimmer, leaves underfoot crunching softly.

At the next turn began the track proper; he waited again for her to catch up and noticed then her bare feet. Why hadn't she brought her shoes? He'd tossed his old boots in the dinghy; she probably hadn't even thought of it — but then she hadn't known where she was going. Maybe he should have told her.

He watched her limp towards him, her lips pressed together, determined. What was it she wanted from him? Apart from the obvious, which he wanted too, as soon as possible. But it wasn't enough; he wasn't offering her anything. He'd made a mistake: he'd done something completely amoral, thoughtless. She'd lose her job because of this one moment of madness when he'd rung and left the message for her to join him, a moment when the insanity of the whole escapade, from the nicking of the truck on, spilled over to screw up her life as well.

He hadn't thought that she would come; that was the thing, that was how he could forgive himself: he hadn't believed she'd come to Waikowhai. If a cop came marching around the corner now with his blue dickhead hat and night stick, marching along down the bushy hillside, he would give himself up without a second thought. He bent to untie his laces.

'Here, you wear these,' he said, handing them over. 'They stink and they're about ten sizes too big, but they'll make your life easier.'

She kissed him, quickly, on the cheek.

'Thank you, darling.'

It was their first endearment. He smiled at her and her face, open to him as she sat on the ground and pulled on the boots, was happy and excited and full of feeling. She wasn't thinking past him, he realised — she had thrown her lot in with his.

'Come on, not much further,' he said, and led her on to the place he remembered from when he was a boy, where the bush cleared for a moment, where the house had been. There was a great clump of arum lilies under an ancient macrocarpa; a chimney and fireplace still with the grid in it; a sheet of corrugated iron clinging to a cross-strut of framing, leaning against the massive trunk of a puriri. Nasturtium wound around the trunk of an old pear tree, hung with lichen. He spread the blanket on the springy grass by the chimney, and they lay down together.

So this is what it's like, thought Nola, this is how it feels to know the door has blown open onto the world of adults and sex, that I won't be stopping him, or him me, he will have me, I'll have him inside me . . . but she wasn't prepared for how a woman can go out from herself as the man comes in and she felt herself go, fly up into the dome of the sky above his labouring back — she observed how he was moving, like a fish, an eel, a whip. This is what it's like, she thought, this is what it's like, only it hurt a little — delicious, sharp and swift — drawing her back into herself so that she could look up into his face as he bent to kiss her, and all the layers of her life flew apart suddenly, billowing like a fast bright spinnaker speeding her future towards him.

During the night she woke to find him sitting up beside her, a cigarette burning in his hand and the whisky flask at his mouth.

'What are you thinking about?' she asked him.

'Nothing much.'

His words were slightly slurred and she couldn't see his face. Was he looking at her?

'Bernie?'

'Go back to sleep,' he said softly. 'Sleep's the best thing for you.'

She flung her arm across his thighs and breathed in the smell of him, a smell that somehow made her heart leap and soothed her at the same time, the perfume of the whisky and the tobacco, the sweat of his skin, the smell of the sea in the weave of the cloth of his clothes. Obediently, quickly, she slept again.

In the morning they ate their bread and drank some water from the canteen, an ancient tin bottle he produced from the duffel bag, something from the war. It was perhaps his father's, thought Nola — the water tasted of rust. Bernie drank it down and they set off for the boat.

In the late morning they rowed back to shore and Patu and Bernie took a rifle up into the hills. Brett had rigged up a hand-line on the boat earlier that morning, and after he had cracked open some cats-eyes for bait he and Nola took themselves out to the point. They sat on a flattish rock and the boy, intent on the silvery pucker where his line pierced the surface of the sea, was quiet — at least until a great tug and lurch on his line had him leap to his feet, his mouth open.

'Nola look Nola — I've caught something — Nola get ready I'm bringing it in — watch out — it's not a shark, it's too small — she's an eel, she's a fighter — she's a bloody big fat hooer!' And he landed a small rock cod, about four inches long, pink and gasping. He squatted to it.

'How long will it take to die?'

'Not long,' she answered, wanting to reach out and touch him, to stroke his tow, salt-thick hair. Perhaps, when this was over, when the cops found out the true story — that Bernie had only gone to the house to collect his son, a child that Kev had beaten, and that Kev had attacked Bernie first, and that everything afterwards was an accident — perhaps, if Bernie loved her as much as she loved him, then they could become a family. She could be a mother to his boy, a better mother than his real one.

She did put out her hand then, and laid it on his shoulder, but the child flinched away from her, losing his balance, one foot striking out for the kelpy edge of the rock and submerging to the knee. When she steadied him, he flung his leg up again, scraping it on the sharp limpets and barnacles: a streak of blood welled and ran on his shin.

'It's okay,' she said.

Under her hands his arms were stiff, his gaze still fixed on the fish as if he wanted to pretend he hadn't flinched and shifted and cut his leg, that the moment before hadn't happened.

'That must sting like jingo,' she said after a moment, noticing how he'd paled, how his freckles stood out. He said nothing. There was only his avoiding, shielded eyes, the rise and fall of his skinny chest under his faded shirt; and then suddenly, from up in the hills, the muffled report of a .22. He lifted his head towards it.

She let him have his way — she would conspire with him that the cut leg was nothing — and let go, turning her attention instead to the mullety, lifting and clinking on the anchor chain in the middle of the narrow bay. It was a perfect late-summer day, the sky high and blue, not a breath of wind. It seemed as though there was a hint of melancholy in the air though, thought Nola, as if the season had decided that as it must fade out soon, it may as well do it with grace. That's what she thought about doing the last beauty contest, the Miss Auckland next May. She'd do it with grace, for Peg. She missed her mother suddenly — would she be worrying? Perhaps the police had been around to see her; she would be out of her mind. Tomorrow she would persuade Bernie to find a telephone — there might be one further down the coast at Katherine Bay.

In the afternoon Patu and Bernie returned with two rabbits, a bush pigeon and a large rat that had been shot for sport when it ran ahead of them on the track down to the beach. Brett claimed it instantly, lifting its upper lip to examine its long yellow teeth. Kneeling on the hard sand where the bag was laid out, side by side, he turned the rat over, looking for the bullet hole.

'You shot him in the arse,' he said, grinning, and his father laughed, scooping up one of the rabbits by its ears. He took it down to the water's edge to skin and gut it. For a while Nola watched him, saw how quick and practised he was, his knife slipping easily from sternum to tuft and flicking out the intestines and bowel. She would have liked to ask him to slow down — she wanted to see the heart and lungs in their cage of bones — but he squatted over the rabbit, working with a steady, swift rhythm as if he were unaware of her presence. His profile was grim, she thought: his lower lip tucked under his upper teeth; a scowl troughed his brow. He wouldn't have borne interruption.

She and Patu found wood for the fire, then she rowed out to the boat to fetch plates and knives, the water tank, the iron spit.

Patu roasted the rabbits and pigeon over the fire. He was a consummate bush cook and the meat, by the time they laid their starving hands on it, was rich and chewy, greasy, delicious. Nola ate hers seated on a driftwood log on the smoky side of the fire. The wind was gusting mostly from the west, and now and then a salt-laden puff of carbon would catch her full in the face, but she was too hungry and sleepy to move. Opposite her, Patu and Bernie sat side by side on a low pohutukawa branch that spread out along the sand, the same one Brett had used for a horse during cooking, and talked. It was the first real conversation she had heard them have and she realised their friendship went back years, that they had known one another in the prison. She had just assumed — not that she'd even thought about it — that they had met as mud-hook mates when Bernie bought the mullet at Waikowhai. They were talking about a man called Green.

'Who was Green?' asked Brett, who sat higher up the horse's neck, where a branch forked away at a place he could wedge his plate. There was a long silence and then both the men began to speak at once.

'Mate of Kev's,' said Bernie.

'One of the last men hanged in New Zealand. A murderer,' Patu said, his mouth gleaming with fat, and then when Bernie didn't go on, he said, 'We took him down.'

'Down where?' asked Brett.

Bernie was about to answer. He took a breath and opened his mouth, then reconsidered and closed it again, just as a great swirl of smoke leapt up and flung itself into Nola's face. With her eyes closed, she heard Patu begin.

'The scaffold. We shackled his legs and arms, dressed him up in his canvas coat and hefty boots and stood by while the doctor gave him a shot of dope.'

'Why? What's a scaffold?'

He shouldn't be telling Brett this story, thought Nola. She got up suddenly, and came around to the weather side of the fire.

'That's how they used to punish murderers,' Bernie said.

'How? Why did he wear big boots?'

'To weigh him down when he fell through the trapdoor,' Patu supplied.

Under the tree, level with his knees, Nola reached up to pat him on the thigh. 'Brett —' she began.

'Why did he fall through a trapdoor?' asked the boy.

'When he was hanged. By the neck.' Bernie moved his feet sharply, kicking sand into the fire.

'Until he was killed?' asked the boy. 'So he was dead?'

'They don't do it now, Sonny,' said Patu, turning towards them with one of his rare smiles. 'You don't have to worry.'

'Of course not,' said Nola, briskly.

'Might be better for me if they did,' Bernie said quietly. Abruptly, he stood, startling Patu who nearly dropped his plate, and strode away towards the point. Nola went to follow him, but Patu called after her.

'Leave him alone.'

She stood for a moment with her hands on her hips — Bernie was already on the rocks, taking giant steps over pools and puddles — and watched him go. How it grated, this always being presented with his back view. She took the plates down to the water for rinsing. The tide was coming in.

'There comes a time when you have to leave yourself alone, a time when you have to shut the lid on something and put it away,' I tell Tamara in the car, on the way home from the Tamaki Estuary. For years I wondered if things would have turned out differently if I had persisted with Bernie, if I'd followed him and maybe even tried to persuade him to set sail back to Auckland that evening and confront whatever waited for him there — but instead I forced myself to be intent on the plate brims slipping under the small curling waves and my earnest rubbing at the grease with sand. Only once or twice I glanced across at him, as he sat for a while in almost the exact same place Brett and I had fished from, before he picked himself up and went further, out of sight around the point; a swift, distant figure passing between two misshapen rocks like half-washed-away watch-towers. The segment of blue between them was darker than the water in the bay: deeper, colder, over rocks.

As I stood with a cup in one hand and tin plate in the other and watched him clamber away, I saw him as he must have been ten years earlier, dressing that man in the canvas coat, putting the come-alongs on his wrists, tying the boots on. Maybe the dope was administered first so that there was no resistance. Maybe Bernie bent to tie his laces. Maybe the condemned man tried to kick him away.

Patu went off too, in the opposite direction, around the other point with the fishing line. Brett and I swam and lay in the sand, and when neither of the men had returned by nightfall we rowed out to *Ngaire*. In the cockpit the boy and I hunkered down with half a tin of sweetcorn each, slopped onto the half-clean plates. He had something I had never seen before in a child so young (until Carl, that is): his stillness. A peaceable sense of adult companionship surrounded him, something solid and comforting — even though it's sad, perhaps, for a child to be like that. Carl was still because of his blindness; but perhaps even more so because it was a trait bestowed by his father. Both of Bernie's boys had it.

That last evening near Miners Head I thought Brett was like a little old man, remarking on this and that as things occurred to him: the slap of the water on the bottom of the boat, the roar of the night insects from the bush above us, the appearance of the first stars. He didn't seem to be perturbed that his father hadn't returned. Together we wedged ourselves into the low portal of the cabin and gazed out at the changing sky, watching the light vanish across the surface of the bay towards the shadowy, steep-hilled coast. At about the same time we turned in and went to sleep, but I was roused by Patu yelling out from the beach that he'd build up the fire and sleep ashore.

When I came back below I tossed and turned for ages on the hard, narrow bunk — Brett had the one with the squabs — until I gave up, lit a candle and took it up the cockpit, which had been invaded by sandflies and mosquitoes. To get away from them and the pong of kerosene — at least I thought that's what it was — I took the candle up top and wedged it in.

It was too dark to see anything on land; even the strange rocks at the point or the frothy heads of the pohutukawas we'd eaten under. All had vanished into the soft, windless gloom. The moon was tiny, almost waned completely, but there was a great wodge of stars. Patu's fire gleamed one red point low above the water, just the embers now . . . I watched it and longed for a book, something to take my mind off Bernie. Why hadn't he come back to me? Obviously all the love I believed I had for him wasn't enough to overwhelm his troubles; obviously I was just another problem, or on the way to becoming so, an addition to all the troubles he already had. I decided I had to find him and tell him how he could sort his life out.

'Sure he would've liked that,' says Tamara, and laughs.

'It's not what happened, anyway,' I say. 'Lust took over.'

'So you rowed ashore,' prompts Tamara. 'Why wouldn't you?'

We're stuck in a column of traffic on the Southern Motorway, just past the Penrose on-ramp, the fumes miasmic in the gentle spring air — almost as strong as the smell that night on the mullet boat, which I rowed away from towards my lover, or so I had cast Bernie, like a character in a D.H. Lawrence novel. I used Patu's fire over my left shoulder as a marker, and although *Ngaire* must've squarely filled my gaze, I never observed the candle still flickering on the cabin roof, wedged into the neck of a DB bottle. I remember the shape of the boat on the dark water, her broad hips and short-necked mast, the lumpy sails furled on the boom, but the candle must have been hidden from me.

I pulled the dinghy up on the sand and trudged to the fire.

Bernie was there, curled up on a sack, his arms in the tattered jersey folded across himself, on the other side of the fire from Patu. Maybe he'd decided to sleep on the beach because he didn't want to wake me, even though I had lit the candle partly as a sign for him, to show I was waiting. I lay down beside him, prised his arms open and enclosed myself. At first I thought he slept so deeply he wouldn't wake, but then his arms gave a tremendous involuntary lurch. Perhaps he dreamed he was falling, or reaching for something — it knocked the breath out of me and woke him. He kissed me on the top of my head, my brow, my cheeks, and we would have made love then and there, that close to Patu, if I hadn't stood, half undressed, and forced him to his feet and away to the far end of the beach. We half ran there, laughing. He had got my trousers off me before we'd got there, yanked them down so that I stepped out of them, leaving them on the strand line, sprinting away up to a pohutukawa limb-enclosed soft haven of sand.

'That night, I reckon, was the night I conceived our Carl.' The traffic is moving again.

'The night of the fire,' says Tamara.

CHAPTER SIX

Years later she persuaded herself it could not possibly have been her careless candle that had set the fire — beer bottle and flame in an amber slide and spin from the cabin roof to the boards below — because if it had been, then surely the explosion that woke them an hour before dawn would have happened much earlier, before she'd even reached the shore.

This was the order of things: how the morning of that day began. There was a cockleshell at her temple. A twig dug into her cheek. The whorl of her ear was full of sand. Dribble from the corner of her mouth had hardened to an itchy trail of cement on her chin. The slick of juices between her thighs was paste-like with grit. A sandfly had bitten her on the eyelid, which had swollen and proved difficult to open. It was still dark. These things she was aware of, even before the bang — a violent, stinging whip of the air that ricocheted off the cliff walls around them.

Bare-arsed, she ran for the water, out-sprinting Bernie who for some reason was trying to get his pants on, and struck out into the dark, placid bay for the mullety. Early on, only a few feet from the shore, the black bobbing shape of the dinghy loomed up at her. It must have lifted off the beach on the incoming tide. For a moment — while she swam past it, seeing it blurrily with each breath as she lifted her face to the air every fourth, lung-bursting stroke — she contemplated climbing into it, but her body swam her on, urgent, determined. She lifted her head: *Ngaire* was still a hundred feet away. She swam on towards the leaping orange shape, flames chewing now even along the bowsprit.

Through the roar of the fire she could hear the men calling her from the beach: they faded in and out through her surfacing, breathing ear. From behind her now there was a splash and frantic arms breaking the surface of the water — one of the men was following. Patu's voice called out once more from the beach alone, her name — it must be Bernie swimming.

She pushed on, thirty, forty strokes, and when she stopped again it was close enough to the fire to feel its tremendous heat on her face and shoulders. All around her blew a plague of burning smuts and flakes, settling on her head and shoulders and blackening the already impossibly dark stretch of perhaps five or six feet of water between her and the burning boat. Bright beyond the stern, diesel flared on the surface, an unearthly, brief, blue-flamed slick.

The colossal noise that had called her out was lessening now; the salt-thick sails were eaten; the charred mast fallen away to the port side of the boat, its final unburned tip floating there. She could see a chunk of it, suddenly, through a window in the fire, opened up and framed by the flaming timbers of the boat. The varnish on the unburned wood gleamed a strange prosthesis pink, flesh-like in the leaping light.

The swimmer behind her was increasing his speed. Patu bellowed again from the beach; neither of their names this time, but inchoate, agonised, disbelieving.

There — something floated closer, between her and the boat, a lunge away. She flung towards it, her eyes closed against the shuddering fire, and went under, the water seeming to lose its buoyancy as she surfaced: it wouldn't hold her up. She kicked hard against it; against herself for wanting, for just a second, the sea to close once more over her head . . . She couldn't do this, she couldn't bear to see him — but it was in her hand now: his floating mop of tow-coloured hair. She hauled him towards her, her other arm going around his torso, depressing the shining, round, air-puffed shape of his shirt-back as she flung him face up. She looked at him once and wouldn't again — that same prosthesis pink, a little of it; the rest of his face mostly black, his cheek on one side burnt away — she saw a flash of white teeth, saw his eyes blackened, gummy. Turning onto her back, she took the boy's head between her hands, gently, and drew him to lie above her. As she swam, her legs forcing them both through the water, she heard the main timbers fall in the hull, the ribs of the mullety giving in and falling to the sea.

Bernie had arrived, finally, gasping at her shoulder. She turned her head and watched him see his son, swimming on, kicking away. Chest heaving for air, for his son's life, he flung his head back and opened his throat to haul in breath, which escaped almost immediately, skimming over his vocal cords in a high, eerie keen. He came closer, clumsy and thrashing, reaching out to try to take the child from her.

'No,' she managed — and kicked away from him again, Brett cradled against her. She was the better swimmer and she knew he wasn't going to listen to reason. She had to put a distance between them. She kicked on and he called out angrily, 'Nola!'

'Come on. Back,' she said then. 'Come on.'

Waist-deep, Patu waited for them. He lifted the boy in his arms while Bernie struggled up to his feet. Together they laid him on the sand, just above the water line.

It was warmer in the shallows and Nola lay there for a moment, catching her breath, remembering suddenly that she wore no pants and deciding to do something about that — anything, rather than join the grief-stricken men hunched over the little body. She was frightened suddenly. She hadn't been before, during the swim out to the fire. Impossibly, this was far worse: Bernie sobbing and swallowing — it sounded at times almost as if he was coughing or even gagging — crouched over in the sand, one hand reaching out for the boy's shirt, kneading and patting. Patu was shaking his head, struggling on his arthritic knee to his feet to stand with his palms outstretched, as if he waited at the end of a long path for a running child to embrace him.

Quietly, she pushed herself away, walking on her hands in the dark shallows until the water deepened again and she breaststroked along the curve of the beach to the southern end, where they'd spent the night. There was a new, soft fuzz of light above the hills that stood between their side of the island and the sunrise. She headed up the beach, finding the trousers only after twice mistaking them for a pile of seaweed. She hauled them on, tying her white uniform belt as she hurried back towards Bernie to tell him about the candle, that it was all her fault. But as she drew closer, half running, Bernie turned suddenly and moved away, swiftly, towards the cold campfire, stomping into his boots and grabbing up his rifle and knife.

She went after him, calling, but as soon as he heard her voice he quickened his pace, doubling back up the beach along the cliff edge towards the opening of the gully track. Anger flushed through her, stinging at her temples and clenching her fists.

'You bugger!' she screamed after him. 'You ruddy bugger! Come back!'

He was running now, a distant shadowy figure, making the turn into the cleft, disappearing.

She sat suddenly, on the sand, dropping down where she stood. At first she heard only the roaring of her anger and saw how white stars flickered in her eyeballs, pressed hard against the bone of her kneecaps, her arms tight around her shins. Then she wanted to cry, her throat burned from the smoke and the swimming. The abandoning world was completely silent, absent, cold.

But the stars gave way to Brett, running that last time up the long asphalt path to the dental clinic, the flash of his legs against the grey of his shorts; his wan, sleepy face in the brown back seat of the Vauxhall that night on the way back to his mother's; his tough, stubby little fingers baiting hooks on the rocks; his wicked, elated grin over the dead rat. To thoughts of how he must have woken early this morning and found himself alone and the cabin roof on fire.

Or not. The candle may have guttered hours before. He may have woken, called for her, struck a match to light the kerosene lamp. He might've dropped it still flaring and watched the fire take hold around him.

Whichever theory, he must have had long enough to realise he might die. It burnt into her brain, whiting it out, as if she'd looked too long directly into the sun.

The thudding in her blood pounded away like footsteps up a long corridor. This was what she and Patu would have to do. They would have to bury Brett and walk out, down the island towards Fitzroy, or to a farmhouse. They wouldn't wait for Bernie, or go looking for him.

Standing up, she walked slowly towards the little body on the sand, as with each step she felt the child's father fall away, go out from her entirely, fly up from her chest and leave her for ever.

When he reached the point in the track where the left turn led up towards the site of the old house, Bernie turned right, climbing a steeper hill through thick, scrubby bush. At the top he climbed a tree to look down on them on the beach. They hadn't moved. Patu stood by the boy still, his hands clasped now, as if he were praying, and the girl was huddled into herself further on, nearer the campfire. As he watched, she stood up and turned back towards the old man. He would find some way to get help for them, then he'd make himself scarce. He could hide here for months, years. It had taken him until the kid was laid out on the sand to believe he was dead, and very quickly after that to know that nobody would blame Patu or Nola — they would blame him.

Maybe it was the old man's fault. He should never have mentioned Green; as soon as his name came up at the campfire Bernie knew it was hopeless. As soon as his name had passed Patu's lips, Green had risen up before him, invoked in the sand, stoop-shouldered in the canvas coat, with his helpless, terrified face: a twenty-year-old kid who'd killed only the once, his unfaithful girlfriend, and was unlikely to kill again. Bernie could see that, even then, at the time. For a while he'd talked to him when he was on duty, late at night in his cell, and the boy had opened up to him. But then Kev had put a stop to it: he'd wanted Green for himself, the star of his mob, the jewel in his crown.

Pushing on, unbuckling his machete from his belt, he remembered again how Green had been while they readied him, how he hadn't pushed at them or cursed, not even in the desultory, half-hearted way you might expect from a broken, remorseful young man. Fear had pushed him under, glazed his eyes. The doctor's dope seemed hardly to touch his sides.

All yesterday evening, after he'd strode away from Patu and Nola and his boy, he hadn't been able to shake him off. The weighted tread was just behind him, and despite the late summer heat he'd felt chilled to the bone. It was inevitable: something unnatural and evil was going to happen; he'd reached the end of the line. That was why he hadn't gone out to join her on the boat when he'd returned to the beach at nightfall.

Nola had come to him, of course: ready, warm, giving. Too ready. Too warm. He wasn't worth it. He hoped she'd grow to hate him, to hold him in the same contempt in which he held Kev — the low-life who'd tracked him down after he was released. He'd come to the house bent on revenge for Green, as if Bernie were personally responsible for his death. If he'd been home, then he could have explained that it was a mix-up, that usually wardens who'd got to know a prisoner personally didn't accompany him down, but he'd been assigned the job, his earlier friendliness with Green forgotten. But he wasn't home, and

Kev found Kay home alone and courted her. At least Bernie supposed that was what had happened. How much courting Kay would've required he didn't know; not much. At the time she had a big prescription for diazepam — she was heavy-limbed and monosyllabic, a pushover. Even now she was fonged up most of the time, according to Brett.

Brett. As quickly as the boy's face rose in his mind he dismissed it again, shoved him away. That hadn't been Brett on the beach: it was something else. Brett was elsewhere. He forced his attention to his boots, slipping, wrenching, grabbing at the steep uphill incline. If he got to the ridge he could follow it down, put the mountain at his back, follow it down to Katherine Bay. Tataweka, that was the name of the mountain — he saw his grandfather's face, the hard, stained mouth forming the word — Tataweka: the highest point on the north end, the mountain that shadowed the mine.

Breathing.

He could hear something breathing and moving in the bush ahead of him. It came as hard as his did, rasping and uneven, but the ascending footsteps were lighter, quicker, the bush giving way more easily to a less opposing body. He strained his eyes through the dense trees. Was it a pig, perhaps? There were pigs on the island, and goats. Sheep too, that went wild and grew wool long enough to cast them. He couldn't see anything, just the dark trunks of the trees, the matting of branches and vines, a boulder large enough to be a rock face, a single narrow shaft of early light up ahead.

As quickly as it had begun the breathing stopped — and as it did so, so did the dawn chorus around him. He held his own breath, strained for any sound at all. There was nothing. He was too far away from the coast now to hear the sea.

It was a child, he realised: a hiding child waiting ahead for him to pass by; maybe one of the Maori children from the local tribe. Perhaps the child was frightened; perhaps he should call out and reassure him, or her. He tipped his head up to see how much longer it would be until the sun was strong enough to pierce the bush, strong enough for him to see more. A small gap wreathed a patch of high cloud, a slow billowing of pink and silver.

There was a sudden exhalation, loud and close, as if whatever it was had held its breath and hit the time limit on its bursting lungs — but it came from behind him.

'Hello? Who's there?'

His voice sounded broken, hoarse from his collapse on the beach. He'd heaved like a pansy he'd known in the prison who'd howled every night in his cell, as if he were grieving for the whole world. He turned, faced down the hill, and as he did so felt a warm puff of air on the back of his neck, soft as an insect, delicate, with trailing legs — he even put his hand up to brush it away, but realised in that instant that it was breath against his clammy, sweaty skin. There was no footfall, no bending branches, no room for it to pass, no proof of its existence and passing but the breath . . .

There. A sheen of a shoulder at waist height, a flash of grey drill: Bernie wanted to put his hand out to stop him but the hackles were rising on his neck in a stinging prickle, a primitive swelling in the flesh at the root of his neck. Every muscle in his body tensed and he felt himself draw into the core of himself, ready to spring, to strike out, to drive the wraith away.

The sun dribbled watery strands of tepid light through the canopy above him. The bush was alive again, though he had no recollection of hearing the birds resume.

His face wet, he went on in the direction his child had taken, up the precipitous slope, towards the sky. He had put the child away from him one last time.

Tamara has a toothache and I'm driving her to the dentist.

She tells me she's had the toothache for ages and kept it quiet, though I doubt it somehow. It's not in her nature to suffer anything quietly. Now, as we drive across Grafton Bridge towards her dreaded destination, she sits glumly beside me clutching the underside of her jaw. I've had a look with a torch — it's a class 2 cavity, occluso-mesio-buccal in an upper-right premolar, with some associated inflammation of the gum. For a moment Tamara was all for me having a poke around in there with a needle or the end of a match, in the hope it would save her this journey.

'What does buccal mean?' she'd asked. 'I like that word. Buccal.'

'The cheek side of the tooth,' I'd told her. 'It's quite deep.'

'Buccal. Buccal. Occluso-mesio-buccal.' She drums her fingers on the dash.

A long column of children already in their summer hats and T-shirts cross Symonds Street and begin to traverse the bridge. A few of them look up at the clear plastic arched screens fitted at the top of the rails to prevent suicides jumping to the motorway hundreds of feet below. I wonder if those children know what they're for, as they pass us waiting for the lights, pointing and squinting upwards in the bright spring sun. Children these days know too much.

Tamara winds her window down further to listen.

'Check that sound,' she observes after a moment, dropping her hand from her jaw. 'Why is it do you reckon American children are quieter than the no-necks here, but the grown-ups are ten times as noisy?'

'I didn't know that was so,' I say.

'It is,' she announces. 'I've conducted a survey. We get louder, you get quieter. You got any ideas why?'

'Confidence. Overcrowding. Less anxiety — or more of it.'

'You, for instance, can be very quiet. You can say nothing for hours on end.'

'It's nice to be quiet sometimes.'

'Don't mean you're a sad old girl.'

'Not at all. Usually we're not together this early.'

'Usually I'm still snoring at this time.'

'Always you are.'

'Habit. All those years of bars and clubs.' She pauses for a moment before she goes on decisively. 'That's all over.'

'Really?'

'Yeah. Never again. Nor weddings or parties.'

'You'll want to play again.'

'Lost my chop.'

'Nonsense.'

'Lost the desire to entertain.'

'So you'll just play alone in a cupboard somewhere?' I ask her, and she laughs wryly, but says nothing.

She won't be able to resist it. Curled in a patch of sunlight on the edge of the seat, Tamara's hand lies with its Fate Line and Line of Sun a deep parallel in the fold of her palm, the palm of a born performer. A triangle terminates the Line of Sun at the base of her ring finger. She will be saved by that triangle, perhaps: it will help her apply her talents practically, ensure her success.

For the rest — her conic hands, her long fingers and out-size thumb, the music and expression of her, the vivid star on her Mount of Jupiter — at least I can reassure myself that Tamara has the talent to match her temperament. More and more, on the job, I see right hands that bear little resemblance to the left, hands full of selfishness and discontent: dipping Lines of Head; melancholy Mounts of Mercury; Life Lines wreathed with travel and restlessness; crosses stymieing am-bition on Mounts of the Sun. I see these signs on hands that give no hint of the artist, the musician, the writer, and very oft-en afterwards clients will supply the details of their prosaic lives, lives they would find far easier if they decided just to be content with their lot. The artistic temperament is one to aspire to, in our culture of wilful dissatisfaction.

'So what happened?' says Tamara. 'Tell me on the way. How'd you get off the island?'

'There was a ketch anchored in the next cove. When the sun came up it made its way around the point. A man and his wife rowed ashore. They'd seen the fire, they said. The flames had leapt high above the point but there was no moon to sail by and their anchor had only just stopped dragging after hours of knocking along the bottom, and they were dog-tired after a hard day's sailing south from the Bay of Islands and they weren't getting any younger. They were about in their early sixties.'

The ability to drive and talk at the same time diminishes with age. As we begin the crawl into Karangahape Road I narrowly miss the rump of an Audi.

'Shake it along,' says Tamara.

'Then they saw Brett on the sand, with Patu's handkerchief

wrung out in the sea and lain over his face. The husband rowed out to the ketch and returned with a sleeping bag, which we unzipped and wrapped Brett in, and Patu carried him to the dinghy. The wife was crying and holding my hand. Patu refused to come with us — he went to find Bernie.'

'Stick with the you part — don't give the story of them.'

'Of Patu and Bernie on Great Barrier?'

'Nup. Stick with the truth.'

'You have a very prescriptive idea of what the truth is.'

'So these creakers sailed you home?'

'To Westhaven. The man rang the wharf police. They sent two officers down to the boat and I told them as much as I thought wise. I said nothing about Kev and only told them Bernie's first name. When they asked me for his surname, I said I didn't know it. I didn't care what sort of girl they must have thought I was, going out on a boat with a man she hardly knew. They took me down Quay Street to the station, where they kept me overnight, locking me up after letting me phone Peg.'

'So they already knew.'

'Of course. They'd talked to Miss Kipps and to Peg, who'd reported me missing on Monday night. Peg'd told them every-thing: how the boy had come to my clinic with a black eye and bruising; the fight with Kev around the milk truck; the fact that Bernie and I were stepping out together. They must've talked to Kay. And I suppose they examined the body to ascertain the cause of death, to see if its lungs were smoky and deflated, or drowned full of water, rather than killed instantly by the fire and falling timbers, or whatever. Eventually they handed him over to Kay.'

'You have a funeral?' We're passing a huge articulated truck and Tamara is almost yelling. I wait until the lights change before I reply.

'Yes, but I didn't go. Didn't feel I could. For months Kay would ring me late at night full of booze. Sometimes she was abusive, other times wheedling and whiny. "Have you had a few drinks, Kay?" I'd ask. Try as I might I couldn't like the woman — I could only pity her and grieve quietly for her child. I went through a phase of listening to her and soothing her down, then I got to hanging up.'

In Mercury Lane I back into a parking space and Tamara undoes her seatbelt.

'We here already?' she asks, clasping her jaw again.

At the dentist's I take a seat in the waiting room. Hunch-shouldered, Tamara the tragedienne is led by the nurse to the chair in the clinic. Without turning my head I can see her scuffed Doc Martens, the frayed hems of her too-long jeans. There is the strong, familiar smell of methylated spirit; the almost sepulchral silence; the squeaking of the assistant's white shoes as she moves about, making things ready.

The dental clinic is on the second floor of a grand old corner building. On a low table gleams a pile of glossy maga-zines, but I don't pick one up. Instead I take a seat at one of the high arched windows, which gives a galleon's view of blue sky and a reeling flock of seagulls coming in to roost on the roofs and awnings opposite. Once, you would've been able to see the port from here.

'Bad weather at sea,' Peg would always observe solemnly, if ever we saw seagulls flocking inland. 'Bad weather at sea. It's closing in.' As a child I loved it; I felt cosy and warm and snuggled into her, imagining the near sea grey, cold and rising.

Tamara emerges eventually, with one side of her face so deeply anaesthetised she looks as if she's had a stroke.

'I don't want to go home,' she mumbles as soon as we're

out on the street.

'Neither do I,' I say. 'Is your tooth hurting?'

She shakes her head.

'Let's go for a walk then.'

We make our way along Karangahape Road towards Rendells. This is a part of the world, a rare oasis, where Tamara and I may move as part of the crowd. We fit right in. Nobody stares at Tamara on my arm; at her beaded and carved cane, which is not painted white and never will be; nor at my lurid red hair greying already at the roots, my circa 1974 satin coat of many colours, my short, tight navy pencil-skirt, my high heels. I consider my legs to be still very good, my finest feature. This morning I will buy myself a new pair of nylons from Rendells: something transparent but with a shimmer to it. And something for Tamara: some nailpolish perhaps. Blue or green or lilac. Some fake nails. Yes, I'll do her hands for her, ready for her return.

She walks bravely, steadily, beside me, not saying anything, her ears open to the traffic; to a pair of cheap-suited, arguing Pakeha businessmen who pass bombastically by; to a young Indian mother cajoling a toddler back into his pushchair; to the clip and flop of many heels on the pavement. In one shopfront — one that only just evades being boarded up by continual fast turnaround leases to failing retailers — is Jimmy with his hat out before him.

'Baby face!' he sings when he sees us. 'You got the cutest little baby face.'

I've never seen Jimmy this far east. Usually he hangs out around Three Lamps, at the other end of Ponsonby Road. He was a favourite of Carl's, who would often stop to hear him sing a line or two, then offer a coin.

Tamara pulls up short, the unparalysed corner of her

mouth hooking up into what would be a broad grin if only it had its mate to respond.

'Baby face,' sings Jimmy again, encouraged by our pausing. His own face is about as far from a baby's as you could get: sad, fallen, heavy with dull-witted bewilderment. He's forty-ish, fifty-ish, Polynesian, a big, shambling, roll-shouldered man, who sings in a smooth sweet tenor.

'There's not another one could take your place,' sings Jimmy, speeding his beat, looking me in the eye, his own eyes all yellowed whites and milky brown. 'Baby face —'

'My poor heart is jumpin', you sure have started somethin',' Tamara responds, deep and rich, her head thrown back, opening her throat. 'Baby face —'

But Jimmy has lost the words and is standing with his mouth agape, watching her. Tamara sings on, oblivious, while Jimmy takes a step towards us and an old lady with a trundler stops to watch too, smiling.

'I'm up in heaven when I'm in your fond embrace,' she sings, and I join in, handing Jimmy a two dollar coin from my purse. 'I didn't need a shove 'cause I just fell in love with your pretty baby face!'

Tamara laughs, loud and ringing and too long under the awning until the old lady moves away. Gazing at us intently, Jimmy bends to gather up his old beret with the coins inside it, rolls it up and shoves it in his pocket. He wants to follow us.

The road is clear of traffic suddenly, stopped at the Pitt Street lights at one end and Queen Street at the other, so I draw Tamara in close and we cross to the other side. Flop-footed in his outsize jandals, Jimmy tags along.

'We'll have coffee at the Alleluya,' I tell her, steering us into St Kevin's Arcade, under the lofty roof and past the shop selling past centuries' magazines and china and starched linen, under the old leadlight sign pointing down a flight of stairs — To Myers Park — past the tight, white glass buds of the Art Nouveau lamps below it, across the brown tiles that replaced the mosaic that was there when I was a child. The dark, candlelit interior of the Wyrd Sisters shop opens on our right, the lofty ceilings open higher still to the mottled clearlight gable roof, and we negotiate our way through the scruffy tables and chairs to the most distant table. 'Step up,' I tell Tamara, and we do, onto the low sill in the wide, multi-paned bay window.

'This is the table above the trees. There's a pohutukawa and a rimu. And lots of phoenix palms further down in the park.'

'I know,' says Tamara. 'We sat here before, Carl and me.'

'I'll have to go to the counter to order our —' I begin, half standing again, but Tamara goes on, 'That vag still with us? Where'd he go?'

'He stopped at the opening of the arcade, by the bag shop.'

'What's he doing?'

'Standing there. He's put his hat out. He's forgotten all about us.'

'The night he died, Carl sang with him,' Tamara says quietly. 'I tell you that already?'

'No.' I wait for her to go on. One long dark hand comes up to the table from her lap, crabwalks towards the sugar jar. She says nothing.

'Actually, you didn't.' This is something new. 'Did you tell the police?'

Tamara shakes her head slowly. 'Forgot. Everything that happened after — it made me forget it.'

'When? When did you see him?'

'Went along Ponsonby Road after the gig looking for

something to eat. He was right where Skew parked the van.'

'So at this stage Skew wasn't so out of it that he couldn't drive you home? Two espresso, cold milk on the side,' I tell a passing pierced and passive waitperson.

'Skew? Nah. He had a blast out the back of a bar later on . . . Anyway, Carl sang with him and then got Liu to run back with a scoop of fries for him, after we'd got our burgers. Then he followed us.'

'Where to?'

'The Alhambra. He waited on the bottom step till we left, fairly late. We were all pretty wasted — I held on to Liu, Carl had Skew and I caught Skew say, "Out of the way, Jimmy."'

'He was still there?'

'Could hear his thongs flopping along the lino floor behind us. Outside it was cold, still, a quiet Tuesday night. We waited for the cab. Liu went off almost straight away — lives in College Hill, nearby. Skew was going to wait with us for the cab. But after a few minutes we heard him say, "The fuckin' cunts!" Then he ran away down the road.'

'That was when his van got towed.'

'And must have been when Skew got his dumb-ass self arrested. He got ornery with the tow-truck driver, who rang the cops.'

Our coffees arrive. I add the milk and sugar to both and show Tamara where hers is.

'Don't fuss,' she says irritably, and tries to take a sip using the unparalysed side of her face. She won't go on with the story now. We both know what happened next.

A van pulled up — you and Carl thought it was a taxi. A voice said, 'Where to?' Carl said, 'Grafton, Claremont Street, near the hospital.'

Someone got out onto the roadside and helped you in and you supposed at first it was the driver, who'd slid across a bench seat. But you realised later it happened too fast. It must have been one of the others helping you up the high step into the van and find a seat, low down. Carl lost his balance and fell onto his, a mattress jammed shoulder-to-shoulder with young men.

'Carl,' you said, in an undertone. Everything was very quiet. There was a strong smell of dak and sweat, but he was down by then, and the voices had broken out again — questions directed at Carl. 'You blind, bro?'

One voice said, 'Put the lady in the front,' and someone, maybe the young man who had helped you up, helped you down again, to let you take his place in the cab. From the street you called again, louder this time — 'Carl, get out — this isn't a cab,' — but the strong arm around you pushed you up onto the step, the door was shut and the van lurched away from the kerb and down Ponsonby Road.

Skew, who was shoving the tow-truck driver at that moment, saw — he thinks — a battered, pale-blue panel van pass by. He looked up just as the towie lost patience with the skinny old fool and decked him.

The rearranging in the back went on for a while, the getting comfortable. One of them told you you looked like that famous actress, the one with the dreads: Whoopi Goldberg. You said, 'Give me a break. She's at least twenty years older than me.' You felt your sunglasses leave your face, heard how they were passed around and tried on, the laughing at one another. Then the one next to you said in a higher, lighter voice, 'Can't you open your eyes? Go on, open 'em up' — and you felt hands on your face, the soft hands of a man only just finished with being a boy; you felt his intent breath on your face as he gazed at you. Then he saw your stick, the paua and beads set into it, the intricate carving.

'Cool,' he said, and you felt it leave your grasp. It was passed around, it seemed for an age, while the van twisted and turned around the streets.

They did try to take you home, but they were hopeless: zapped, stoned. You wondered if was just joy smoke — maybe they'd been doing P. But they seemed too mellow for that. Scattered, sure, but not scattered enough.

'Used to live there with my granny,' one of them said, and you'd thought then that they did know the way. They drove around the inner city for twenty minutes or so, you estimate, before they gave up.

Then the van was driving fast, so fast it shuddered. 'We on the motorway?' you asked, and the boy beside you said that you were. You asked for your stick back. 'I need it to get around,' you said, and it was passed back to you from the rear of the van, jarring as its rubber tip struck the windscreen. You thought to yourself you were glad you didn't have your Walkman with you, or a selection of your CDs. Maybe you'd never've got them back. This part of the journey you thought went on for half an hour or more. A joint passed around; someone in the back set up a rap, two or three voices joined in.

'We're out of petrol,' the driver said then, a guy they called Vale. 'Got some money?'

There was a general rummaging, a digging into pockets. Someone in the back farted loudly and several voices giggled, high-pitched, stupid and infectious — and you remember you smiled, you couldn't help it. They were just kids. The one who had helped you up counted out eleven dollars fifty.

The van went off the motorway, headed down a steep incline, then you were stopping on the flat at a service station. Vale got out. There was the aroma of petrol and a change in acoustics from the open door on the driver's side and the overhang of the forecourt. Carl said, 'We'll get out here, if you don't mind.'

'Yeah,' you agreed, 'Thanks all the same,' and you fumbled with the door.

'May as well be sitting here all by myself,' Tamara says, scowling. 'Tell me what happened next. When did you know you were going to have an expense?'

'Not for ages. Months. I thought my periods had stopped because I was grieving. And anxious.'

'About Bernie?'

'About the Miss Auckland contest. And Bernie. Of course I was anxious about Bernie. I was in love with him.'

'Did they catch Bernie? What happened to him?'

'Patu got him to walk out with him after a couple of weeks. They could've stayed hidden for years. That part of Great Barrier is easy for a man to lose himself in — all heavy bush and steep hillsides. Kev died the day they walked out. He was in a coma, but it was as if he was waiting for Bernie to surface, to make sure he faced the music.'

'Did he do time?'

'Four years. Manslaughter.'

'That's not long for taking a man's life.'

'Manslaughter, not murder. But yeah, you're right. He could've got more — six years, maybe. But the judge went easy on him: reckoned the fact his wife was carrying on with someone else was provocation. Also, Bernie pleaded guilty.'

'Did they blame him for the boy's death?'

'No. Patu and I were both witnesses. It was an accident.'

'It was your fault. The candle. Did you own up?'

I'm shaking my head, not that Tamara can see me. I never even told Bernie. I never told a soul except Tamara.

'The boat was leaking fuel,' I say, despising myself for it. Why would I plead innocent to her? 'If Bernie and Patu had fixed the leak the fire would never have happened. It had been raining. And who's to say Brett didn't wake in the night and try to light the lamp? Maybe that's what happened. Maybe he dropped the match and set the cabin alight.'

'Maybe,' says Tamara. 'Maybe he did. More likely it was your fault.'

'Let's not begin apportioning blame here, Tamara,' I begin, an icicle dangling from every word, and I'm about to go on when I notice a muscle in her forehead twitching, just above her left eyebrow.

More likely it's Tamara's fault we've lost Carl. More likely if she'd stuck around he'd still be with us today . . .

'Could you . . . um . . .' Her voice is thin, wavery. '. . . get me another coffee? And tell me . . . tell me about when you were a freshwater trout and went in the beauty show.'

'That's what you want next?' I'm just as tentative, just as churned up. I can't even laugh at 'freshwater trout', though it's a good one.

'Uh-huh,' she confirms. 'The beauty show now. Lightly and politely.'

CHAPTER SEVEN

It was all in the papers, of course, and Peg kept saying it was a miracle she was still allowed in the competition at all. Girls in the contest had to be of high moral character, whereas Nola Lane had been written up as the girl who'd escaped with a murderer to Great Barrier, where there had been a further tragedy, and although she was innocent she'd been tarred with the same brush, and mud sticks, and all of that, said Peg, and she'd had to have a long conversation with the producer of the competition. She'd given him to understand that Nola had been taken to the island against her will and had been very unhappy ever since, and that the one bright spot on poor Nola Lane's otherwise gloomy horizon was the fact she'd been selected as one of the seven finalists.

'P for Peg and P for persuasiveness,' said Peg.

Privately, Nola would've been glad if she had been disqualified, but maybe the papers would get hold of that too, and she could see Peg was set on this. 'It's time to stand up and fight back,' Peg said. 'Time to try to get over all the unpleasantness.' When Nola pointed out that the show's producer, Jim Black, would now add abduction to Bernie's long list of crimes, Peg did a good impression of surprise.

'Oh!' she said. 'I didn't think of that!'

They were in the bathroom of the house in Glenlyn and Peg was leaning into her small reflection applying eye-liner. The appearance of her daughter behind her, in a yellow nylon nightie, was mercifully a lemon-coloured blur in the rectangle of glass affixed to the medicine cabinet. These days she never knew what she'd see if she met her daughter's eyes — the only guarantee was that it would be deep and turbulent: misery, or longing, or impatience, and occasionally something that verged on sheepishness, or guilt. Peg told herself she should have viewed this as inevitable at some stage, what with all the talk about teenagers and angst. To be sure, Nola was no longer a teenager, but only just, and this was perhaps a delayed reaction. She had always been such a good girl, the perfect daughter, an ideal foil for a mother like Peg.

'You're lucky there, Peg,' people would say when they'd lived in town, neighbours or friends from the Grafton Theatre. 'You're awfully lucky with that girl, Peg.'

They'd extol her virtues: her love of hard work, her skill on the tennis court, her altruistic career choice, the way she didn't run around with boys.

And here she was, turned tumultuous: that darker strip in the fuzzy gold reflection was a deep frown in Nola's other-wise smooth and creamy brow. The nose, Peg knew without looking, was a disaster zone, still discoloured and uneven from the blistering it received on Great Barrier — more than one might expect from just a bit of sun. There had been a blister-like sore on her shoulder, too, and another on her arm, but they were healed up nicely now. The only cure for the nose would be industrial-strength make-up.

The scowling face in the north-western corner of the mirror moved away and Peg began on her second eye, surprised to note that her hand was shaking. The front door opened: Nola had gone out to collect the mail and the morning paper. A few minutes later Peg saw her pass the open bathroom door down the hall towards her bedroom, still in her nightie. The door closed emphatically, almost a slam.

'Nola!' she flung out into the hall after her. 'For heaven's sake! Don't go back to bed! You'll be late — we have to leave now!'

In Nola's bedroom it took a moment or two for Peg's eyes to adjust to the gloom. Beneath the gleam of the white nets, the still-shut shining Venetian blinds were an impervious carapace to the daylight. On the dressing table a gold chain linking three china dogs picked up the only available light and winked at her: Don had given Nola the dogs for her eighteenth birthday.

Peg felt an unaccustomed pang. Don had always made a point of being here on the mornings of Nola's competitions. He was strict with her about controlling her nerves; he would coach her on her gait and posture, the angle of her head; he would drive them in his Holden. You could always be sure that Don would organise himself to be here overnight if Nola had a contest. Sometimes Peg entered her for things just for that reason: to engineer a Night for Certain, not one Out of the Blue at the beginning or end of a business trip. There might not be a bottle of Worth or duty-free gin, but she could enter a short-lived fantasy life where Don achieved a utilitarian husbandly aspect, which suited him more than the romantic lover did. He fixed dripping taps, pumped up the Prefect's tyres, set a rat trap and disposed of the body in the morning. Besides, could a man who favoured houndstooth hacking jackets done up over his big belly, and pork pie hats in an opposing check, ever be romantic? Circumstances had forced Peg to believe he was, though he better suited the other role.

Sitting on the edge of her bed, with the pink eiderdown wrapped around her shoulders, Nola was holding a letter. The torn envelope was on her knee and she was crying.

Crying was the last thing she should be doing to her eyes on the morning of the competition.

Without being asked, she handed the note over.

Don't come to see me, love. Set your sights higher. You've got your whole life ahead of you. B.

'Well,' said Peg, after a moment. 'It's sensible advice, isn't it?'

'Yes, but . . .' began Nola, trailing off, plucking at a pink and white sprig on the sheeny quilt.

'But what? He doesn't expect you to wait for him, and neither should you. Look . . .' Peg sat down beside her, extended a skinny cream angora-clad arm. She felt hot, clammy — the day had promised cooler than it was. She'd have to change again, just as soon as she got this girl organised.

'I told you at the time: don't go falling in love with him. Didn't I? I warned you. He was the type of chap to have a bit of fun with, nothing more —'

'A bit of fun?' Nola blazed, her face full into her mother's. 'What kind of mother are you to tell your daughter that? You're a terrible mother!'

And she got up, flounced off to the bathroom and slammed the door.

'Don't forget to shave your legs,' Peg called after her.

Passing a short while later, in a cooler blouse, Peg suspected she could hear Nola being ill. Nerves. Peg suffered stage nerves herself, though as she explained to her pale and silent daughter on the way across the bridge, her variety always had her going at the other end.

'What are you going to do with yourself, Mum?' Nola asked as she parked the car in Shortland Street outside the television studios. It was the first thing she'd said since they left Glenlyn. 'Why don't you do a bit of shopping and catch the bus home? Then you can come back later to the Town Hall for the actual show.'

Peg shook her head, the wide brim of her tulle-swathed hat flapping like the wing of an ailing albatross. Nola looked at her mother more closely: she had prepared herself for this day as though she were mother of the bride. The ridiculous hat, which had roosted on the back seat on the way over, was last year's with this season's trimmings; the little apricot suit could have been one of Miss Kipp's. The nails were pearly pink; the seams of her old-fashioned silk stockings perfectly aligned on her skinny shanks; a pair of navy blue gloves sat at the ready at the top of her cream Oroton handbag: Peg was immaculate.

'It's not that I don't want you,' Nola said desperately. 'It's the rules. We were told not to bring our mothers in. It's going to take hours. It's all really technical.'

Peg narrowed her eyes and relieved her daughter of the burden of the ballgown, wrapped in a sheet.

'When did you ever care about rules?' she asked, and would have gone on to impress upon Nola that she was coming in, no matter what, but Nola had exploded.

'Always! Always, always, always — until about two months ago. It was me who went down to the landlord to pay our rent when I was only about six years old because I knew the rule that said if you don't pay the rent you're out on your ear. Remember that?'

'Shsh!' went Peg, lifting the gauzy brim of her hat and looking up the steps of the television building to see if anybody was listening. She was reassured by the observation that the brick walls were thick and the fact that they were late. Everyone would already be inside.

'We should get in and get started on your make-up.'

'Gwen will do my make-up, Mum,' said Nola, muted now, but hard. 'We've got Gwen — she's a proper make-up artist. Bye bye. See you later.'

Hooking the little case that held her bathing suit and shoes over her wrist, Nola bent forward and took the gown from her mother. Under the hat Peg's face looked crestfallen, her mouth forming a little moue, not for a kiss but to suppress anger and bite back any heated words.

'I just want you to do well, Nola dear,' she said in throbbing, martyred tones. 'I want you to win.'

Nola shrugged.

'Unlikely,' she said, and turned to go up the steps and in through the grand double doors.

Pulling on her gloves, Peg watched her go and tried to quieten the fluttering anxiety in her chest. Her daughter seemed suddenly to be a stranger to her — a giantess of a stranger, beyond normal human dimensions — mounting a staircase that led to fame and fortune and independence. The doorman gazed for a moment at her loveliness and didn't even notice the old bird standing on the footpath below, her face tipped up towards her vanishing daughter more in awe than in anger. She remembered a dislocating moment when Nola was about thirteen, when they'd gone to Newmarket for some shopping. Peg had looked across Kirkpatrick and Stephens and wondered, 'Who's that beautiful young woman?', then realised in the next instance that it was Nola, who'd drifted away from her side to look at a pretty eiderdown: pink and white, with a sheen to it, the same one that kept her warm at night now. It had been Nola standing there in the big store on Broadway, pensive, a leg slightly crooked at the knee, a long finger to the corner of her mouth. This must be how it happens, Peg had thought: how your children slowly become something other, apart from you, not immediately recognisable. The idea had filled her with panic.

She would not panic now. She smoothed her dress over her narrow hips and set off down the hill towards Queen Street and Smith and Caughey's, where she would visit the tearoom for a restorative cup and a puff on a Cameo cigarette.

Two of the girls were already finished make-up and Nola met them coming out of the dressing room on their way to the studio to look at the backdrop and cameras. They were friends, models from the same agency. They'd shrieked and jumped up and down like Americans when they'd been selected from the initial fifteen contestants. Now they smiled at her as they linked arms.

'You'd better hurry up,' they said.

Gwen sat her in a chair in front of a bank of mirrors. It was just like the movies, with a row of lightbulbs set into the wall around the glass. Nola's stomach churned.

'Have you got foundation on?' Gwen peered at her. 'Or is that the sun?'

'Sun,' said Nola. The chair rocked a little. So did the walls and her reflection. She was going to be ill again.

'You girls,' Gwen was saying, 'so silly. All this sunbathing. You'll be old before your time. I'm a voice in the wilderness now, but one day you'll me remember me telling you and you'll wish you'd listened . . .'

As she talked she smoothed stuff on. Nola looked up into her face and thought perhaps Gwen had never gone out into the sun at all. She was the colour of soap, and smelt like soap; her beige hair set in a firm helmet around her heavily made-up skin; her eyes at close range blurring into sea anemones, with their white shadow and dark eye-liner and false lashes; her pale orange lips like the roe of scallops; and the powder she wore suddenly having another, more base and overpowering smell, which was at once fishy and a little faecal, and brought an image to Nola's mind of the mess she'd had to clean up one day after a five-year-old lost control of her bowels in the dental chair — and she was up, her hand over her mouth, while Gwen pointed wildly towards the ladies'.

'Nerves,' she heard Gwen say at her back to the white-smocked assistant.

But it wasn't, Nola thought, banging open a cubicle door and hunching over, retching, her eyes streaming miserably. She wasn't nervous at all. She just felt . . . what? She couldn't find the words for it. As if she weren't here? As if this contest were already somehow in the past; as if it were already only a memory, something historical, something she had left behind.

If she wasn't here, then where was she? she wondered, her knees sinking to the cold linoleum, and knowing at the same time that these thoughts were crazy: they belonged in the realms of fantasy; they had the logic of a dream, a nightmare. But the answer came as her empty stomach heaved again: she knew where she was. She was sitting beside Bernie in his prison cell, which she pictured as barred and bare, like the cells in matinee westerns, with a striated view of a sheriff in a Stetson hat, his dusty boots up on his desk. Chastely, holding Bernie's hand, Nola sat on the hard wooden bunk beside him and knew that he was cold at nights, with just that rag of sack to cover him.

The image shifted, changed; the cell melted away, and it was another bunk they sat on, the low bench in his boat. And there was nothing chaste about the way his hand moved between her legs, or how his hot breath flared on her neck.

'Miss Lane?' A woman's voice was calling her from the other side of the door. 'Are you all right?'

Nola struggled up, straightening the belt on her new shirtwaister, checking with bleary eyes that it was still clean.

'I think so,' she said, opening the door.

'I'm Miss Lowe.' A plump, short lady was standing outside. 'Mr Black's assistant.'

She was about forty perhaps, with no facial lines other than a deep indentation on each side of her mouth, which gave her the appearance of a ventriloquist's doll. A bad-tempered one, maybe. Nola pictured her on Mr Black's lap and quelled a hysterical urge to laugh. Miss Lowe's eyes, deep-set, brown, gazed at her with mildly irritated concern.

'Are you still feeling unwell? Have you got a temperature?' A cool hand unfurled towards Nola's forehead. 'The other girls have gone over the road to Miss Kay's hair salon and you should follow them, if you're able.'

Nola supposed she was. At the basin she rinsed her mouth and splashed water on her face, before following her officious guide up the many flights of stairs to street level.

The fresh air revived her a little, and she made a resolution as she opened the door to the salon to enjoy this last contest. How lucky she was, she told herself, to have got this far. How many girls would envy her this: all this pampering and attention; the fact she was going to be on the television. She wondered if there was a television in the prison. It was unlikely, but she hoped there was, because then Bernie might be able to watch her. This would all be worth it, if Bernie was watching.

'Hello, I'm Sonia,' said a pencil-thin and pallid hairdresser, before leading her past a row of roaring hairdryers, where three of the contestants were seated, a blast of shampoo-scented hot air rising from their shoulders. How serious their faces were under the monstrous helmets, thought Nola; how intent they were on their dog-eared copies of the *Woman's Weekly*. She hoped one of them would win. None of them could possibly care less about it than she did.

Miss Lowe had stopped at the counter and was on the big black telephone, smoking a long brown cigarette and looking anxiously at her watch.

'Oh, look,' said Sonia breathily, folding the cloak around Nola's neck, 'she's on the phone to the studio again. They lost you for a minute. There was quite a panic.'

'But I wasn't lost,' said Nola. 'I knew exactly where I was,' and she gave herself up to the blissful strokes of the brush.

By mid-morning she wondered if Bernie would be able to

recognise her under her mask of make-up, to tell her apart from the other girls who shared her colouring, shoe size and vital statistics. Here they were in their bathing suits, arranged around a real playing fountain set into the studio floor, posing for the cameras that were being dragged around on chains as though they were dangerous and recalcitrant beasts. The girls were exhorted to lean a little over the sparkling water, to trail their hands in its limpid depths. It's all so stupid, thought Nola, and chastised herself a moment later, just as the fountain gave out a loud and rather rude burping noise and ceased to spout. Three technicians rushed to examine in its inner workings.

It wasn't stupid at all. It was a serious business, and it was being broadcast to the nation, for the first time ever, from Invercargill to the Cape.

'My parents went out and bought a television set specially, so they can watch it,' said Carmel O'Malley beside her, a brunette, this year's Rose of Tralee.

'Oh, lots of people have,' said the girl immediately beside her, whom Nola remembered from last year's Miss Blossom as Miss Easylay, sponsored as she was by a firm that manufactured carpet tiles. 'My uncle has an appliance shop and he said lots of people have bought a set just so they can watch us.'

'Ooo, don't!' said another girl, nearer the front, her shining legs being arranged at this moment by Miss Lowe in an alignment designed by Jim Black, who stood beyond the camera. 'Makes me nervous to think of how many will see it — it's not just the crowds who'll come to the Town Hall tonight, is it, Miss Lowe?'

Miss Lowe shook her head, straightened and stepped backwards, heavily, into a camera. It swayed on its stand for a second or two before crashing to the floor. On the run, the cameraman swore — under his breath but loud enough for them to hear.

'Relax now, girls,' called Mr Black in exasperated tones as the camera was righted and Miss Lowe's offended dignity soothed. 'You may as well take a moment or two.'

Nola walked around a little with the Rose of Tralee.

'Odd, isn't it?' Carmel said. 'Getting around in your togs and high heels?'

Nola agreed, and agreed also that they were starving, and that it would be fab if they could nip out for a pie.

It was question time when they'd finished with the fountain. The MC arrived: a short, bearded man who was usually on the radio announcing the names of records and plays from the BBC. He came up to Nola's shoulder and affected a light, jokey tone.

'My, you have a lovely posture,' he told her. 'I'll bet you walk around at home with a book on your head.'

'I would rather put the book in my head,' said Nola, waspish, and not intending to be funny, though it earned a laugh and a thumbs-up from Mr Black.

'Good, good, very good,' said the MC doubtfully.

They were taken in taxis up to the Town Hall, where people were queuing out the door. Nola kept an eye out for Peg but couldn't see her, not in the few seconds it took to sweep around the building to the Green Room. The nausea that had plagued her earlier had vanished, and in its place came the nerves that the other girls had dispensed with. Her jaw ached, her blood felt as though it had frozen in her veins.

It was bathing suits first and ballgowns second, and she

could only imagine the expression on the judges' faces, invisible beyond the bright lights. Famous among them was another radio personality, Marina, and Colin Kay.

Backstage she struggled back into her girdle and slip, hands shaking, legs dissolving. Miss Easylay, whose real name was Carole, helped her drop the gown over her head. It was a copy of a dress Peg had found in a *Vogue* and had made herself: cream silk, a semi-fitted bodice with pin-tucks, rouleau straps, no visible waist and a deep frill from knee height to the floor. It was a wedding dress, a nightie — Nola hadn't liked it from the start. At least there were no zips or buttons or hooks and eyes to slip around in her sweaty fingers, only a collar necklace of heavy silver and turquoise that had belonged to Peg's mother. Carole, already dressed in a pale pink sheath gown, helped her with the clasp. She looked like a giant, pale-pink tongue-depressor, thought Nola, as Carole leaned in close to her ear.

'You're lucky you're still in the show,' she said softly, so that none of the other girls could hear. 'My mother thinks it's a scandal.'

'What?'

'You know what I mean,' said Carole meaningfully. 'You shouldn't be here. They can't possibly let you win,' and she was walking away, wobbling slightly on her bow-trim stilettos.

They crossed the stage one by one, twirled and joined the line at the edge, and it was while she was standing there, aware that unlike the other girls she was not smiling — she could not smile — that she saw a familiar face in the second row, gazing at her adoringly. It was a broad, doughy face, one given more to sulking than worshipful adoration, with thin brown hair scragged back into a ponytail. It was Karen, Kev's daughter, sitting beside another girl Nola didn't recognise. A school friend maybe, or a cousin. Karen didn't look at the other girls at all, only Nola, her eyes travelling from the peeping toes of her matching satin-covered shoes to her neckline and face. Their eyes met and although the girl's expression didn't change, a slightly predatory look came over her. Nola shivered, enough for the girl beside her to turn her head slightly in her direction. Where was Peg? Where was Mum? she wondered, like a child, and risked another look out into the auditorium. She couldn't see her.

The judges had come onto the stage and were announcing the winner. Leonie stepped forward and Nola watched as she was crowned and the music swelled and the audience clapped and cheered. The other girls were clapping too, she realised, and she joined in quickly before anyone could think she was disappointed.

She wasn't. Not at all.

In the Green Room she hauled on her coat, stuffed her things back into the little suitcase. She would have torn off the false eyelashes as well, but worried they'd take her eyelids with them. Gwen had used a powerful glue to keep them on all day.

Carole was sobbing in Carmel's arms, the new Miss Auckland was wreathed in smiles, the other girls were chatting and laughing. One of them, as Nola went towards the door, bent into the clustered group and Nola was sure she heard her say 'Bernie Tyler' — or was it 'murderer'?

She looked away, tied a camouflaging scarf around her head, and went out into the crowd.

On Queen Street few of the dispersing audience seemed to recognise her now that she was down off the stage, away from the bright lights. Besides, if they did, what would she say if they offered her their condolences? She could be like Rhett in *Gone with the Wind*: 'Frankly my dear, I don't give a damn.' She would like to say that. She would relish the opportunity.

As they'd arranged, Peg was waiting for her under the awning of the Catholic Bookshop. She was pulling on her gloves and deep in conversation with a girl in a gymslip. The girl's white calf muscles gleamed in the lights of passing cars, the brown ponytail was coming away from its rubber band.

'Everyone has something beautiful,' Peg was saying as Nola drew closer. 'If you look hard, you'll find something.'

The girl was disbelieving, Nola noticed as she came level with them.

'Not where I come from,' she was saying. 'Not us.' She swung her heavy head around to Nola and glared at her.

'Hello, dear,' said Peg, 'Never mind. Are you all right? Not upset?'

'Not at all,' said Nola. 'Just glad it's over. Hello, Karen.'

In the street light Nola could see that Karen had blushed, though she didn't take her eyes off her face.

'How are you getting home?' Peg asked the girl then. 'Would you like a lift with us?'

'Don't live around you any more,' said Karen. 'Not since —' and she waved a hand in Nola's direction. 'I've gone back to live with my mum. Just up there. In Greys Ave.'

She moved off then, without a farewell, crossing the street and walking purposefully towards the foot of the hill. Peg tut-tutted.

'Did you see how dirty that girl's frock was?' she asked. 'I'm surprised she had the money for the ticket.'

'Must've scraped it together somehow,' said Nola wearily.

She was feeling nauseous again. What was wrong with her? 'Come on, Mum. I've had it.'

'Who was she?' Peg asked as they waited outside the Civic to cross the road. 'She seemed to know who I was. She knew I was your mother.'

'No one,' said Nola, not out of cruelty or for any reason other than that she couldn't bear to have to explain. The words 'Kev's daughter' refused to formulate themselves in her mouth. 'Just a kid. The older sister of one of the children from school.'

Peg looked at her sharply as they set off across the street. Did she know there was a connection with Bernie? Nola wondered wearily. Everything was connected to him, yet nothing was. She felt giddy with it, and her legs ached from a day in unaccustomed high heels. Outside JLC she stumbled a little, the bright lights of the department store blurring and blending. Peg linked her arm with hers, patted her hand.

'Well done tonight, darling,' she said. 'I am terrifically proud of you, you know. You do know that, don't you?'

'Thanks, Mum,' replied Nola, muted.

In the window was a display of babies' clothes: a full machine-knitted blue layette, modelled by a bald baby doll fashioned in an alarming shade of pink, as if it had severe sunburn. The doll's eyes were disproportionately large, bulging; its hard legs jutted out encased in soft wool. Its fixed stare lodged itself in Nola's mind, though she only glanced at it for a second, and she realised, suddenly, why she felt so ill and exhausted.

You're going to have a baby, said the shop doll, its blue, unrelenting eyes blazing at her back as she pushed on, quickening her step, so that Peg had to hurry to keep up. Perhaps the further away from the window she got, the less true it would be.

'Nearly there,' said Peg, as they turned the corner into Shortland Street. 'Nearly there, love,' and her voice sounded comforting, soothing, and Nola wished she could roll the years back to when she was an infant and her mother could offer her all the solace she needed.

Tamara has a weakness for Indian sweets and to that end we leave our table in the old arcade and make our way along Karangahape Road towards Rasoi.

Jimmy has moved along, disappeared. We stand at the window of the restaurant, the stainless steel plates on the other side laden with bright granular balls and cubes.

'What is there?' asks Tamara. 'What can I choose?'

'Pistachio barfi, mango barfi, rainbow barfi, date barfi, ginger barfi, coconut barfi, Penda, Mohan Thaar, Suji Laddoo, cashew barfi.' I read aloud the carefully written tags on the white plates.

'Pistachio barfi is bright green,' Tamara says, surprisingly. 'That was Carl's favourite.'

'You came up here a lot, then?' I ask. 'To K Road?'

'Yup,' she says, and leans gently into me. 'Let's go in the shop.'

While she orders a lurid and sticky selection I think of how very often, after a late night and a midday rising, she and my son would leave the flat without any explanation of where they were going and I would never enquire. Carl and I had led entirely separate lives after the death of Ned, his second and last seeing-eye dog, a trauma that gave Carl the impetus to go to

Australia and stay with one of his muso mates, start a new life.

'We loved the big old second-hand record shop — you remember that one? It's gone now. Demolished. And we loved the old clothes shop. We'd come up here with Sina and she'd help us choose new gear. You remember the gear.'

Once Tamara played the Temple bar in a cheese-cutter so moth-eaten and stained it could only have come off a corpse. She said it was one crazy rim and that she liked the way it held her brains in: it left a dent in her forehead.

'Why else'd you come up here?' I ask her, though I have my suspicions.

'For the atmosphere, the people we knew, the fans who'd front up to us on the street. And the wafts of incense from open shop doors, the smells of spices from the Sri Penang. We liked to blow our dosh in there. And of course the Indian sweets.' Tamara's fingers close around the bag and she waits passively for me to pay. She's broke, of course, with the band evaporated and her work gone. Even so, even when she was playing Tamara was always one for suddenly falling still and silent while everyone else dug into their pockets.

'And Bernie? Didn't you meet Bernie up here sometimes?'

'Now and again.'

'You never said. I guessed, but you never said.'

'Carl said not to. Said it'd upset you. Said —' and Tamara leans her head close to me, so close her hair prickles my nose, 'Said it was easier all round if we kept it a secret. If we told you you'd go on and on and on, and we'd have to listen to it — said he'd rather not have to listen to it, there was no point in arguing back, because you'd never understand.'

The Indian man is holding out my change and I take it from him with a shaking hand. 'Never understand what?' I take a step away from her. Her breath smells sour suddenly, sour with spite and vitriol.

'How he loved Bernie. How they liked to go to a bar together, or a cruise in one of Bernie's cars, how they talked. May not have been much of a father to him, but he was his mate. Uh-huh. That's for sure.'

'He could've told me that. I knew that.'

'And we played gigs in his old club sometimes. Just me and Carl, just the horn and the piano. Cool jazz. That's what Bernie likes.'

Tamara smiles. The upward inflection in my voice, the grip of my hand on her arm, they all speak to her of vindication. Carl was right. *It would only upset her. She'd go on and on and on.*

'There was talk of Carl taking over the club, before Bernie retired. Bernie wanted him to have a reliable source of money. Kept telling Carl music was a young man's game and he wasn't a young man any more, and that hadn't he always been good at figures? But Carl wasn't interested, so the old man sold the business just before he retired. Still has some interests, though. Still owns the building his very first club was in. One time he took us there and we went inside, upstairs. It's an electronics shop now.'

'And?'

'And zip . . . He's an old man. He liked to talk about his life, like all you creakers do.' Tamara puts a large, crumbling pink sweet into her mouth and chews thoughtfully.

'Did he ever . . . ?' I begin, but lose the impulse to ask. Why should I care if he ever gave me a thought, much less mentioned me?

'Ever what?' asks Tamara.

'Nothing.'

'Maybe you shouldn'a done what he told you. Maybe you should've gone to see him, then Carl could've had a daddy from out front.'

'But I did,' I tell her. 'I took Carl to see him in prison, in the autumn of 1962, when he was five months old.'

'Tell me that,' says Tamara. 'There anywhere to sit down?'

The shop has a line of red booths down one wall, all empty. We slip into one at the back, side by side. I should be going to work, but work will have to wait. This is how it was for Bernie and me the day he met his son.

CHAPTER EIGHT

At first, when he filed into the hall with the other men, Bernie pretended not to see her sitting on the far side, with an empty chair to one side of her and two to the other. His eyes scanned the wide ring of chairs set around the room, crowded with women and children come to see their men. There were male visitors too, brothers or fathers, the rarer mate, or adult son.

But she had seen his eyes rest on her and the bundle in her arms and the carrycot like a small coffin on the floor beside her; she saw the small jerk of his head as he looked away again. It gave her time to take him in, to see the many ways he'd changed. There was more grey at his temples, his brow was more lined, his little pot was gone, his shoulders were thinner: he was exactly as she'd expected, as she'd imagined. The rest of his hair seemed darker, but maybe that was just the contrast between that and his skin: after months inside his face had paled, the years of working under the hard sun on new roads gone from it. At a midpoint between two screws he stood himself against the wall and folded his arms.

He still wasn't looking at her. She lifted a hand, waved urgently, briefly — and smiled — she felt her lips part over her teeth in a rictus of pleading. Still he ignored her, and a blush rose stingingly to the peaks of her ears. She felt the heat of blood spreading on the surface of her throat and she concentrated on resettling the golliwog against her son's sleeping body. Above its staring button eyes, its black wool hair was set with saliva, stiff as hair-spray.

After another moment, or two, or five — was it as long as ten minutes? — one of the wardens approached him and said something, too quiet for her to hear from the other side of the broad, noisy room, and Bernie looked directly at her.

The last of all the men to join his family, he came across the expanse of shining, scuffed floor towards Nola in her hand-knitted suit the colour of moss, her hair cropped and set in lacquered fair curls. He hadn't recognised her at first, just as he'd worried that he wouldn't. Then, by the time he'd picked her, he realised enough time had gone by for her to realise he had failed to know her, and that she'd be hurt by that — a thought that struck him dumb — so he'd crossed his arms and leaned back against the wall and looked off into the middle distance, until a screw came and whispered in his ear, 'There's a young lady giving you her full attention, Tyler.'

She looked like a young Anglican from the Remuera Young Wives' Club, squeaky-clean: she was putting on a face then, she was coping. He could take his hat off to her; he'd been right: she didn't need him. Above the white shawl her red cheeks flared, and he pitied her for that, but he could only make himself raise his eyes as high as the child, or what he could see of it, the rising gleam of its forehead in the soft woollen folds. Leaving a gap, he took the second chair along from her, angling it towards her slightly.

'This is Carl,' she said, and there was something in the way she said it that was reminiscent of the films, of the theatricality of the old girl Peg — something grand, which he didn't like. He couldn't understand it, or believe it.

'He's five months old,' Nola went on, quieter now. 'He was born in October.'

He didn't know any of the men around him. Until now they'd kept him apart, alone of all his kind in the exercise yards, and fed him in his cell, many of the cons being old enough to remember him as a screw. It wasn't long ago: only three years. There was talk of sending him to New Plymouth, to the prison for homos and cases difficult to keep safely confined — men like him, screws gone bad, crooked cops.

Until now it had been easy to keep him apart.

Until now he hadn't had any visitors, not even Patu, who'd gone away up north to his tribal land.

A young bloke two or three along from Nola slipped Bernie a sideways look, and across at the baby. The woman with him was looking too — an older lady, his mum or aunty maybe. Bernie leaned back in his chair and folded his arms again.

'Would you like to hold him?'

He shook his head.

The night before Peg had said, 'You're making a mistake. He won't want to know.'

'But I want him to know,' Nola had replied, going on with the setting of a sleeve into her hot-off-the-needles suit jacket, dark green flecked with amber. 'I'm going to wear my new suit. And I'm going to tell him what's what.'

After lunch she drove through the quiet, rainy Saturday afternoon, under dripping trees and telegraph wires, across the Harbour Bridge in the Ford Prefect, Carl drowsy in his carrycot on the back seat, and while she drove she comforted herself with the thought that at least he knew she was coming, he was prepared to see her and a baby. A baby. She'd sent him a note, the second in their brief acquaintance. She would tell him the rest in the kindest way possible, the most humane.

Alongside the railway line she drove, up Boston Road, and parked outside the high, grey stone crenellated walls of the prison, the dark and sinister Victorian folly that every Auckland child believes for the shortest time of their lives to be a fairy-tale castle.

'Bernie?' She held the baby out to him.

'I don't want to hold him,' he said in an undertone. Nola froze, and a quick glance at her face told him she was panicking now — this didn't fit in with her plan. She swallowed, nervously jiggled the already quiet baby for a few seconds, then put him over her shoulder.

She shouldn't do that, he thought. She'll stir him up.

'I was going to have him adopted, but I didn't think I had any choice. Had him in Bethany and I'd made up my mind . . . to . . . I'd decided to give him away. But I've kept him. In the end I had to keep him.'

She spoke so quietly and quickly he could hardly hear her over the noise in the room, the voices reverberating off the high ceiling.

'Up to you,' he said. What did she want? Congratulations? She'd stuffed up her life, good and proper.

Murmuring gently, insistently, reassuringly, she was lying the baby down again flat in her arms, unbuttoning the chin strap of the baby's knitted pale blue helmet and pulling it away from its head. Five months. He wasn't sure, but maybe Brett had moved around more at that age, waved his arms and legs. There was a resemblance, though, he could see it — something of Brett and himself in the forehead, the square shape of the brow. The head was bald except for a patch of gold fuzz at the crown. His chin and cheeks were anyone's.

He was just a baby; it looked like any baby.

'Long way off sitting up yet,' Nola said, somehow encouraged by his silence, and sat the baby up against her stomach. Still not quite under control, surprised by the sudden change in posture, the head lolled slightly to one side.

There was something odd about the eyes. They were half open, one lid dipping lower than the other. Maybe it was taken with the shine on the wooden floor, with the weave of Nola's lap, with his feet —

'He's blind.' That quick, low voice again. 'They think he can see a little bit, but it won't last.'

'He's small,' Bernie couldn't help himself, 'isn't he? Small for his age. I wouldn't know, I wouldn't have any clue about . . .' He trailed off. If they'd been allowed to meet alone he might have been able to think of something to say. If they'd been allowed to meet alone, in another room, it would have been completely different.

'Nobody would have wanted him. Not a blind boy. He would've grown up in an orphanage.'

Bernie's hands flew out from where they had cupped his

elbows and retreated again, as if for a moment he had wanted to hold the baby but changed his mind.

'You're right, he is tiny. He was early. But it wasn't caused by that, his being early. You know, until only a few years ago they were blowing premature babies' retinas out with too much oxygen in the incubator atmosphere. That's what blinded them, you see. But not Carl. No, no. He has something else.'

The baby lifted his hand suddenly, upward to his mother's chin in the direction of her voice, thwacking her chin and startling away again. She smiled and lifted him, turning him around so that he could nuzzle into the crook of her neck, patting his back. Her hands were all over him. Bernie watched them, white and plumper than he remembered, rubbing the back of the baby's head, gently squeezing his little legs. The baby ground his mouth against the diamond-shaped patch of her skin inside the collar of her blouse, and then began to rock, his head banging back and forth, his fingers kneading her jacket. Nola made no move to restrain him. If anything, her patting and prodding seemed to encourage it. She was still talking, long medical names that meant nothing to him, while the baby made a noise that went with his rocking: a soft, rhythmic wa-wa-wa that sounded monstrous, abnormal.

'Don't let him do that,' he said sharply.

She broke off mid-sentence. He didn't want to know, then. She'd thought that if she talked quickly, got it all out at a rapid clip, the words she'd gleaned from the doctors and books from the library — 'hyperplasia of the optic nerve', 'unilateral partial aniridia', an absence of iris in his right eye (the one that drooped) — if she'd said it all very fast he might listen, and his mind would be set at rest. He would know she had everything under control. She stared at him, silent.

'Don't go on,' he said then. 'It's enough to know his eyes are buggered.'

Nola turned the baby around and his head snapped up, his back arching against her arm in a sudden attempted crash-landing to her lap.

'Don't be a cretin,' she muttered under her breath, nestling the child in close.

'What?'

'Why wouldn't you want to know? You may as well. You may as well know everything you can. I'll show you some diagrams.' She leant to the bulging bag at her feet and began rummaging in it.

'May as well know what?'

She'd called him a cretin. A pulse of anger thrummed through him, the first for months, firing along his spine, push-ing against the claggy slime of despair that was his constant, numbed state. He watched her, still rummaging in the bag, the child in her other arm transfixed by the lightbulb in its wire-wove cage above them. One eyelid fluttered like a moth's wing over its white eye. Bernie tipped his head up towards the light too, on for the dark, rainy afternoon, and watched thick cigarette smoke wafting in the beams. He closed his eyes.

'Damn,' said Nola's voice. There was a chink, something made of glass being set on the wooden chair between them. A baby bottle. He wouldn't open his eyes to see.

'I put them in here somewhere, to show you . . . here.' There was the rustle of paper.

It was a trick: he opened his eyes and in one swift move-ment she passed the baby into his arms — why didn't she just put him in his carrycot? — and bent to her bag again, lifting it onto her lap and plunging in an arm. It was knitted in the same dull wool as her suit — vast, with bamboo handles. Maybe she'd got a job lot of it. How was she coping, then? For money?

'Have you gone back to work?' he asked her. 'Did they give you your job back?'

'After a bit of argy-bargy. They weren't that keen, but Mum went in to bat for me. And they're short of dental nurses, you know, so they let me have a year's leave. I go back in August, after the holidays.'

'So you're all right? For money?'

'I've got some savings. And Peg makes a bit. People still come to the house to have their hands read. Their palms, you know. She's good at that.'

Nola was still searching through her bag. A faint, acrid smell wafted up from it, as if she'd spilt some milk in it. Or maybe the smell rose from the baby.

The screws on the other side of the room were watching him. Had they thought he wouldn't do it, that he wouldn't hold his son? He looked full into his face, saw the little nose waffling at his strange pair of arms, at the smell of Bernie's skin and breath, saw the dribbly, perfect mouth with a first tooth crowning, just inside. Nola took out two folded nappies and placed them on the chair beside the baby bottle, half full. She wasn't giving him the proper milk, then. Maybe she should. Maybe that's why he was so small.

She rummaged on.

'Nola. Forget it,' he said sharply and the baby startled, throwing its arms out, brow puckering. Poor little chap, poor little bloke. He stroked one of the fine, spindle-fingered hands.

'Eureka!' said Nola, loud enough to make people stare. She put the bag down, swept the things on the chair between them into it, and shifted sideways to sit on the now empty seat, smoothing the paper carefully on her lap. It was an intricate, carefully copied cross-section of an eye in an array of coloured lead, the iris blue, 'aqueous humour' grey-green, the retina red as a matinee curtain, the optic nerve in jagged yellow running away at the back of it all to carry the impulse to the brain.

He nodded, watched her finger point out to him the ink-labelled parts, heard an enthusiasm in her voice that reminded him of his brief career at school. He didn't like it. But he nodded anyway, and sat with the warm weight of his son in his arms, while she talked on and on, explaining the meaning of hyperplasia, how quickly the thickening of the nerve would advance, the name of the specialist at the hospital, how there could be an operation for the aniridia. When at last she paused to draw breath, the baby drew in a lungful too and howled once, queryingly, piercing enough to make the hall fall quiet.

'He doesn't know I'm still here when I stop talking, you see.' Nola folded the diagram, tucked it into the pocket of his prison shirt, her fingers hot for a moment on the other side of the thin cloth, and took the baby from him. 'You can keep it if you like. The cross-section.'

He shook his head. It was ghoulish and girlie. What would he do with it? But he left it there, poking out of his pocket, neatly folded like a dandy's handkerchief.

Should he check with her that she got his note? he wondered, looking at her chin, tilting now, under its fine patina of silvery powder. She'd gone to a lot of trouble for him, all that get-up: the hair, the brooch, the fashionable suit — not that he liked it much. If he asked her that — whether she'd got the note — then he was letting himself in for the story of how it was for her when she read it. He'd sent it last May, which would have been about the time she must have realised she was going to have a baby.

The poor kid.

'I've had some telephone calls from Kay,' she told him, settling the baby in her arms and digging the bottle out of the bag again. This was what he'd dreaded, ever since she'd sent him the note telling him of her imminent visit. Even more than seeing Nola saddled with a baby, he'd dreaded hearing her talk about Brett.

Here it comes.

'She's usually drunk. She goes on and on.'

He couldn't think of anything to say to head her off. Instead, he concentrated on the baby's wet, pink mouth closing on the teat, the fingers fluttering at his woolly sides.

'She thinks it's all my fault.'

'No,' he managed finally.

'She thinks I should have brought Brett home and let you go to the Barrier on your own.'

'You know it wasn't your fault.'

'Has she been here to see you?'

'Of course not. Why would she?'

'She keeps saying she's going to. She's all on her own now. Kev's children have gone back to their mother.'

'She'll be all right,' said Bernie, though he suspected she wouldn't be. He pictured her thin, frantic body hunched over the phone in the hall of the Prospect Road house: the house he'd bought with money inherited from his father, the money his father had carefully saved all his working life — money he should have spent himself, enjoyed, in his last years. He'd left it all to Bernie and his sister. Now it was gone.

'Did she always drink like that?' Nola was asking. What did she want to know that for? Maybe she was just making conversation. She wasn't even looking at him, but at the baby, like he was.

'No,' he said.

A screw whose eye-line met the clock called out. It was almost four.

'Nearly time. Five more minutes.'

Carl had gone to sleep, his droopy lid closed, the other half fallen over his unseeing eye. There was a soft pop as Nola pulled the teat from his mouth.

'Bernie?' she said quietly. 'I want to ask you something.'

Already, obediently, the families around them were packing up their belongings. One little girl, obviously a regular visitor who knew the drill, had scooted over to wait by the door, dangling her doll by the hair. The young chap beside them stood holding a paper bag bulging with the regulation six pieces of fruit.

'I want to know if you think . . .'

'What?'

She was biting her lip, two shiny white teeth leaving scoop marks in her thick, pale lipstick.

'I want to know if you think I did the right thing.'

She was asking him more than that, Bernie realised. It wasn't just about the choice she had made, it was a demand of some kind. If he said he agreed with it, she might want to come again; she might see him even more as some low-life who needed rescuing. That's all it had ever been about. A girl like her — a clever confident girl — having a roll in the hay, a roll in the dirt, before marrying a doctor, a dentist, a successful businessman.

How had she done it, he wondered: how'd she faced this one down? Keeping the baby wasn't something she'd done on a whim. For a moment he envied her her state of atonement with her conscience. He would never feel like that again.

'I wouldn't know,' he said finally.

'I'll get him the best I can,' said Nola, bending to gather up the handles of her bag. 'Oh. I meant to tell you,' she went on, not looking at him, 'I got your note after the trial and I agree with you. You're absolutely right. I won't come again, unless you want to see Carl.' Standing now, with the baby's helmet freshly buttoned under his chin, her capacious bag sagging to mid-calf, she asked, 'Would you like me to write to you?'

Say yes, he willed himself, but as he stood he seemed to be absorbed suddenly into the moving bodies around him, into the dull winter-clad backs of the families moving towards the exit door. He felt hollowed out, his insides gone over with a grader. He couldn't even nod.

'Goodbye then,' said Nola, glancing down once at the sleeping baby in her arm and giving him a gentle squeeze. Then, suddenly, unexpectedly, she looked up at Bernie and smiled, a wounding flash of what could have been forgiveness, even empathy.

He hadn't thought she'd forgive him. If she had, then possibly she hadn't had the depth of feeling for him that he'd imagined, especially that last night together, screwing on the beach. Women don't make love like that unless they're in love — all appetite, open mouth and muff, body soft and endlessly yielding. He remembered how she'd reached up for a branch while she straddled him, hauling herself up on it and at the same time hooking her heels under his buttocks and lifting too, so that he arched and arced inside her, while the tree above them rustled and creaked and swayed . . . How had she known to do that? What gave her the idea?

She had guessed a little perhaps of what he was thinking — she had read it in his eyes — because she was shaking her head minutely, her smile changing, curling up at one corner.

'Hooray, Bernie,' she said, and turned away to join the mass at the far end of the hall, the baby grizzling in the carrycot as it bumped against her legs, her hastily repacked bag spilling nappies.

He spent the rest of the afternoon lying on his back in his cell, cursing himself for responding to the loudspeaker in the exercise yard. If he hadn't, if he'd just stayed out there under that measly patch of sky, he wouldn't have her face whirling in his mind, in all the guises he had known it, whether he closed his eyes or kept them open. Here she was decisive, driving him to the local doctor; here she was curious, coming aboard his boat the first time; here she was waiting for him to kiss her; here she was loving him; here she was weeping; here she was bravely heading for the water that morning on the beach.

And here was the little face she'd brought to see him: the collapsed eye, the paucity of expression, a lengthy second sentence that awaited him on the outside.

'We should go. It's late night out west at the mall tonight and time is ticking on,' I tell Tamara. 'I'm losing business.'

We cross back to George Court's corner and find the car. I like to open the stall by lunchtime and work through until ten-o'clock closing: if I average one reading an hour I do all right.

We head out of town along the North-Western

Motorway, the swampy inner harbour on either side, the factories of Rosebank Road now rising on our left, towards the sprawl of Henderson and the shopping centre.

'So your mom said told-you-so when you got back?' she asks, her scummy boots up on the dash, though I've asked her five hundred times not to do that.

'From the prison?'

'Uh-huh.'

'No. No, she didn't. She just gave me a hug,' and I have Peg in my mind so clearly, suddenly, coming down to meet the car when she heard me zip up the driveway, double-declutching into second gear — at least my driving had improved by then. She took one look at me through the rain-speckled windscreen and, the second I clambered out, wrapped me in her arms and I howled and cried and I sobbed and wailed and gnashed my teeth until little Carl joined in too, and we had to shush him and lull him and carry him upstairs. Sometimes I wish I could still cry like that, just give myself up to it, but mostly I'm glad I've grown incapable of it. What came first, I wonder, a consciously willed protective atrophy or the natural dulling of my ageing heart?

There are cruise ships now that resemble malls more than anything else: massive floating hotels with shopping centres set into them, monoliths that steam from port to port, disgorging hardly any of their mostly elderly passengers. This mega-mall, the one Tamara and I now make our way through, with its shining floors and acres of vertical glass, its smell of plastic and new cloth, of warm sugar and coffee and hot fat drifting across from the Food Hall . . . this mall could perhaps resemble one of those new ships — but never the *Mariana*, which Carl and I took from Auckland to Suva to Honolulu. How her wooden decks and passageways creaked and shuddered, that old dear, how she banged about in a high sea. The shoppers are not so different from the passengers then: teenagers, harassed mothers of toddlers, businessmen, tradesmen, retired men with money worries suffering through an outing with their wives. In the 1970s a cruise on the *Mariana* was affordable for so-called 'ordinary people'.

Maybe I'll tell Tamara about that next, of how soon after Peg's death I took that phone call from Alf, an old friend of hers from the Grafton Theatre, who'd landed a job as Entertainment Officer on the *Mariana*. He was wondering if Peg was there, and would she be interested in a job as a hostess and reading the passengers' hands, and I said that I was Nola, and he said he remembered me hanging around backstage at St Andrew's Hall while Peg rehearsed her parts in Grafton productions. I told him that Peg had died a month ago and that I was pretty good at hand-reading myself. He said he hadn't seen the death notice in the paper, that he'd been away at sea. And then, after he'd offered his condolences he gave me the job straight away. Just like that. We all went on that first cruise, all three of us. Carl was nearly fourteen, I was thirty-five and Bonzer was seven. Did Carl ever tell Tamara about Bonzer? I wonder.

My stall is tucked into the lee of an escalator, outside the mall's purveyor of vitamins, doorstop sandwiches, joyless cakes, dried pulses, unguents, essential oils and herbal remedies. That is where I store the fittings for my stall, and often my customers pay a visit there first. I sometimes observe them watching me through the lettered glass while they make up their minds to have a reading. *$30 for Half an Hour*, reads my sign, and underneath it could say *Cheaper than a Shrink*. I might have it added on.

At the rear of the stall against the elevator case I place a chair for Tamara, who inserts an entire rainbow barfi into her mouth, takes her Walkman from her bag and plugs herself in. My clients can see for themselves that she is blind, and for their continuing sense of privacy the thumping beat of her jazz selection renders her deaf as well. When she first started coming to work with me after Carl's death I worried that I would lose business, but, though it is heartless to admit it, Tamara adds to the exotic ambience. I don't go in for crystal balls or incense rolled by the hands of underpaid Indian children, but my little stall is hung with velvet curtains as red as that long-ago retina in the diagram I gave to Bernie. The sign, headed *Palmist*, is gothic, black and gold, a hint of the occult: a concession more to an idea of successful marketing than to my own instinct for my practice, which is as scientific as anything I once did to juvenile teeth. We are lit from above — my stall has no ceiling of course — and we are observed by the downward-escalator riders, should they care to look.

The curtains are thrust aside and my first client enters with her hands already outstretched. A heavy-set woman in her late fifties, she is faintly moustached, vastly bosomed and sweaty, with an aroma of onions and garlic. She sits opposite me, on the other side of my little table with its red beaded lamp. Tamara wags her head to whatever it is she listens to and thrums her long fingers on her skinny thighs in their denim cases, thick with dirt and ash. The woman, the customer, glances at Tamara once and away back to me, her small, square hands palm up on the table. I take them, squeeze them gently and turn them over. They are hard, muscular, warm, the texture of the skin dry. There is dirt under her nails, a healing graze in a scatter of little scabs above her wrist.

'Rose prickle,' she says, and I think, from her accent, she is perhaps Greek. 'Thorn.'

I tell her of her energy, her practicality, her methodical employment of her time, and she nods — it's true. She works hard.

'It is good to work hard,' she says and she shoots a glance at Tamara, now humming quietly with her music — soft, higher-pitched than the register she uses when she's singing properly. It could very well become distracting if she keeps it up, both to me and my customer. I turn the lady's hand over.

'Can I ask you your name?' I ask her.

'Effie,' she says, shifting her buttocks on the protesting chair, and her palm tells me the same story as the back of her hand.

'Perhaps sometimes you should think about what you want out of life, Effie,' I tell her, 'instead of doing always what other people expect of you.'

I tell her of her even nature, her sense of fairness in any dispute, her physical vitality, her good health continuing into late life. Here is a woman who is gracious in love, generous and generally well respected — though perhaps she sometimes holds on to opinions that she knows in her heart to be wrong. This is the closest I come to articulating the bigotry I see, which, given a convergence of lines and her short square fingers, is instinctive to her. On the percussion of her hand her marriage line is singular, long, deep and red and there are four or five children: vertical striations above it.

'Five,' she supplies as I pat her hands and lay them in her lap, giving them back. 'And twelve grandchildren,' she tells me, digging in her purse.

While we wait for the next customer Tamara and I have a

cup of tea out of the thermos. Fingers rustling in the now greasy paper bag, Tamara selects a Penda, a chewy disc yellow with saffron, and chomps on it in time to the tinny thumps emitting from either aureole, and while I watch her I worry about how independent she will be, back in Chicago, a city she hasn't lived in for ten years. She is far less forthcoming about her family than she has been about her former lovers. There is a mother who rings sometimes. Those conversations, at Tamara's end anyway, are short and dutiful. There is a younger sister, Serena, who is on her own in the projects with a couple of kids. The phone conversations with her can go on for a couple of hours. Sometimes they argue and shriek, other times Tamara slumps over the phone helpless with laughter. And there is a brother, Xavier, whom she hardly ever mentions. Once Carl told me Xavier was trouble, mixed up with a gang called the Supreme Cobras, in and out of prison.

'In Chicago,' I try, leaning forward to pull the earplugs away, 'in Chicago, will you stay with your sister?'

'Don't want to talk about it,' she says, too loud, jamming the plugs back in. 'I'm busy.'

Maybe she is concentrating deeply, maybe despite her resolve never to play again she's getting new music down.

But I want you to talk to me, I think. I want you to talk about the future. And the past. I want more of the detail of what happened that night when you and Carl got the lift in the van along Ponsonby Road and ended up at a service station. There may be other clues — sounds, smells, sensations — hints that haven't yet come to light. I don't think you've combed the story through enough. I want the ending.

You arrived on the forecourt. Carl said, 'We'll get out now, if you don't mind.' And you thanked them, and opened the cab door because it was right beside you and easy to operate, a kind of handle you'd met before. You grabbed it, a cold chrome lever, pulled it up, leaned your shoulder into the cracked vinyl padding and pushed — the door flew open and you stepped out. You felt along the battered side of the van. Where was the handle for this door, the door that would let Carl out? Until now fear had been intermittent — you had been frightened when you realised your mistake, then reassured when the boys drove around looking for my flat, frightened again when the van had hurtled down the hill. But now, now at this moment, you were calm, clear-headed, beyond panic, determined. You found the handle, one you squeezed, pulled back the door — 'Carl?' And as he answered — 'I'm here' — the driver's door opened and someone, probably Vale, got back in the seat. You said, 'Carl?' again, and possibly held out a hand in the hope he was reaching for you. A voice from the depths of the van said, 'Jeez, she's ugly, your girlfriend, isn't she, Bro?' and someone laughed.

The key turned in the ignition, the engine turned over, died. 'Carl?' You felt with your stick for the step up, put up one foot as the key scraped again and the young, strong foot kicked at the pedal pumping through the new gas. You heard the handbrake click, squeak, give way and the van surged, bucked into gear and swung away. You flung yourself backwards to save yourself, landing on your coccyx and your elbows, rolling onto your side, the stick clattering and banging beside you on the concrete, rolling into an oily puddle. There's still a recalcitrant smear of grease on an eye of paua.

One of the men from the service station, an Indian you thought, by his accent, hurried out from his glass booth, lifted you to your feet, helped you inside.

Why didn't you tell them then what had happened? Why didn't

you tell them Carl had been abducted? Why didn't you ask them to ring the police?

Instead, you allowed them to sit you down, you told them where you lived and that you had no money, and after a long delay and endless discussion among the staff, the first Indian man got another man, younger, the same accent — his son? — to drive you home in a car that smelt of petrol fumes and nostril-excoriating air-freshener, and on the journey he didn't talk, and neither did you.

The police have gone to every service station at the foot of any incline in the outer city and not been able to find one run by men you described. They've shrunk the boundaries to the inner suburbs, ring by ring, in case you drove around for far less time than you remember; in case your recollection of the time passed driving around is way out, the clock sped by fear.

I have another customer, a pretty, blonde teenager with a sensitive, waffling nose and eyes wet and pink from crying. Or maybe she's an allergic type, a weak constitution. Her hands are soft, flabby, the nail on her right forefinger yellow with nicotine. Her lines are pale, chained, short, the mounds uniformly flat. The most distinguishing feature is her Line of Heart — short like the others, but rising from the Mount of Saturn: high on the palm, indicative of a hard, cold nature, and contempt for the opposite sex. I encourage her to exercise more, to take an interest in the people around her, to be motivated by more than greed and personal gain. I don't mince my words, as Peg would say. The girl pays me, scowling, and leaves in a huff.

The earplug wires coiled in her lap, Tamara has crossed her arms, leaned her head back against the vibrating escalator case and fallen fast asleep. She stays so throughout the next reading, and the next, and while I read and wait for the fourth of the day, which I decide to make my last. I can work late next Thursday and the Thursday after and the Thursday after that, after Tamara has gone. Right now I want to take her home, keep her away from the dope, decline a glass of wine and encourage her to have an early night.

In the car on the way home we suffer through another of her crying jags and once she's tucked herself up in bed she calls me in.

'More Carl,' she says, like a child. 'More Carl, when he's older.'

She wants him formed, closer to how he was with her than what he was to me as a baby, on his way towards his adult life. If she'd had his baby she'd want stories of him as a little one, she would want to enter that ancient dialogue between mothers and daughters-in-law where the father is compared with the son: the relative ages of milestones reached, first words, steps, all the tiny achievements that attain such importance in a young mother's mind. But she never did have his child, possibly never would have, even if Carl had lived. She's not the motherly type, and it would have been difficult for them. Too difficult. Would I have had to live with them permanently, to help? I look around at this room, the room they shared. It is chaotic, because of the packing and sorting, but it was always chaotic, with clothes discarded and clean mixed up together, apple cores, toast crusts, coffee cups, cassette and CD cases missing their contents, Tamara's roach ends, empty water bottles, bits of rubbish. I used to resent it, especially since I went to such trouble to keep the rest of the flat clear of obstacles. The bedclothes, black satin, haven't been washed for weeks.

'Hurry up,' says Tamara, yawning, 'else I'll nod off before you've even started.'

'All right. I'll tell you about a time when he was fourteen, at the beginning of my time on the ships. Carl came on that first voyage, before he went away to boarding school. Hang on a minute.' There's a photograph I need to aid my memory, although already, as I hurry out to the living room to put the piano stool at the foot of a tall cupboard and climb up to slide out a dusty carton, already that day is breaking in on me when we all gathered, all the ship's entertainers, on the *Mariana's* stadium to pose for the photographer.

And here it is, the photograph. Alf — dear old Alf who pulled a plethora of strings so that I could bring Carl — stands in the front, white-shoed and -trousered, in his nautical blazer and striped tie. There's womanising Dave the suave magician; Raymond the MC who wore a scratchy nylon toupee even in the sticky tropics; backing singer Gloria with her blonde wig and tambourine; Jo, Mick and Malachy, the black trio supposedly from Alabama but actually from Birmingham; Colin the comedian, a buck-toothed, big-noting squirt from Melbourne; bow-tied Warren dangling his trumpet from his thumb; bandleader Roger with his baton triumphant — quite a crowd of us, about forty-five including all the band members, dancers, hostesses. As I carry the black-and-white picture back to the bedroom, most of the faces that shine up at me are male. We stand on the bathing deck, the officers' quarters above us, squinting in the bright sun up at the photographer, who as I remember was balanced on a chair on top of a table brought out from the Pool Bar.

'What've you got?' asks Tamara, sleepily.

'A photo.'

'Is it on the ship?'

'It is.'

'Carl in it?'

'No.'

'Why not?'

'He waited off to one side with his dog.'

'Ned?'

'No, his first dog. Bonzer. He was a beaut dog, something special.'

'He took his dog on the ship?'

'Of course. They were stars. Especially after Alf heard him playing the piano and stuck him in the floorshow, a couple of spots a week.'

'What'd he play?'

'A couple of his own that he was working on then. And some standards — Miles Davis, Oscar Peterson. Also versions of some hits of the time — Judy Collins, the Hollies, Bread. A hilarious take on "Venus", which he sang himself. Mostly easy-listening.'

'Yuck,' says Tamara, jazz snob. 'Poor kid. They dress him up?'

'We got him a suit made overnight by an Indian tailor in Suva — pale blue with a white ruffled shirt to go under it.'

'Tell me,' says Tamara, 'all about how he was then, from inside his skin.'

CHAPTER NINE

The first night he played, on a patch of the ocean between Suva and Honolulu, Carl was more nervous that Bonzer wouldn't find the piano than that he'd stuff up his numbers when they finally got there.

'Find the piano,' he said to the dog, the moment his mother had stopped fussing over the frills on his shirt front and smoothing the lapels on his suit jacket, which she'd told him was pale blue satin. Pale blue: a colour he imagined to be cool and smooth, slippery on the tongue, curly with 'l's. His mother's breath smelt sweet and strange, of the new drink she'd taken up on the ship, fizzy, made out of sugar: black rum and coke, a pirate's drink.

Bonzer set off across the slippery dance floor; was that pale blue too? Carl wondered, listening to the skittering of Bonzer's claws under the greeting applause . . . rain on a tin roof. Bonzer's claws like the click of Peg's steel knitting needles on a winter night, but he wouldn't think of Peg now because he didn't want a lump in his throat, or his chest, and he tightened his left hand on Bonzer's harness handle, keeping the dog slightly ahead of him as he'd been taught by the man he'd got him from. One half-hour lesson was all he'd had, if you could call it that.

Watching him, Nola wished it was herself leading her boy to the piano, and began fretting again over the legalities of accepting Bonzer in the first place. Boys Carl's age were never officially given dogs. This one had come from someone Bernie knew, the brother of his business partner, Raymond Rose. The brother had passed away.

'He's a good dog. Black lab,' Bernie had told Nola in the first contact they'd had for a year and a half. 'He's well trained. I thought Carl could use him — and Raymond'd like him to have him. You can have him for free.'

'Doesn't he have to be returned to the Blind Foundation?' Nola had asked, worried.

'He came here from America with the Rose's brother three years ago — he's outside the system.'

Maybe he hadn't heard her question.

'They all come from Australia. All the dogs here. They're trained in Oz,' she'd interrupted.

'I said America, not Australia.'

'Yes, I know.'

'You're not making any sense, Nola Lane. Again.'

Nola sighed. This was the way of it every rare conversation they had — into the suffocating realms of irritation and misunderstanding. She didn't say anything.

'D'you want him or not? Put Carl on.'

So she had, and Carl couldn't believe his ears, and the dog

was delivered that afternoon, but not by Bernie. He'd been very busy, since he got out of prison, with his business interests: setting up a 'gentlemen's club' at the red-light end of Karangahape Road. It was Raymond Rose who'd brought Bonzer, with a scribbled list of commands he'd heard his brother use and a brief demonstration of how to hold the harness.

'Find the piano,' Carl said as they moved away, a command Bonzer had been taught that afternoon. In the bright lights over the band on the dance floor he would be black moving on black, towards the white upright bolted to the floor, himself walking steady beside him. Nola slipped around to a place at the nearest table, a seat Alf had reserved for her, and just as well: it was a full house.

Bonzer drew up by the piano, smooth and elegant, so that Carl had only to release the harness handle and slip sideways onto the stool. He laid his hands on the cool, frictionless keys and waited for the signal from the bandleader, a sharp tap of his baton on the metal edge of his music stand. It seemed an age in coming and while he waited he realised his palms were sweaty, so he lifted his hands again and wiped them on his trouser-legs, quickly, just as the rat-a-tat-tat sounded swift and light — and he thought for a moment he'd forgotten the order, but of course he hadn't.

He shut off his mind, let his hands and ears do all the thinking for him — and played through his repertoire: all those songs and standards he'd learned off Nola's records and the singles he'd begged her to buy after hearing them on the radio. He heard how the sound was dulled since their practice that afternoon in the empty bar; how it was absorbed by the listening bodies, how it surged over the grit of low chatter, around the occasional eruption of laughter that tore through the shift and surge of the music. This was a bar, after all; it wasn't a concert: he couldn't expect them to be silently appreciative. Especially not when they were drinking this rum and coke, a drink that made his mother chatty and sometimes very silly.

The action of the piano in the Emerald Bar was stiffer than the pianos he was used to, the one at home and the one belonging to the nuns at the Cluny convent he went to for his lessons. He would like Sister Bernard to be here, the nun who shared her name with his father, only it was pronounced the French way: Bearnar. He would like her to be listening to him and sharing his moment of glory. Sometimes Sister Bearnar would check outside the door to see if any of the other nuns were within earshot, then she would play herself, and she could really swing, Sister Bearnar, the great bulk of her setting the piano stool creaking, that piano stool that was solid under his still wiry frame — just as this one was as he started into Gershwin's 'Summertime' with a wailing saxophone taking the vocalist's part and he felt, rather than heard, Bonzer spring to his feet. There was a second's pause before he howled, his head lifted, and his mouth, as Carl discovered when he took his hands away from the keyboard and felt for his dog, connecting with his muzzle, had formed a perfect O.

The audience laughed and stamped their feet, as if they thought this was part of the act, and Carl played on, hoping that Bonzer would stop soon — and the band played on too, taking their lead from Carl. When they'd gone another twelve bars and still Bonzer sang, Roger stopped them with another percussive tap of wood on metal. Applause lifted around them, building to a crescendo, cracking and banging like the plastic bags his grandmother had saved and pegged to the clothesline in a high wind, wrapping him around, depriving him of oxygen. He felt his chest heave and his shoulders slump and when Roger came to urge him to stand, to bow, he kept his face turned away from where he hoped the majority of the audience were, though it seemed they were everywhere. He wasn't a novelty act, a sightless freak with a singing dog; he was a serious musician. Next time, if there was a next time, he would leave Bonzer shut in their cabin in the crew's quarters.

His mother came to find him, ice tinkling on glass in one hand, cigarette smoke rising from the other.

'What a show-stopper!' she said, her voice breathy with laughter. He took a step away from her, pulling his arm free from her too-tight grasp, silently raging. She needed to understand that Bonzer's behaviour was not amusing. Carl was too young to have a dog anyway: you were not supposed to have one until you were twenty. He was proficient with the long cane and should have stuck with that; they'd only brought the dog with them because Nola liked to be the centre of attention. He hated her.

He called his dog to him, took up the harness and left the bar as soon as he knew his mother's attention had shifted to a man who stood beside her; the possessor of a voice who'd said something about the money and fame that could be earned by 'the boy's double act'. He was often hanging around his mother, the owner of that voice: it was Dave, the Australian magician.

'Bed,' he told Bonzer, and the dog set off down the corridors, alleyways and stairwells at a steady pace. What would happen if they got lost? Carl wondered. Would Nola notice any time before midnight? When the magician was around, her body lightened, as if she'd suddenly turned into a person-shaped éclair filled with whipped cream, and if she was holding Carl's hand or arm he would have the oddest sensation that her bones were melting like candle wax, her skin growing hotter.

The dog had stopped and Carl would have asked him to go on, but he heard muffled footsteps on the carpet coming towards him. The corridors were narrower here, on C deck, and it wasn't possible to pass three abreast.

'Are you all right?' the person asked. 'Do you know where you're going?'

'Yes,' he said, 'my dog does. Excuse me,' and he heard a slight intake of breath as if the woman, possibly an old lady by the quality of her voice and the strong scent of Tweed (both of which reminded him of Peg) was offended by his lack of gratitude for her concern. Let her be. He didn't always have to be grateful; he didn't always have to be the sweet little blind boy, the son of tall, beautiful Nola who had suddenly taken to dying her hair red and draping herself with long clattering necklaces and medallions in an effort to be witchy and mysterious. She wasn't mysterious to him.

They went down another flight of stairs, passed between the whirring blank expanse of wall at the air-conditioning plant and the disinfectant smell from the open door to the hospital on his left — a smell that reminded him of his mother's old dental clinic — and it was only a few more steps from here. Bonzer stopped and turned him towards the door. He felt for the number, 27, and they were home.

As soon as he was inside he flicked on the light, out of habit. How many times had his mother or grandmother come into his bedroom at home and said, 'Why are you sitting in the dark?', a question that up until now had seemed curious rather than insensitive. It was insensitive. He felt for the edge of his bed and sat down, fury churning in his stomach like the aftermath of a bad curry, the curry he'd eaten with his mother and Dave when they'd gone ashore in Suva to get his new suit. He wanted his life to change; he was ready for it. Ever since he was five years old he'd spent his weeks at Homai, a school for blind children, coming home only at weekends. At first he'd hated it, so sick with longing for Peg and Nola he couldn't eat or sleep. But he got used to it. He'd learned to read Braille and use the long cane; he'd made some friends. Now, some mysterious people had decided it was bad and old-fashioned for children who couldn't see to be herded together, and the residential school was to be disbanded. Nola had told him she would make up her mind on the cruise about what he was going to do next. She said she was too stressed and tense to make a decision. She said he'd probably go to another boarding school, which had made him cry.

'I've had enough,' she'd said more than once. 'I've had enough of everything.' She'd taken leave from the dental service but she wanted to give it away entirely.

He unbuckled Bonzer's harness and tossed it on the floor. Too hard: he heard it strike the opposite wall. 'Scarcely enough room to swing a cat,' Peg would say, if she could see it. He lay down, closed his eyes and imagined how it would be to be surrounded by sighted kids. There were some children on board the ship — he'd heard Dave talk about performing in the Junior Club.

'You should bring Carl along,' he'd said, and Nola had replied, 'But he'd miss out on so much,' and Dave had said, knowingly, 'Oh, yeah — the sight gags,' and Nola hadn't said anything. Nor had she taken him.

Would the ordinary schools have talking books like the ones he borrowed from the Blind Foundation? he worried, as Bonzer jumped up on the bed beside him and laid his long body along the length of Carl's, sighing heavily when Carl hooked his arm over him. Would there be teachers who would carry on with teaching him Braille?

The lump under his pillow was his transistor radio. He drew it out, fiddled with the dials, but the reception this far down in the ship — were they even below sea level? — was bad. Or maybe they were too far away from land to pick anything up. He left it on anyway, listening to the swelling and ebbing static, the hints now and then of human voices under the fibrous mat of hissing and prickles, and dreamed of a vast, blue whale shape coming to nudge at the other side of the ship wall, half beast, half machine.

How long his mother had been in the cabin he had no idea, but his radio had been switched off. To do that she must have leaned across him and slipped her hand under his pillow. Bonzer still lay beside him and Carl could tell by his breathing that he was awake too. Someone was whispering from the other berth.

'What the hell was that? Christ, my foot feels dislocated.'

'The harness. I've told him not to leave it on the floor, but —' Nora giggled. 'Do you want the light on?'

'Won't it wake him up?' the visitor asked. It was a man.

'Doesn't make any difference to him.'

So it was still dark, then.

'More romantic with it off.' It was Dave, and he didn't sound at all romantic but comically wheezy, his whisper nothing like his speaking voice, which was deep and rich. Maybe Dave had a good singing voice, thought Carl. He might be a baritone. He'd ask him tomorrow. 'Can you sing, Dave?' he'd ask him. 'Shall we work up a duet?' That would keep him away from Nola.

'Oh, I see,' Nola giggled again.

'Was it rubella?' Dave asked, conversationally.

Everyone asked that. It was the usual reason for blindness in people his age, after the epidemic.

'No. I think . . .' Nola began, and stopped. She came and bent over him — he felt her breath on his cheek, heard her strike a match and blow it out again. Sulphur tickled his nostrils. Sulphur was hell and sulphur was the smell of Rotorua, where Peg had taken him once years ago.

'You think what? Is he asleep?'

'Yes.'

'How can you tell? His eyes are open.'

'He's my son. Of course I can tell. His face looks different.'

'What were you saying?'

'I think it was caused by mercury. From all the contact I had with mercury making silver amalgam for fillings.'

'Like the Mad Hatter,' whispered Dave, but Nola was on a roll, now that she was on the subject, and went on as if she hadn't heard him. Carl hadn't heard her talk about this before. Her soft voice was spongy with anxiety and drink, as if she were about to cry.

'I would have ingested it from breathing in the vapour. And from wringing out the squeeze cloth. We were supposed to use pliers to do it, but sometimes if I was in a hurry I did it with my hands and I — oh . . .'

She was quiet for a moment, her breathing deeper, and Dave was making a soft moaning noise, slightly muffled as if something was in his mouth. Nola's mouth was in his mouth, thought Carl, the bad curry feeling returning. They were kissing for far longer than was necessary. He'd learned about this sort of kissing in a film he'd heard once at the Civic. There had been a long pause in the action and the sound of someone eating a sticky boiled lolly and he'd turned to Peg and said, 'What are they doing?' in a too-loud voice and the people around them had laughed.

This kiss went on and on and on. Go back to sleep, he willed himself, though his head was swimming with what he'd heard.

'It was an accident of birth,' Peg had said whenever he'd asked her, and she'd always follow it up with, 'You're just the same as other kids. You just haven't got your sight.'

Mercury. When Peg and Nola read palms they would talk about the Mount of Mercury, the soft swelling at the root of the little finger, the size of which dictated desire for change, travel and excitement. A person with a round padded mount was often blessed with devastating wit, they said.

'No —' Nola hissed suddenly, and there was a shoving sound, a hand pushed along fabric, a falling away, the kind of fabric that squeaked on contact, nylon perhaps. Her pantyhose? Carl suppressed the thought as Nola whispered urgently, 'Not here. Not with Carl in the room.'

'He wouldn't know,' said Dave, forgetting to whisper.

'He's blind. Not deaf.'

'Bloody hell! Bring me down, why don't you?'

Now, Carl suspected, Dave was not whispering on purpose. 'You really know how to show a bloke a good time.' His voice was sharp with sarcasm.

There was a silence then, and Nola's voice, her quick, soft 'Sorry', came at the same time as Dave's feet met the floor and the bed creaked as he stood up.

'We could go to your cabin, ' said Nola quickly.

'You forgotten? Colin will be there. We share, remember?'

'We could ask him to leave.'

There was a pleading tone in his mother's voice that brought a lump to his throat. What did she like about this man? He wore an aftershave so strong it scoured out your nostrils and might have woken Carl if their voices hadn't. Maybe Dave was good-looking. Part of Carl's brain was still thinking about mercury. He wondered if other people did that, or if it was just him, able to have several thoughts in his head at once. Mercury as a substance was slippery, shiny, you could push it around with your finger. One day, when he'd gone into the clinic for his mother to check his teeth, she'd put a couple of drops in the palm of his hand.

'That'd be the same as putting it out on the Tannoy, wouldn't it? He'd tell the whole ship. This is our little secret.'

'Why?'

'Why what?' He sounded impatient and very close. Carl had the idea that he could touch him if he only reached out a few centimetres.

'Why does it have to be a secret?'

'Because I'm married,' said Dave, 'as you well know.'

Nola was quiet for a moment.

'Where's that bloody harness thing?' Dave went on. 'I don't want to stand on it again.'

'I didn't know you were still married. I heard you were separated.'

'We have an arrangement, you know. Doesn't pay to push it. I like to keep things quiet.'

'I wear a ring myself,' said Nola. 'Have done since Carl was little.'

They were kissing again. Carl put his fingers in his ears.

'If I'd told you I was married,' Dave went on, in a slimy, soppy voice, making noises in between as if he were sucking an ice-cream, 'then you wouldn't have kissed me.'

'Maybe,' came Nola's whisper. 'Maybe I would have.'

Carl couldn't stand it any more. He sat up. 'Mum?'

'Shit!' said Dave, and then, 'Excuse me, sonny. You gave me a fright.'

'You shouldn't kiss my mother,' Carl told him, one hand on Bonzer's head for an ally. 'I don't want you to do that.'

'Carl —' began Nola.

'You're being silly, Mum. I'd like you to go now, Mr Sherman.'

'That's enough, Carl,' said Nola, and her voice sounded closer, from higher than before. She'd stood up. 'I'm going to take Bonzer for his evening stroll up on deck so that he can — you know.'

If it had been only the two of them there she would have said 'go wees', thought Carl, but with the magician beside her, listening, she went on being stupid.

'When I get back I'll expect to see you in your pyjamas and in bed. It's very late. Come on, Bonzer.'

She clicked her fingers, the dog sprang off the bed and the three of them went out. After a while Carl got up, rummaged under his pillow for his pyjamas and lay down again. It was too hot to get under the covers.

Somewhere on the stairs or alleyways between D Deck

and A Deck, Dave took Nola's hand and led her out onto the Games Deck in the stern. The dog trotted beside them, tail wagging, keeping close to Nola. She told Dave about how Carl had come by the dog, how they'd had the brief lesson from the tattooed bereaved brother, how clever Bonzer was. Dave walked quickly, not talking, nodding in cursory greeting to the few passengers they passed this late, many of whom seemed the worse for wear after a night in any one of the ship's five bars. One man flattened himself against a wall like a starfish as they passed, his eyes bulbous and rolling, his lips wet. Further on, they side-stepped a puddle of vomit.

'Yuck,' said Nola, lifting her long hostess skirt.

'You must've seen a lot of that, being a nurse,' Dave said.

'I was a *dental* nurse. For children.' Hadn't he listened?

'Don't have those in Aussie.'

They came up into the night. Dave leant against a railing and undid his tie, white to match his suit. For a moment it caught the wind and unfurled, streaming out of his hand like wake. He rolled it up and stuffed it into his jacket pocket.

'Come here.' He drew her towards him, his lips on hers. He kissed like a man who'd kissed hundreds of women, practised and slow, and Nola was excited by this — this was what she wanted: to be one of a long list of adulterous affairs this man had. She wanted him not to remember her as anything special, because she wasn't — not Nurse Nola running scared and full of dread from her dreary life in the suburbs, her mother dead after a long, debilitating illness and her son the perfect barrier to romantic attachments. His hands cupped her buttocks, pulled her closer and she positioned herself one leg on either side of one of his, pressed herself up against him.

'Come on,' he said in a strangled-sounding voice, and led

her further around the corner to the lifeboats.

He's done this before too, thought Nola, and she liked that idea, that this was part of his shipboard routine — pick a hostess or a passenger, seduce her, keep her a secret and discard her at his own convenience — a pattern as predictable as the order in which he performed his tricks. See the coloured scarves knotted together flying from his pocket, the mirror box, the vanishing coins, the sedated rabbit in the false-bottomed hat.

The lifeboat he chose was about parallel with the cinema, she thought, watching him loosening the ropes that held the cover on. There were no portholes or windows that they could be observed through, something that must have recommended this place to him, this cramped and probably uncomfortable lovers' lane.

'I know some other places,' he told her. 'We could go somewhere inside.'

'This is fine,' she murmured, slipping off her shoes and climbing in. There was a delay before he followed her and when she popped her head up, like an absurd bird in its rocking nest, to see what was keeping him, she almost laughed out loud. He was folding his suit for fear of smudging it, standing in the moonlight in his Y-fronts.

'Hurry up,' she said, and then, experimentally — it was the kind of thing a Harold Robbins heroine might say — 'I'm aching for you,' though they surely wouldn't have giggled the way she did then, high-pitched and nervous, as he put one foot on the railing and the other into the boat and pulled her down onto a mattress of life-jackets.

It was true — he knew lots of tricks and she was a fast learner. Afterwards he thought she'd already known them.

'Christ. You'll do anything,' he said admiringly as he tossed the French letter overboard. 'Where'd you learn to screw like that?'

She lit a cigarette, blew smoke at the tropical stars and considered her reply. *Not from Carl's father*, she could say, or *From books*, or *It comes naturally* — but she chose instead, 'Round and about.'

'We'll have to do it again sometime,' said Dave, by way of farewell, beginning to clamber out.

Smiling, she pulled on her panties and hauled down her dress, fluffed up her flattened, lacquered hair and climbed down to join him. The black bounding shape of Bonzer was there too, with his enthusiastic nose.

'Keep it away from me,' said Dave, his warding hands spread in front of his white suit-pants and she had an impression of how he might be with his wife: fussy and demanding.

'He's just pleased to see you,' she said, keeping up this new persona — tough, bright, hard. Dave was fooled by it, just as she wanted him to be.

'They say dogs are like their owners.' He was picking up his folded jacket before Bonzer could stand on it. 'He's as keen as you are.'

'We haven't had him long enough for any kind of osmosis to have occurred,' she said, as coldly as she could, taking the dog by his collar. 'See you tomorrow.'

She left the light off in the cabin and got into bed, making Bonzer stay on the floor so that he didn't wake Carl, who was on his back snoring lightly. Maybe the snoring was a sign he was growing up: he sounded like a sleeping man. He almost looked like one too, she thought, his jaw longer, the shoulders under his pyjama jacket not the narrow, boyish ones they were even a few months ago. It was happening too fast, perhaps, his growing up and her growing desire for a new life, forcing them into uncharted waters.

It was hours before she slept. Her heart thumped and she felt giddy; sensations that brought to her mind an image of herself as a child on a manicured lawn, a park perhaps, her arms outstretched, spinning and spinning and spinning until she had to lie down on the bristly ground and gaze up at the whirring sky, watching intently until the clouds stilled and the sun hung steady again. Some children, the moment the vortex stopped, would spring to their feet and do it again and again, to stay for the longest time possible in this altered state.

Once had always been enough for Nola. But not now, not in her new life. She had changed, an alchemy brought on by this very boat — she reached up and stroked the shuddering laminate wall — she was thirty-three and it was time to put herself first for a change.

The past fourteen years seemed, as she lay in her narrow berth on this particular night, on this particular slowly shifting spot on the Pacific Ocean, to have been a colossal waste. Not of time, nor of effort — look at what Carl had become — but of herself. She was seized suddenly by a desire to get up, switch on the light and scrutinise her face in the little square of mirror screwed to the wall. How many wrinkles? How many broken blood vessels, that delicate red tracery a map of too many frustrations, too many lonely nights on the sherry and fags while she waited for Carl to grow up and then for Peg's suffering to end?

'I wish I could click my fingers and he'd be five and off to school,' she'd said to her mother he was about three months old.

'Don't wish his babyhood away,' Peg had replied. 'You might not have another one.'

They'd been that day to a paediatrician, a patrician silver-haired man who seemed to know that Nola wasn't married, despite the ring. She'd felt Carl's failure to make 'mid-line contact', to bring his hands or feet together, was her fault, her sins visited upon her child. It was Peg who'd asked the obvious question.

'Is it common for blind children to be slower than the sighted in this regard?' she'd asked, rather tersely, folding her gloved hands over her handbag on her lap.

'Oh, absolutely,' said the paediatrician from behind his wide kauri desk, the groomed trees of his Remuera surgery garden shifting and flashing in the window behind him.

If only she'd been tough then, as tough as she was now. Back then, a certain surliness was Peg's province: Nola could never have competed with her. They'd gone home, lain the baby in his crocheted bouncinette on the carpet and drawn his hands together. The sensation startled him: he flung his head back, flailed and screamed.

'Clap hands,' said Peg.

The baby yelled.

'Pat-a-cake, pat-a-cake, Baker's Man,' sang Peg loudly over the screaming, persisting with bringing his hands into contact, cranking open the fists stiff as the peel of a green-skinned orange.

I wish he was older, Nola had thought, watching them. I wish we were past all this.

In her narrow berth Nola pushed the memory away, rolled over and curled herself up.

She was still asleep when Carl left the cabin in the morning without Bonzer, dressed haphazardly and intent on breakfast.

On the first morning out of Auckland, on the way to Noumea, he and Nola had eaten in the Ruby Grill with the passengers rather than in the crew dining room. It had been Alf's treat, and there had been pineapple. At the thought of it, Carl's mouth flooded with saliva. It was the most delicious thing he had ever tasted. He remembered how the juice had slipped down his throat, lively with sunshine and singing to his tastebuds of high waves breaking on the reef, of the cry of sea-gulls wheeling high above the warm rind of an island beach. He remembered how the fibres of the fruit burst between his molars, how his fingers had held on to the prickly skin, which seemed to be made up of circular patterns with a spike in the middle like a hard version of a mother cat's stomach with her rounds of nipples. Pineapple skin was the skin of a robot cat; pineapple juice was the song of every pirate that had ever ridden the Pacific.

'Excuse me,' he asked an approaching set of footsteps, 'am I going the right way to the Ruby Grill?'

The voice that answered was American, male, kindly. 'I'm going that way myself — you can come along with me.' There was a sticky moment when the man tried to take his arm.

'I'll just walk beside you, if that's all right,' said Carl.

'Where's your dog?' asked the man, and Carl could hear the edge of a laugh, the fringe of it poking out from under the word 'dog', and he stiffened, the hilarity of his audience's response breaking over him all over again, a cold dousing at the end of a warm shower.

'Having a lie-in,' he said, and the man roared with laughter, slapping flesh on flesh (a palm on a thigh? Two hands meeting mid-air?) as if Carl had cracked the best joke ever.

On B Deck they were joined by two children, who ran up

behind them on soft bare feet and grabbed hold of the American's arms. He groaned a little with the impact.

'Why didn't you wait for us, Dad?' they asked, and they sounded like Will Robinson on *Lost in Space*, a programme he and Peg used to watch in Glenlyn. They had that same nasal, querying tone and almost as much to be envied for: they were real, paying passengers away for a holiday; they were on board with their father; and most of all — they were American. America. The smooth, varnished elegance of the word, where Bonzer came from, and all the music that country burst with, showing itself for a tantalising second between each towering letter.

'America,' breathed Carl as they made their way up the last wooden alleyway to breakfast, where the long brown tendrils of bacon smell reached out and tickled at their nostrils.

'What'd you say?' asked one of the children from slightly ahead of him. 'Are you blind?'

There wasn't a breath between his first question and his second.

'Shshsh,' said the father, taking hold of Carl's shoulder. 'How about you sit yourself down and I'll bring you what you want? This here's a buffet breakfast.'

He said 'boofay', which Carl liked. He would say boofay himself from now on.

'No, thank you, sir.'

They lined up with the other passengers.

'Can you see the table yet?' asked Carl. 'Is there pineapple?'

'Let me describe it to ya,' said the American. 'By the way, I'm Mr Haldane.' A warm, dry hand took hold of Carl's and pumped it up and down a few times.

'Need to work a little on that handshake, boy,' Mr

Haldane whispered, then raised his voice to go on. 'And these two here are my daughters, Randy and Rudy.'

Randy and Rudy, thought Carl with astonishment. Why would anyone call their daughter Randy? Or Rudy? Which was ruder? Maybe Mr Haldane didn't know what it meant.

'Rudy?' he said, 'I thought you were a boy. You have a boy's voice, like Will Robinson in *Lost in Space*.'

One of the girls, either Randy or Rudy, threw her voice up towards the low ceiling, roaring with laughter the way her father had, rollicking and loud. Carl waited for the slap of the thigh, the mid-air clap, but there was none.

'Right,' said Mr Haldane, 'down to business. It's a two-tiered buffet table with the full range. We have on the fruit side grapefruit sliced in half with a cherry on a toothpick right through the middle — very pretty, bright red on the yellow . . .' He paused for a moment and Carl predicted the question to follow.

'You know your colours at all?'

'Yeah. I can remember them, sort of.'

'Good, good,' said Mr Haldane. 'Makes my job easier.' He took a deep breath before plunging on. 'There's cantaloupe with a slice cut out to show the flesh inside —'

'What's cantaloupe?'

'Melon.'

'Watermelon?'

'No — different. Not as juicy, more flavour. There's a box of dates with a paper doily fringe; there's apples, grapes and pears. In the bain-maries there's all the cooked food, you know, the full English breakfast: bacon and eggs and sausages.'

The queue shuffled forward. Rudy and Randy were giggling and shoving each other. Giggling at what? Carl wondered, knowing about the shoving only because one of them lurched into him. He felt her soft breast squash against his arm, her smooth, shampoo-scented hair brush across his cheek.

'Sorry,' said either Randy or Rudy.

'You girls stop that,' said Mr Haldane. 'Oh, nearly forgot. There's a coupla vases of orange chrysanthemums. Flowers, you know. You don't eat 'em.'

'No pineapple?' asked Carl, and he heard his voice crack and break with emotion. Behind his eyes a sudden pressure rose, as if he would cry. He'd so looked forward to the pineapple. It was going to soothe away everything — his mother's new, strange behaviour, his humiliation last night, his longing for Peg, which rather than lessening seemed to grow sharper every time he was reminded of her.

'Oh, yeah. Didn't I say? Two of 'em, top tier, standing on their toes on cute little pedestal dishes. I'll grab you some. Randy, you take this young fella to find a seat and I'll bring him over a plate.'

'Just pineapple,' Carl instructed as a warm, bare arm hooked through one of his. 'That's all. Lots.' He allowed himself to be led away.

'Shall we take one of the booths?' Randy asked him. 'There's one free. Let's grab it.' She hauled on his arm to draw him up as if it were a pair of reins. Once he'd gone riding with the children at Homai and they learnt to pull on the leather straps to bring the moving, hairy flanks beneath them to a halt. He neighed, softly, experimentally, to see if Randy would get the joke.

'Say what?' she said.

'I felt like a horse. When you stopped me then. The way you stopped me.'

'Oh.' She wasn't laughing at all. She sounded apologetic, uncomfortable. He felt her lean against him gently.

'There,' she said. 'To your left. Just slide along.'

He did as she said. The surface of the bench seat was smooth and shiny, plastic or vinyl, and squeaked under the cotton of his shorts.

'Keep going,' she said. 'We gotta make room for Pop and Rudy.'

Pop and Rudy and Randy, he thought. It was fantastic. He slid further, squeaking. From all around them came the clatter of forks and knives on china, the chatter of other early break-fasters. He listened to hear if she was still there, if she was still breathing softly, close by on the other side of the table. Perhaps she'd gone off to get her own meal.

'You always been blind?'

She was still there, then.

'Yes. More or less.'

'You can't see nothing at all?'

'No.'

'Where're you from?'

'New Zealand. Auckland.'

'We're from Portland Oregon. You heard of that?'

'No.'

'I ain't never heard of Auckland either till we went there on the ship. We had a holiday in Australia and now we're cruising to San Fran. Mom and Pop just got a divorce so Pop's taking me and Rudy on a trip to make us feel better.'

'Do you live with your father all the time?' asked Carl, curious. Maybe that would be a solution, he thought. Maybe now that Homai was closing down its hostel he could go to live with his father, get to know him. His mother needed a break from him: she said she was suffering from stress. Just before this job came up on the ship she had to go to the doctor with a nervous rash.

'Nope. Wish we did. Allas have a better time with him — he gives us lotsa stuff.'

There was a pause and Carl had the sense she was scrutinising him closely.

'How old are you?' she asked.

'Fourteen.'

'Same,' said Randy. He felt a finger, redolent with coconut-oil-scented suntan lotion, brush the end of his nose and he flinched. 'You're kind of cute,' she went on. 'I heard blind guys are the best kissers.'

Carl turned his face away from the direction of her voice and felt the blood creep up his neck again to heat his cheeks. Where was the pineapple? he wondered. He supposed Mr Haldane was loading up trays for his daughters as well. He could hear his voice, louder than any others, giving instructions to a non-responsive waiter who was presumably complying.

'Some of that, one of those, a bit of that,' came the voice.

There was a percussive banging, back and forth, which heralded the egress and ingress of hurrying feet. With each bang there came a puff of the smell of frying — bacon, eggs, sausages — waiters coming in and out of the kitchen. It was rhythmic, catching. He drummed his fingers on the table, syncopating the beat.

'So?' said Randy. 'Don't you want to kiss me?'

Kiss her? Did she really say that?

'Most guys do,' she went on airily, 'blind or not.'

A faint whirring accompanied a gust of cool air that slipped through a gap in the front of his shirt. He felt for the buttons — two were undone, but there were no opposing buttonholes free. He must've got it mucked up when he dressed. Another hand brushed his, took over his fumbling. Randy was leaning over the table, her breath smelt of toothpaste. He remembered a book Peg used to read him, an American one, about Little Bear, who got up in the morning and brushed his teeth before he ate a sticky breakfast of pancakes and maple syrup. Maybe that was another difference between Americans and New Zealanders, who clean theirs after they've eaten their porridge or savoury mince.

'What are you thinking about?' Randy's voice was lower, huskier, still close. 'I know. Wonderin' what I look like, maybe? You can feel my face if you want.'

'S'all right, thanks,' he managed.

'Shy, ain't ya? I've got blue eyes and long blonde hair and tits to make your mouth water. There. All done up now.'

He felt her move away and heard the pouf as she sat down, forcing air from the squab. A plate chinked as it was placed on the table, and another and another, and Rudy was squeezing in beside him.

'There ya go, sonny. Right in front of you,' said Mr Haldane.

What did she mean, *tits to make his mouth water*? The pineapple wasn't as fine as he remembered it to be.

In an attempt to be helpful, Mr Haldane had had the skin taken off, which made it hard to get a purchase — the chunks slipped around his plate, evading him. The air around the table smelt of fried food, which sat in his nostrils and did battle with the fresh, acid smell of the fruit. Talking with their mouths full, their breath coming in bacon-scented puffs, Randy and Rudy planned a swim in the pool immediately after breakfast and invited him to come along. He wished now he'd brought Bonzer with him. He was out of his depth; he wanted to return to the safety of the cabin and his mother. Bonzer would have been a good excuse to make a getaway.

'Excuse me,' he said, the moment he'd swallowed the last piece he could catch. 'I'd like to go now.'

His cane had fallen to the floor under the table. The family all dived for it at the same time, Randy and Rudy banging heads under the table, which made them laugh hysterically for some time. His fingers itched to take hold of it. After a moment, when Mr Haldane said, 'That's enough, girls,' Carl held out his hand and took it from them and made his way back to the cabin.

He considered he knew the ship now — he had the corridors on D Deck and all the decks mapped out in his mind. He imagined the ship: its high outside walls shuddering through the expanse of ocean on either side of it, water that leapt and surged, uninterrupted, as far as the horizon, the other side of which defied even the sighted. They were blind to it; it hid itself from them.

The first day out of Auckland he had stood with his mother on the deck and she'd described to him how the land folded itself away behind the blue sea, how beyond the Gulf the waves were bigger and rougher. With the wind whipping around their heads she told him how she could see a gannet, and began to describe a vast bird with a yellow head, who folded his wings against his body and plummeted from a great height to seize an unsuspecting fish many feet below.

'I know about gannets,' Carl had interrupted. 'There's a

story about them, how in old age they go blind from all that clever diving so they find a younger bird to go fishing with. They fly out together over the sea and the old bird feels the whoosh as the younger one dives and follows him down. After a while the young bird gets the jack of it and one day at low tide he leads the old bird over the rocks and pretends to dive and the old bird goes splat. Breaks his neck.'

After he'd finished the story there was a pause before he heard his mother's voice, choked-sounding, as if she were holding her breath.

'Who told you that?'

'Dad did, and —' Carl began.

'He shouldn't —' His mother's voice was lifting with the wind, which was gusting, blowing about more.

'Mum, it's all right! It's an interesting fact — I like facts about nature. It's all right, Mum. I don't see myself as a gannet. You can relax.'

She'd laughed then, given him a hug, squeezing him hard. They'd stood at the deck-rail together while the wind grew louder and stronger and they found they could yell out into the pummelling gusts at the tops of their voices, and their voices were thrown back at them, cracking over their heads, disembodied.

Carl wished he could go there now, and howl out into the wind, but it was a calm day and the trick wouldn't work. Instead, he holed up in the cabin with Bonzer and waited for the evening to come. He was to play again with the band, this time leaving Bonzer on his bed.

'I won't be in the audience tonight,' Nola told him as she helped his with his bow-tie. 'I've got four palm readings booked in the Topaz Lounge. Half an hour each. I'll come up to the Emerald Bar as soon as I can.'

She'd been heavy-handed with the perfume, he thought. Her Madame Rochas. Oh, but it was lovely, though, the scent of that and the Helena Rubinstein powder she put on her face. He bent forward and kissed her suddenly, just as they were leaving the cabin.

'What's that for?' she asked, surprised.

'Nothing.'

He could tell her there was an American girl called Randy who wanted to kiss him, who wanted him to put his hands on her, who had tits to make his mouth water, and that he was scared to death of her. But he wondered if his mother, now that she was carrying on with the magician, would encourage him to take Randy up on her offer. Worse still, she might want him to report back.

'Make sure you go straight to the cabin after your last set and take Bonzer up on deck,' she said at the threshold of the Emerald. There was a pause before she let go of his arm.

'That is,' she went on quickly, 'if I'm not back in time to go down with you.'

'Seeing randy old Dave again, are you?'

Maybe Dave would like American Randy, he thought; shame she wasn't older or he wasn't younger. Dave would probably know how to handle a girl like her: a girl with *tits to make your mouth water*.

'Mum?' he reached out to where she had stood a moment ago, into empty space. 'Mum?'

She'd never done that to him before, just walked off without answering a question, or telling him she was leaving. He felt with his cane for the edge of the door and stepped into the room. Roger would be looking out for him, he hoped —

he'd come soon to lead him across to the piano. It was still early, the crowd sounded thin. Some clinking of glassware came from the bar area, a few voices, the cigarette smoke levels an eighth of the choking atmosphere that would thicken up later.

He waited and stewed. Why had she taken offence and stalked off? He'd only described Dave as he was. Also, he realised a little shamefacedly, and wondering if it was worth the test, he was finding out if his mother knew the meaning of the American girl's name, or if it was another thing he'd imagined or got wrong. Language was often problematic like that. Music was so much safer.

Here, finally, was Roger, taking his arm and leading him to the musicians grouped beside the dance floor. Gratefully he sank onto the piano stool, laid his hands on the welcoming keys, and knew that no matter what the future brought — another boarding school, but with sighted boys; or life as before with Nola; or his new exciting idea of going to live with his father; whatever — as long as he had a piano to play he would always be at home. He felt it come, the way it always did: roaring in at him from somewhere behind his head and wrapping him around, the magic of his flying fingers and cool, oddly empty head and swelling heart, and he played and sang until midnight, as though his life depended on it.

Tamara is asleep before I finish and I finish telling the story before it ends with Randy's seduction of my son in a storeroom, which, judging by the time they spent together after that — kissing in the pool, at the table, in our cabin, their faces or hands joined — probably happened

more than once. She was his first love: a shipboard romance.

For another half hour or so I sit quietly, listening to her soft breathing, with the photo of the *Mariana's* entertainers on my knee. Dave and I stand side by side in the third row back, and I remember how, just as the photographer called 'Smile!', I linked my little finger with his, not that you can see it. Warren's dangling trumpet obscures our hands, which would be blurred in any case: Dave pulled away as if I'd burnt him. He was a man of the kind, I discovered, that the world abounds with: the kind that doesn't like to confuse affection with sex. His smooth handsome face stares up at me and I wonder where he is now, I wonder if he is still alive. He would be nearly seventy. What a lovely liar he was — I found out on our third and last cruise together that he wasn't married at all, but told the story as a safety device. It prevented the ladies from getting too involved, he reckoned. There had been several hostesses or passengers since me, by that stage, but somehow Dave and I had remained friends. Or at least drinking buddies. Full of rum and coke, I roared with laughter when he told me the true story, then staggered off to my cabin and fell into my usual alcohol-soaked and dreamless sleep.

Now, while Tamara snores, I tidy the room a little, pick up the rubbish and dirty cups, before I go to my own room and lie down. I wish now I still had the capacity for booze I had in those days, so that a coma would wrap me around and anaesthetise me. I wish I hadn't stirred that time up. My anticipation for telling it was almost as intense as it had been when Carl and I were packing to leave all those years ago. Then, I felt as though I stood at the top of a mountain and surveyed every possibility my life held, an array of walled gardens bathed in sunlight, and I had only to choose which I wanted. Just like Mr Haldane's breakfast boofay.

When finally I sleep, I dream of searching for Carl, just as I have every night since I lost him. The terrain I move through is unfamiliar and everyone I meet tells me they just saw him a moment ago, and gives me complicated instructions of where to find him. A Tibetan monk shows me a map in red ink, but the lines and calligraphy vanish the moment he hands it to me and he leaves me, without a backward glance, standing on a cliff-edge holding a blank piece of parchment that flaps and cracks in the cold, spiralling thermals.

When I wake, Tamara is sitting on the chair beside my bed-room door. It is only just dawn; the moth-holes in my curtains show as tiny silver stars. I can make out her profile, her outline lumpy with her old dressing gown and braided hair. What woke me? Perhaps one of her jaw-breaking yawns. She's yawning now as I watch her, luminous strands of saliva stretching and breaking.

'Tamara?'

'Uh-huh.'

'Are you okay?' My question is barely out before she starts.

'Why didn't you let Carl go to his father? 'Stead of which he spent all those years in a boarding school while you galli-vanted around on ship after ship carrying on with who knows who, never sparing a thought for Carl banged up in yet another institution, homesick and lonely, persecuted by the bully-boys for his poor blind eyes — you didn't even let him go to Bernie for the summer vacations; you insisted he stay in this shit-hole of a flat with a paid caregiver because of course by then you'd sold your house with the garden that he loved, the house in the suburbs that no longer fitted with your new fruiting life —' She

pauses for breath, hauls in a jagged chestful, gives out a strangled sob and falls silent.

My head aches. Dawn rages are worse than any others at
any other time, because the rest of the day is ruined. This is
true for everyone. Carl was a fine one for waking up bleak and
hopeless and despairing for the world. As he grew older I responded to it less and less. In the kitchen I would sing along to
the radio so that he knew I was there, but if he challenged me I
would ignore him. Character-building, went the mantra in my
mind. It's character-building to let him sort it out by himself.
It's my motherly duty to let him sort it out by himself.

Tamara has stood and taken a step towards my voice. She
looks scary, unfamiliar, her hands spread in front of her more
threatening than tentative, more aggressive than exploratory.
Her upper lip is stiff with a sneer, her shoulders are shaking
with fury. Maybe if she comes as far as the bed she'll rain blows
on me; she wants someone to blame.

'One thing at a time. I couldn't have let him go to his
father because of the company Bernie kept. He might have had
a big house in a wealthy suburb by then, but it was still full of
prostitutes and low-life —'

'Snob!' shouts Tamara.

'And Carl may well have been homesick for the first year
at the boarding school but he got used to it: he was used to
being away from me at Homai anyway. It was just the new en-
vironment he had to get used to and by the time he left he was
one of the most popular boys in the school —'

'Who're you kidding?'

' — and he was reluctant to leave, in fact — '

'Only 'cause the place was mapped to him by then — '

'— and that was when Bernie came in useful, giving him

his first gig in one of his clubs. By then Carl was old enough to navigate through the questionable morality of all —'

'Snob,' says Tamara again, but more quietly this time.

'And by then I wasn't going away so often. Alf had retired and hand-reading had fallen out of fashion. By the late seventies fewer people were interested in it, let alone believed in it.'

'You never are wrong, are you? You never make the wrong decisions. You're so fucking up yourself —'

'And what were your other accusations?' I'm angry now. I swing my legs out of bed, count off on my fingers. 'Selling the house in Glenlyn and having a paid caregiver. Well, if you could've seen the house — it'd gone to rack and ruin. I couldn't keep up with the maintenance. Hell's Angels had moved in on one side and a drunken bloody wife-beater and his miserable family on the other. We were burgled three times. I wasn't strong enough — I couldn't cope, and I thought, well, I was happier here in town as a very young woman so I thought I'd try it —'

Tamara gives a strange cry, raspy and smoky, and buries her face in her hands.

'What?'

'"If you could have seen it". You should listen to yourself. You're so fuckin' insensitive.'

'For God's sake! It's just a turn of phrase. I only meant it as a turn of phrase.'

'Shut up!' Tamara in full voice could shatter glass.

'I'm sorry, Tamara. This is ridiculous. I'm going to have a shower.'

I dress slowly, reluctant to face her again, one ear on her

movements around the flat. Her last day in New Zealand and Tamara has planned to spend the afternoon with Sina and Liu. At four o'clock we'll be leaving for the airport. That is, if she still wants me to drive her.

When I come into the kitchen Tamara is pouring cereal, one finger in the bowl to gauge the level.

'You looking your best?' she asks, the moment she hears my footfall.

'Why?' My voice sounds hard and impatient and I regret it. Maybe she's calmed down already, even more rapidly than she usually does.

When she turns around I see that her face is transformed from its earlier, ugly rage. Instead she's twinkling; a secretive smile softens her mouth.

'Because we have a gentleman caller arriving within the hour. For coffee. He's bringing cakes. I rang him while you were in the shower.'

'Skew or Liu? Who?'

'Skew or Liu? Who, who, who?' Tamara mimics, rap-style. 'It ain't Skew. It ain't Liu. Someone who's got somethin' to tell me and you.'

Silently, I unscrew the top half of the espresso pot and rinse it out. Beside me at the bench, Tamara gives a maniacal laugh.

'Bernie,' I say, because of course it will be.

Now feeling in the fridge for the milk, Tamara doesn't confirm or deny. As I pass her on my way to the stove, I notice she has filled her cereal bowl with cat biscuits, which are kept in a glass jar beside the one filled with muesli. She must be distracted: she's never made that mistake before. I'm almost angry enough to let her take a mouthful. Instead I swap the bowl for another with the right stuff in it and put the other on the floor for the cat, who is winding around my legs and chirruping.

Still standing at the bench, Tamara eats fast and carelessly, milk cascading from her spoon down the front of her already marked sweatshirt. The coffee shoots up just as Bernie's footsteps sound on the wooden fire-escape outside. Tamara hears him too, and goes to answer the door.

'Why weren't you at the funeral?' I hear Tamara's voice, raised and angry, before Bernie has even made it as far as the living room. 'How come you never phoned me back or asked after me since we saw you — when? July? Bernie?'

There's a long silence then, and Bernie's decision not to go into any explanations is palpable, like a sudden drop in air pressure on a long plane journey.

'Nola here?' he says eventually.

I bring the coffee through on a tray and use the pouring out and fussing with sugar and milk as a way of not looking at him. He's looking at me, though: I can feel it. What is he thinking? What a mad old bat she's become; look at her skinny old arse and scarlet hair.

Tamara makes her way to Carl's piano and sits down at it, closing the lid and laying her arms and head down on the cool, polished wood. Only metres beyond the window the flyover roars and flashes with traffic. It's too early in the season for cicadas. Sometimes, midsummer and full throttle, they form a vibrating, bass harmonic with the overhead machines. Once, years ago, Carl pointed it out to me. 'Can you hear that?' he asked. 'Like Tuvan throat-singing.'

'Thanks for leaving the phone message,' Bernie says eventually.

'That was Tamara, not me.'

'Not this morning. On the Wednesday morning. When they . . . when they found him.'

'You know something about it.' Tamara's voice is muffled. She hasn't lifted her head. 'One of the men in the van — he asked Carl if you were his father. Bernie Tyler.'

The cup I'm carrying over to her lurches in my hand, splattering coffee on the carpet.

'What? Why didn't you tell me this before? Or the police?'

'He was the only one in the van who sounded white. Skinny white man's voice and a stink of cologne and smoke and booze. Older than the others.' She pushes herself upright. 'Who was he?'

Bernie shrugs. Tamara cocks her head, listening hard.

'Answer her,' I say sharply.

'Could have been anyone.' Bernie sounds bewildered.

'You got that many enemies?' Tamara's voice bulges with scorn. 'That many people hate you enough to kill your son?'

'We know it was an accident. Carl was hit by a car.' Bernie is doing his best to control himself. He's not used to women talking to him like this. As I hand him his coffee I look into his eyes and see the alarm there. I see also that he is all of his seventy-something years and how his face has mostly set, surprisingly, into an expression of contentment.

'You're trying to tell me . . .' he begins, stopping and clearing his throat and starting again. 'You're trying to tell me there was some bloke in the van who actually asked Carl if I was his father? A bloke my age?'

'How the fuck would I know how old he was? All I know is he sounded older than the others, a mean, high voice. Creepy and soft. He knew you.'

'Personally? Where from?'

Tamara is silent. Bernie looks away from her, to me and back again.

'Tamara?' Bernie asked.

'I heard.'

'Well, then?' Bernie leans towards her, his old man's hands clasped on his knees. It gives me a start to see those hands, knobbly, thin. There was a period of two to three years when Carl was at primary school, when they were all that I remembered of Bernie. It was after I had finally forgotten his face; when he finally began to fade for me; when he ceased to be my last thought before I slept and my first when I woke — and that, finally, only because I had realised that in order to survive I had to consciously dismiss him from my mind. It was not a natural fading, but a colossal exercise of will. Until then I'd revelled in him, remembered every sensual detail: his kiss; the warmth of his shoulder under my cheek; the taste of the skin at his throat; the slide of his dry, warm palms on my hips; the weight and pulse of him. From the memories came fantasies, which became so real to me that they would sometimes break open in the middle of the day, while I bent over a child's mouth, or sat with my mother in our isolated, bleak little house in what now seemed to be the most tedious, bloodless suburb on earth. In time the fantasies became more real than the memories — they became like real memories themselves. Not all of them were erotic; some were prosaic, everyday: Bernie's step on the stair with his arrival home, sitting at the kitchen table with Carl on his lap, his head thrown back in that sudden way he had when he laughed, the flash of his gold tooth; the presence of him, his company.

So I had to dig him out — or lose my mind. He was the drug I had used to escape from the endless round of work and worry about Carl, and Peg's increasing querulousness and ill-health. I learned to recognise him as a symptom of a greater malaise.

But his hands stayed with me.

Not those hands. We could pass in the street and not know each other.

'He was sitting behind me in the van,' Tamara begins, finally. 'Maybe next to Carl. I don't know. He said you'd known his father in jail.'

'In Mount Eden?'

'Yep. Suppose. He just said jail, that's all.'

'And you don't know what his name was?'

'Nope.'

Another silence, with Bernie and I both craning our geriatric bodies towards her. Brow creased, Tamara is thinking.

'Try to remember,' Bernie mutters. 'Anything he said, anything you can remember. It might help me to work out —'

'He said, "It was a man called Tyler who took my father down." Something about his father going down.'

'Green.' It's me saying the name, not Bernie. 'Was it Green's son? The story that you and Patu told Brett on Great Barrier Island — how you took Green down to the gallows.'

'I never told Brett that story,' he hisses at me.

'You did. On the beach.'

Bernie is ashen, yellow-grey, the colour of newspaper left out in the weather.

'Green was a young man. He was unmarried. He was strung up for murdering his girlfriend.'

'Maybe he had another girl, one who had his baby,' Tamara says. 'Some bitch with a vengeance.'

'There's no point in making things up!' Bernie snaps at her.

Twisting her body around, Tamara feels for the top of the piano and puts her coffee cup down. She opens the lid, plays a soft minor chord, adds a seventh, a ninth.

'She was just surmising,' I murmur.

'Get me the phone book.' He's opening his spectacles case, jamming on a pair of reading glasses. 'Can you remember anything else?'

'I'm flying on out of this place tonight,' she says. 'You want me to help you, you be nice. Where's my coffee?' Her fingers feel along the edge of the piano, locate the cup.

'Tell me again the name of the street they found him on,' says Bernie, the directory open at G.

'Church Street, Onehunga.' How could he have forgotten the name of the street?

'That's right,' says Bernie, as if he were quizzing me. 'Church. A corner.'

'What are you doing?'

'Wondering if . . . what if they were taking this person home and if it was Green's son, or some relative, then maybe he's listed in the phone book —'

'We'd only just picked him up before I got out,' Tamara interrupts.

'What?' I can barely contain my anger. 'This is yet another thing you didn't tell the cops. You never said they stopped to pick someone else up. What was he doing? Hitch-hiking?'

Tamara shrugs, her coffee surging against the walls of the cup.

'Don't get pissed at me. I can't help it. It's like . . . it's like I've dropped something and it's broken all to little pieces and I'm feeling around trying to find it all. Prob'ly still be remembering things when I get back to Chi-town.'

'You bloody better not,' Bernie says coldly. 'Lay off the dope and remember it all now.'

'He got in,' Tamara raises her voice over the top of him, 'and something about him made them all laugh — and they went around the van saying hello —'

'D'you think he was a stranger to them, then?' Bernie asks.

'Dunno,' says Tamara belligerently. 'How the hell'd I know that?'

'Then what?' I prompt gently, after a pause. 'They said hello and then what?'

'When they got to Carl, he didn't say hello, or gidday or talofa, or anything like that. So well brought up he said his whole name — he said "Carl Tyler". That's how this dude knew who he was. And he asked, "Was your dad a screw?"'

'But he didn't say his name?'

'No. I already told you that.'

'Then what?' I say again.

'We stopped at the gas station and I got out and the rest you know.'

Bernie slams the telephone book shut hard enough to make Tamara and me jump.

'This is fucking hopeless,' he says.

'Check this!' Tamara wails, holding her blouse away from her skin, a dark wash of coffee spreading over the pink cloth. 'You stupid old nut.'

Amid the remaining chaos of Tamara's room I help her to find another top and take the other through to the bathroom to soak it in a bucket. She comes to find me, rubbing angrily at her already inflamed eyes.

'Don't do that,' I say gently, putting an arm around her. But she flinches.

'You're not my fucking mama,' she says nastily. 'I'm not your fucking substitute.'

'Okay, love.' I go back to my soaking, shutting off the tap. 'You be like that all you like.'

She's silent now beside me, her arms tightly crossed across her body.

'It's all right — it'll be fine. Do you want to see if Bernie would like to come with us?'

No response.

'It's a good idea,' I go on. 'He can drive us.'

'Don't care,' she mumbles, and she crumples suddenly, all the rage and determination of the past two weeks leaving her in a rush. I fold my arms around her and listen, maybe for the last time — hopefully, even? — to her gulping, broken sobs.

'Nola?' It's Bernie, looking around the door, his old face creased with concern.

He reaches out to take my burden, but I'm quite strong enough to hold Tamara up. I've done so plenty of times since Carl's death.

Bernie drives us in his ridiculous car, which draws stares from pedestrians and other motorists and passengers. Tamara brightens up when he tells her we're going in the Pontiac, a 1955 two-door, left-hand-drive Chieftain, lovingly restored by Bernie himself. Before she gets in she runs her hands over the shiny paintwork of the door, and inside she pats the pale, plump upholstery. She slips easily into the back seat, a manoeuvre she must have practised to have it so seamless and swift. She's been out driving with Bernie before, and Carl must've sat where I'm sitting now, in the front seat.

'You know exactly the spot?' Bernie asks me as we wheel around the Royal Oak roundabout.

'I'm not even going to answer that.'

I stroke the white cross, which lies across my lap. We decided not to put his name on it. In the back seat Tamara takes the bend sliding on the bench seat, clutching a small bunch of spring flowers: paperwhite, jonquils and freesias. The living-room-sized car is heavy with their scent.

Down the steep incline we go, pulling up outside the conglomeration of shabby buildings and prefabs that make up Onehunga School, before the broken yellow line that curves around the corner of Selwyn and Church streets. Further down, the road levels out semi-industrial, with the Trident Hotel, a mini-golf centre, factories and car yards. A short distance away roars the motorway that Tamara and I will later take to the airport, and on the other side of that, glinting amalgam-grey under the soft, slippery sky, is Manukau Harbour, where forty years ago Bernie kept his mullet boat.

'They found him right down there, on the corner,' I tell Bernie.

'On the path, or inside the school grounds?' he asks. He hasn't let go of the steering wheel; his knuckles are white.

'The gutter, actually, Bernie.'

'I think I'll stay in the —' Bernie begins.

'No.' I touch him lightly on the shoulder. 'Let's do this. Come on.' But I don't press him on it. He wasn't able to get himself along to the funeral: it's likely he won't be able to do this either. Tamara and I link arms and walk the rest of the way to the corner; she with the flowers, me lugging the cross.

'Someone'll lift it for sure,' she says, letting me go while I try to push the cross into the soft earth on the other side of the school fence, a single metal bar. 'Cross or the flowers or both.'

'Hope not. Here — you help.' I lie the flowers on the ground beside us and take Tamara's hands, laying them squarely on the transverse of the cross, and together we push it in, a good foot or more.

'There ya go, Carlie,' says Tamara. 'That's for you, hon.'

She reaches into her pocket and takes out a little knife, perhaps to cut the string for tying on the flowers. Three Pacific Island children, one with a sparkling new scooter, come down the hill past Bernie's car. They cluster around and stare at us.

'What are you doing?' asks the oldest one, who is about five years old. But her mother appears behind her, a vast woman vastly pregnant. The mother smiles at me.

'That for that fella who died here?' she asks.

I nod, not trusting myself not to burst into tears. Children should never see old women crying. To distract myself I tie the flowers to the cross, round and round with metres of green string. It's only when I'm finished that I glance up at Tamara. As close to the scalp as she can go without drawing blood, Tamara is using the little knife to hack off one of her braids. Squatting beside the cross, she pushes her hair down into the earth, against the submerged shaft. Her lips are moving silently, a private message for Carl.

'You want to . . . say a prayer together, or something?' I ask lamely.

'Yeah.' Tamara stands brusquely. 'Holy Father, fuck you too.'

Behind Tamara I can see a big woman rushing across Selwyn Street, dodging traffic, down the hill, past Bernie who's still sitting sombre in his car. At first I think it's the children's mother of a moment ago, but they've gone on around the corner towards the Onehunga shops, leaving us to it. This woman, I see as she draws closer, is white, and a lot older, in her early fifties perhaps. Scraped up in a rubber band at the top of her head, her peroxided hair is grey at the roots. A yellow satin shirt, balled and scuffed, strains across her bra-less breasts. She wears a pair of brown tracksuit pants and bare feet, despite the chill of the morning, her approaching toenails chipped lurid pink.

'Nola?' says Tamara. 'Are we going, then?'

There is the sound of a heavy car door opening and closing and Bernie comes stiff-legged down the path. Maybe he thinks we need defending from this gargantuan female, though she looks harmless. Perhaps she's not the full quid. She still hasn't uttered a word, her gaze shifting from me to Tamara to the shiny white cross and back to Tamara again.

'You were in the van,' the woman says finally, her voice deep, roughened. 'I remember you.'

'What's going on?' asks Bernie from behind her and the woman turns, fleshily, slowly, as if her bare feet hurt her.

Downwind I catch the scent of cheap, stale perfume and last night's grog, a reek of tobacco smoke and under it all the sharp pungency of sweat and dirt, poverty's dreary cologne. Despite the incline of the hill she stands as tall as he does, eye to eye. Beyond them, on the other side of the road, the door to an old wooden cottage stands open and a young Polynesian man in a beanie comes to lean against a lopsided verandah post, watching.

The woman stares at Tamara and then at me, her mouth slightly agape, the watery blue eyes in her plump face narrowing.

'This is the dude we picked up on Great North Road,' Tamara says. 'Same voice — I'm sure it is. Say something else, mister.'

But the woman is silent, the burnt ends of her yellow hair glinting in the dull, moist light.

'Car?' says Bernie, nonsensically, his throat clogged. He coughs, still staring at her, begins again. 'Karen?'

'I don't know you,' says the woman, folding her arms across her spilling stomach. 'Do I know you?'

'Bernie,' he says. 'Bernie Tyler.'

Is it? Is he right? It's my turn to stare at her now, to see if it is. Karen. Kev's daughter. Don't say anything else, Bernie, I'm thinking, you might frighten her away and I want to know everything she can tell me. Let's just find out if she was in the van, if Tamara's right . . .

'And you're Karen,' he goes on. 'I knew you when you were a kid.'

The woman takes a step away, colliding with me, staring at Bernie, looking him steadily up and down.

'What?' says Tamara loudly, aggressively. 'What did you say? *Karen?*'

'Ohh, yes indeedee,' the woman says, still gazing at him. 'So it is. Bernie Tyler. Well, well.'

'Thought you were a bloke.' Tamara has angled her body towards Karen's voice.

'Never thought I'd see the day,' Karen is saying, her large dirty mouth opening and closing.

A heavy articulated truck comes down the hill and quietens us beneath its cornering roar, shooting black from its skinny smoke-stack above the shining cab. The earth shivers beneath our feet. Karen is staring at Tamara again and smiling, not very nicely.

'You get burned too? How'd you get that scar?'

But Tamara employs the age-old prerogative of the blind not to answer. Instead she inclines her head towards the ground and lifts her fingers to feel the prickly stump left by the departed braid. She's half destroyed my hours of work: part of the severed coil hangs loose at the back.

Karen meets my eyes. There's a hunger there, a terrible loneliness — she's frightening.

'Don't you want to know what happened after the boys . . .' she starts, 'after they dropped me home? After you got out and left Brett behind?'

'Carl,' I correct her gently. 'Carl, not Brett.'

'It was Brett,' she says. 'That's how I recognised him, because he lived in Glenlyn with Dad and me all those years ago and there he was a grown man and I realised he'd lost his eyes in the fire. He wasn't killed at all. That was just a story. He just lost his eyes and grew up blind.'

'What?' Bernie's face has paled. His upper lip lifts in a kind of prehensile sneer. 'What did you say?'

Tamara has taken hold of the back of my jacket.

'I want her to tell me what happened,' she says, giving me a shake.

'Come over to my place, then,' Karen says, gesturing across the road, 'over there. I live in that house. You can have a cup of tea.' She smiles suddenly, her big brown teeth like smutty awnings.

'Why not?' I say. 'Bernie?'

But Bernie takes a deep breath and shakes his head. 'Don't think so,' he mutters.

'Not you,' Karen says quickly, defensive. 'Not you. I didn't invite you. You should still be jail. Why'd they let you out? You killed my father.'

Bernie's face has settled into an expression I've never seen before, though as I look at him it seems it follows certain well-worn patterns. What is it? Resignation, perhaps. And guilt. And an absence: a practised removal of his true self to a place of safety. He seems inviolate.

'I'll wait in the car, then,' he says, and retraces his steps.

The gawky girl Karen was swims up at me through the layers of her flesh. As we cross the road together I hear her girl's voice again on that late summer dawn before the arrival of the milk truck: 'You got my stepbrother in trouble'; I see her up-turned face among the audience of Miss Auckland 1961 and I remember, as if I were there, her alarm when Bernie broke into her house and fought her father. On the broken path between an avenue of mountain paw-paw trees, as we approach the rickety stairs that lead to the sagging porch, she says suddenly, 'You still fixing teeth?'

'No,' I tell her, 'not for years.'

Down the grimy hall we go, which reeks of dog and rot, to a large, dim kitchen out the back. The young man I saw earlier is there, standing at the bench, which is spread with newspaper. He's peeling potatoes; the radio is up loud barking rap.

'Christ, what a stink,' says Tamara, her face wrinkled with disgust. 'And what's that shit music?'

'You don't like it, ma'am?' asks the teenager politely, though sarcastically, and turns it off.

'He was in the van too,' says Tamara quietly.

Karen heaves herself into a cracked plastic chair, the legs buckling a little with her weight, and sweeps a space clear on the cluttered table to rest her elbow. 'This is Matt. He lives here.'

Tamara grips my arm. The other hand is cupped at her waist, something glinting between her fingers. It's the little knife she used to cut her braid off.

'Siddown,' says Karen. 'Maybe Matt'll make us a cuppa.'

'Rather stand,' Tamara mutters.

A plastic bag nailed over a gap in the wall does for a window, the real ones boarded up. The fifty-watt bulb in the lean-to ceiling struggles to cast its yellow light lower than the tops of our heads, and the plastic bag, torn and flapping a little, casts a cool, frosty light over the side of Tamara's face. From this angle the scar bisecting her face looks raw, renewed. She feels unsafe.

'It's all right,' I tell her. 'We can sit down.'

'You rest your bones, old girl,' Tamara whispers. 'I'll stand behind you.'

And she does, one hand on the back of my chair, the other still concealing the knife. When he sees me sit down, Matt fills a blackened pot with water and bangs it down on the electric range. The heating element fills the room with the smell of old burning fat.

'Okay,' says Tamara, louder, 'get on with it, will ya? Haven't got all day.'

'Are you so rude 'cause you're blind? Or 'cause you're a Yank?' asks Karen, slowly and loudly. 'Maybe you should go and sit outside with that murdering old pimp.'

She's kept tabs on Bernie, then. She knows about his career.

'He ran a club,' says Tamara. 'He wasn't a pimp.'

'One of my mates worked for him years ago,' says Karen. 'Fell in love with him, the silly bitch, and he dicked her around.'

One of Tamara's hands slips from the chair back to my shoulder and gives it a squeeze.

'Just tell us what happened after I got out of the van.' Tamara tries a new, soothing and entirely uncharacteristic tone. 'Please.'

'Well. The guys said they'd give me a lift home. I was really out of it — been at the Family and Naval for hours with some of the old girls who still work round there. Old hooker's a good hooker, eh, Matt?'

Embarrassed, Matt looks up for the briefest instant, then goes back to his peeling. Karen chuckles and leans forward in her chair, her small, plump hands clasped on the table in front of her.

'Anyway, could hardly stand up. They wanted to get me home before I chucked up all over their precious van. Told Brett they'd get him home after, but he went wild and thrashed about, whacked a coupla the guys with his white stick. Was that you, Matt? Did he get ya?'

Matt carries on with his peeling. They must be expecting company — there's a mound of spuds in front of him.

'Did he get ya, Matt?' Karen says again.

'Nah. I was in the front,' he says.

'You were the one . . .' Tamara begins, head cocked towards his voice, her hand a vice on my shoulder, 'you're the kid took my glasses off and handed them around. You touched my face.'

'Don't remember that,' says Karen, with a hint of jealousy. She's old enough to be the boy's grandmother. 'That's the night I met Matt, see. And he had nowhere to go, so he's staying with me.' She's keen for us to know this, that the boy belongs to her. 'Lives here now.'

There's a pause then. The pot on the stove is starting to steam. Matt ambles over to the table, peers into a number of dirty cups, selects three and takes them over to the sink, where he runs water into them and shakes them out.

'So, he hit people with his stick?' I ask, as gently as I can, though I feel like screaming.

'Yep. Three of the guys held him down. He was yelling for them to stop the van and let him out. They kept saying they'd take him home later but he wouldn't listen. Knew you'd fucked off, see. Freaked him out.'

Tamara's breathing has changed, as if she's about to start

crying. I fight a sudden desire to pull her onto my lap, to hold her like a child while we hear the rest.

'And when they pulled up over the road to let me out, he got out too.'

'Fell out,' Matt corrects, dropping in the teabags.

'Yeah. Must've. Fell.' Karen concedes.

'And?' From me.

'I came home. Matt helped me across the road. Next morning cops banging on my door asking did I know about the hit-and-run. Didn't, of course.'

'I did, though,' says Matt, 'but cops didn't ask me.' He sniggers softly, nervously. 'Didn't know I was there, eh?'

'Just as well,' says Karen, taking her tea from him. 'You might of got the blame.'

'Can she drink tea?' he asks me, setting down the other two mugs.

The liquid inside is black, teabag still floating.

'Might burn herself,' he adds solicitously.

'Blame for what?' I ask.

'Didn't know it was Brett who died,' Karen says. 'Cops didn't tell me it was a blind fella. Just said someone'd got knocked down on the corner and killed and did I see anything? Never knew it was Brett.'

'Carl!' Tamara yells, all attempts at self-restraint abandoned. '*Carl* — you stupid shithead bitch. Brett died years ago. Carl was his half-brother and he was my darling and you just fuckin' left him there.'

Someone is knocking at the still-open door and calling down the hall. Out of the corner of my eye, somewhere above my head, I see the flash of the knife, a tiny silver blade slashing at the air, and rear away from it.

'What do you mean you were there? Matt?' I say. But Matt is staring at Tamara aghast, a potato in one hand, the plastic peeler in the other.

'Nola? Everything all right?' Bernie has invited himself in.

'Tell me what you mean.' I seem to have lost my voice, I can only whisper and Matt is still doing his best not to hear me. Putting his arm around Tamara, Bernie takes the knife off her.

'It's Bernie, love. Come on. That's enough.'

'Matt? Did you see it?'

'See what?' asks Bernie, growling, threatening, still holding on to Tamara.

'Saw him try to walk across the road, that's all. After the van drove off.' He puts the potato peeler down and turns to look at Karen. He wants her to help him.

Karen pushes herself to her feet, which, now that I look at them closely, are tiny, delicate, quite beautiful and out of keeping with the rest of her. And I remember, suddenly, that long-ago conversation after the beauty contest.

'Everyone has something beautiful,' Peg had told her. 'If you look hard, you'll find something.'

Did she ever find her feet?

'And then what? You saw someone hit him and drive off?' Tamara is shrieking, that powerful voice, those capacious lungs. 'And you just fuckin' left him there. You cunts!'

'She's mad,' Karen says to Bernie. 'Take that bloody nutter out of my house.'

'Not as fuckin' crazy as you are, bitch!' bellows Tamara, trying to break free of Bernie. I can feel her lurching against the back of my chair.

'Nola. Come on, get up,' mutters Bernie. 'You're not going to learn anything more.'

'We didn't see anything.' Matt comes closer, talking fast. 'You have to believe me. We'd gone inside. I didn't think, eh. Never met a blind dude before, eh. Didn't think . . . '

'Nola,' says Bernie, louder, 'get up, will you? Let's go.'

'Leave her alone. I think she's praying,' says Matt, taking my bowed head and examination of Karen's feet for something else.

A mistake, an accident.
Another one.

Tamara, Bernie and I make our way back to the car. Already the flowers have gone from the cross, which is on a lean, as if the purloiner had had difficulty wrenching the freesias and jonquils free. Walking between us, Bernie doesn't notice the theft, or if he does, he doesn't observe it aloud, for which I'm grateful. Better Tamara imagines our little monument pristine.

Not as fluidly as before, banging her shoulder, Tamara climbs into the back seat. The return journey requires a soundtrack: the earplugs go in, the Walkman turned up loud enough for me to hear the tinny top line as we turn up Hill Street towards Jellicoe Park.

'So it wasn't the boys in the van who killed him,' I say eventually.

'How do we know that? They might've been stoned enough to go over the top of him and not notice.'

'Jesus, Bernie. I don't think so.'

'You think because the boy was friendly and made you a cup of tea he's innocent.' Bernie bangs the steering wheel hard. 'Bloody stupid. I should ring the cops and tell them we've found two of the other passengers.'

'Thought you hated the cops.'

'Not at all. I've had a lot to do with them over the years, one way or another. Some of them were regular customers at the club. I could go straight to the top.'

'There's no point. What's the point in that? If those boys make a habit of making nuisances of themselves around the place, then the cops'd be glad to have something to nail on them. Even if they didn't do it. And I think . . . you know, I've always believed, ever since Tamara first told me the story, that they really did have good intentions. I think they did mean to take them home. They were just too out of it to get themselves organised. Maybe they didn't have a map or . . .'

'Huh. Bullshit.' He's not looking at me. Protruding from the short sleeve of his grey nylon shirt, his nearest arm is tattooed. An anchor, faded now but nicely done, too professional for a prison job. Did he always have that? Maybe it dates back to the mullet boat days. I don't remember. I never saw him with his shirt off in daylight.

'Karen. Crazy,' he says now, and shakes his head. 'Always was a stupid cow.'

'Surprised you recognised her.'

'Did you?'

'No. Haven't clapped eyes on her for forty-something years. Not since the Miss Auckland in 1961.'

'The what?'

'Beauty competition. You were in prison. You won't remember.'

'No . . . sorry.'

He remembers nothing, of course. None of the burden of the times I wished he were beside me, or pretended he was. We've shared nothing. If we avoid the most obvious topic we'll have nothing to talk about.

'I . . . um . . . I don't mind the odd bit of whatsitcalled, the swimsuit competition.'

'That's a far cry from Miss Auckland 1961,' I say, irked.

'No doubt it was. You were all supposed to be virgins, weren't you?' He's looking at me sideways, a glint in his eye.

'We only ever made love twice, Bernie. Twice. I don't think it counts.'

'You were one gorgeous girl, Nola Lane. I've never understood . . .' He pauses for a moment while he forces the huge engine into a higher gear and overtakes a bus, '. . . why you didn't find someone else.'

'There wasn't anyone else.'

'You don't mean that,' he says softly.

'Yes, I do. I wouldn't say it otherwise.'

Bernie reaches over and pats my hand and it's all I can do not to pull it away, my old rage against him rolling over in my chest like a waking beast.

'I'm sorry,' he's saying now. 'I wanted . . .' He trails off again.

'What? You wanted what? To be unencumbered. You succeeded there.'

'No. I had a son. Our son. I was going to say I wanted the best for you. I wasn't the best. I thought about you a lot, you know, especially when I was inside. I lay on my bed in my cell in Mount Eden and I thought of you.'

Of course he would have done. For a little while. But Bernie had made a decision not to love me and it wouldn't have been long before his heart followed his mind on its dead-end, irresponsible route.

'I did that quite a bit at first, but you know . . .'

'No, I don't. "You know" what?'

In the back Tamara is snoring slightly.

'How those things are. They just wither away. Eventually. The weight of other things takes over. Life takes over.'

Life takes over. Why didn't it do that for me?

There is a tear wobbling in one of my eyes. I could count on one hand the number of times I've cried as an adult. I'm not going to cry now. I dig in my pocket and retrieve a tattered tissue . . . too late. He's looking at me again.

'Nola, you wouldn't have wanted me.'

'You didn't try. You didn't ask.'

'Every time we spoke you were nasty.'

'I was angry . . . You hardly saw our son.' I just want to talk about Carl. Just Carl. I want as much of him as Bernie can give me.

'I saw him more than you think.'

'Tell me . . .' I begin. 'Tell me about one of those times. Let me have that too, to add to . . .'

'Your memories of him.'

'Yes, that.'

Bernie looks into the rear-vision mirror, adjusts it to see into the back seat.

'Tamara's asleep.'

'I know. Just tell me, now, as we go along.'

'All right. This is the story of how I went to see him when he was six.'

'You never saw him when he was six.'

'Oh, yes, I did.' And he takes my hand again in a comradely way, as if we're a pair of old soldiers revisiting a battleground, only releasing it through the telling of the story to change gear, all the way to Grafton.

CHAPTER TEN

Carl must've enlisted someone to look up the number in the telephone directory, which surely wasn't in Braille yet. From what little he'd seen, Bernie knew Braille was bulky — the telephone book of the growing city would occupy a small room. Whoever the sighted person was, a teacher or the matron, she must've been broad-minded enough not to balk at the idea of a six-year-old putting a call through to the Acme Gentlemen's Club. The only other night-spots in 1968, the Hey-Diddle-Griddle and the Colony, didn't compare with the Acme for noise, nudity and notoriety; this establishment had never been off the scandal sheets since its inception, almost exactly two years to the day since Bernie got out of jail.

Those days, a full three and a half years since his release, a 1960 red and silver Chrysler Imperial was parked in the alley behind the building. As he clattered down the stairs from his office, Bernie breathed in the smell of cigarettes, spilled alcohol,

stale perfume and sweat that was the residue of another successful Thursday-night pay night. The club had its back windows
open and the maroon carpet runner that usually lay along the
side of the bar was spread out on the narrow grassless berm to
dry.

Upstairs, a window flew up at his back and one of the
girls leaned out, her hair wet and shining in bands like black
kelp.

'Where're you going, Bernie?' she called down. It was
Merle from up north, one of the new hostesses. They'd been so
busy over the summer, Bernie had had to take on a whole new
batch.

'For a drive,' he called out. 'Want to come?'

Merle grinned, and he remembered that was why he'd
employed her in the first place, for her easy, sweet-natured smile
with the big white teeth and warm brown eyes — he knew
many of their customers would like that smile as much as he
did. And wasn't it the common wisdom that Maori girls were
good at this sort of work?

Her wet head nodded and vanished from the window, but
not so far back that he couldn't see her slough off her pink
candlewick dressing gown and pull on a blue cotton dress over
a dingy-looking bra. He wondered if she was doing it on
purpose, leading him on. Sometimes the girls did that when
they were new, when they found out he was single. Even though
he was about twice their age, plenty of them seemed to think he
was worth a shot. Fancied themselves as the boss's wife, maybe.

He looked away, turning on his heel on the hard-baked
mud, which sent up fine puffs around his brown leather shoes,
and listened to the cicadas. They were loud enough to be in
their thousands. What did they have to live on around here? he

wondered. There was a church with a tiny cemetery around it a block away, a patch of scuffed grass out the back of the Chinese greengrocer, and the old biddy who rented out the flat above the shoe shop had a windowbox groaning with geraniums and come loose at one end. He could see it against the streaky concrete of the rear walls: lopsided, a gash of red. There wasn't enough of anything green to sustain them, these insects drumming at his head.

Here was Merle, still grinning. She'd squeezed her square feet into a pair of narrow white shoes, which he thought he'd last seen on another girl — Roxanne, was it? — but maybe he was mistaken. There wasn't all that much variety in women's clothes and shoes: if you liked women, and watched them for detail, you saw the same skirts and dresses again and again. Gallant, he offered Merle his arm and showed her to the car. Her hair had dripped a wide semi-circle on the back of her frock and this close up he could see that her ears were pierced for earrings but wore none, and that one of her earlobes was swollen and infected. Neither did she wear any make-up, but he supposed she didn't need it. Besides, he preferred the younger girls without it.

'This is all right, eh,' said Merle as he got in on the driver's side and started it up. 'Nice big car.'

'Big enough,' said Bernie. He'd like one bigger, a Pontiac maybe. Left-hand drive. One he could have a line of girls in the front and a line in the back and take them to the beach for the day, to Long Bay or Piha, and watch them frolic in the surf. He'd get a lot of pleasure from that, he was sure. Winding down the window, he looked up at the back of the Acme to see if any of the other girls were awake. Mostly the blinds were down. In one or two of the darker rooms, the ones still in shadow from the new extension he'd had built out from the new Hawaiian Roof Bar, he could see a light burning, fuzzy in the weave of the blind, but no silhouetted heads. Pity, he thought. He'd have liked to bring another one or two along, particularly as he suspected he'd leave Merle in the car once they got out to the school. She'd be all alone.

They drove through Newmarket towards the beginning of Great South Road and as he swung the heavy car left and glided along past the smooth lawns and bungalows and villas he remembered, as he always did when he came this way, the time he had stolen the truck and driven it south with Brett beside him.

Seven years ago. In the course of a lifetime seven years wasn't long at all, but it felt like an eternity. Half that time had been spent in jail; he'd served four years of a five-year sentence. He could've got six, but the judge rewarded him for two things: pleading guilty and having a wife who behaved like a cat on heat. His lawyer had made a lot of that, and of the fact that Kev had been knocking the kid around, and that kid now lost for ever.

Merle had wound her window down too and was letting her hair flap and dry in the breeze.

'So where're we going?' she asked.

'Out to see my lad. He rung me up. You can stay in the car.' It was the stern voice he used, the one that came in handy with the girls when they'd been fighting or causing trouble. He didn't want Merle insisting on coming in, on meeting Carl. The boy might get the wrong idea.

'Where's he?'

'Out Manurewa. Bit of a drive.'

'You can say that again,' said Merle — happily, thought Bernie, watching her lean back in her seat. How old was she?

Twenty? Older? Maybe she had a baby somewhere up north, a son of her own stashed away with Nana. He wouldn't ask — the girls were sensitive to that kind of question; made them worry they'd lose their jobs.

They'd got as far as Penrose, a flat industrialised area where the Friday morning air smelt foul: of chemicals, hot plastic, oil. There was another journey he'd imagined along this road, one he'd never made. That was a trip in a Black Maria all the way to New Plymouth, but they'd kept him in Mount Eden the whole time.

He checked on Merle again, who was smoking now, luxuriously, her hair wind-churned and wild, still with a little smile curling her lips. He wouldn't ask about those purple stretchmarks he'd noticed when she was dancing on his table the other night, and neither would he volunteer any inform-ation about where he'd spent a good part of the last decade. One thing some of the girls were curious about, especially the older, smarter ones who were looking to their own futures as their beauty faded, was how he got the money together to start the club — did he have a secret stash? Had someone trusted him enough to give him a bank loan? They usually only had the nerve to ask him if they were in bed with him, or at the very least sitting on his knee, and he never answered them. The ones who stuck around long enough got to know Raymond Rose, his business partner, who'd got out a year before he had. Prison was a useful place for meeting men who had an eye for getting hold of a lot of money quickly, though the place was changing now, so he'd heard — changing fast, with the drugs coming in, marijuana and LSD. The hierarchy was shifting and men like Bernie, and even the Rose with his lucrative career in bookmaking and fraud, commanded less respect than the importers and dealers.

Truth was, the club had cost hardly anything to set up. The Rose had put up the cash for a lease; the premises were in a cheap part of town; and the money he'd got from the sale of the Glenlyn house had been more than enough to buy the fittings, supply the bar, put in some beds and curtains and carpets upstairs. The question those girls should have been asking — especially the ones hungry for love, the ones who'd cling to him after sex, who'd stop him in the corridor with kisses and caresses — was why he never loved them back, not a solitary one of them. They knew better than to ask that, of course: he made sure there was no talk of that kind. That was the rules. He wasn't close to anyone. On the odd occasion he went up north to see Patu, went fishing, had a laugh . . .

There was life before prison and life after it, and the only link between the two was Nola.

'Didn't know you had a boy,' Merle was saying.

'I do. Only the one. He's blind.' There. He'd said it, finally. Why had it taken him so long? Merle was the sensitive type, she wouldn't embarrass him.

'Oh!' She swivelled on the bench seat beside him. 'We going to Homai? I've got a cousin out there. She works there, eh. A maid or something.'

'You could go and see her, then. While I see Carl.'

'Maybe,' said Merle, her face as closed and sombre as he'd ever seen it. 'Maybe not.'

'Go on,' Bernie said gently, 'you could spin her a line. Come up with a story, if she asks what you're doing. You don't have to tell her the truth. Besides, is it so bad? You're an entertainer, that's all.'

They had reached the edge of the city, the housing

subdivisions out here as raw and ugly as any he had worked on on the northern fringe. He swerved to avoid an underfed dog, slowed to allow a heavily pregnant teenager to cross outside a pub. Merle was quiet, thinking. Contained in the speeding four walls of the Chrysler there was an atmosphere of disbelief, or discomfort, or something not very pleasant. Perhaps he shouldn't have invited her along, Bernie thought, straightening his collar and tie with one hand, the other on the wheel. It was the one constant of his life: inviting females along for the ride and regretting it later.

He made the turn off Great South Road into Browns Road, heading west. Still, at least she was company, even if she hardly said anything. If she wasn't here, his mind might begin to run along its usual well-worn ruts whenever Carl was the focus: the sins of the fathers — all that rubbish. The younger son struck blind by a vengeful God as recompense for the death of the older one.

Ridiculous and out of character, he always told himself, once he'd lurched from that rut into the next, which was less punitively cosmic and more paternally guilty. Last time he'd seen the boy, the kid had informed him that he'd spent exactly three hours and twenty-seven minutes in his company in the past eleven months. Or something like that; Bernie couldn't remember precisely. Carl had a kind of genius for quick-fire equations.

The car swung heavily into the driveway and drove slowly towards the cluster of low brick buildings. How completely ordinary they were, with their corrugated roofs, their wooden joinery, the net curtains at the windows. Nothing in the architecture betrayed the tragedy of the children's lives within. And so many of them. He could hear raised, excited voices lifting from the quadrangle on the other side of the building that housed the office and the dining hall, where the new jungle-gym was, with its tyre swing and climbing frame.

'Your tragedy, not his,' came Nola's voice in his ear. 'If you spent more time with him you'd stop thinking of your own feelings and concern yourself with his —'

He shut her off. Once or twice he'd tried talking to her about subjects other than Carl, since that was always so problematic, but she wasn't amenable to that. She would interrupt him and abruptly return the conversation to their son — she always seemed to be in a hurry. For what, he had no idea. All the hand-reading nonsense, perhaps. When he'd met her he'd supposed she was a scientific type, and here she was peddling a whole lot of hocus-pocus.

'See you soon,' he said to Merle, leaning into the car. 'Won't be long.'

Merle lowered her head like a penitent. What was up with her? he wondered. Women. Up and down like yo-yos. The trick was not to let yourself go up and down with them.

He went up the path towards the door that opened to a corridor leading to the dining hall. It was empty, but for a maid clearing away the last of the breakfast things. Pausing for a moment, he looked in. She was a Maori girl — maybe Merle's cousin — wiping down the long tables, leaving sheeny stripes on the white surfaces, gleaming under the high, modern gable-style roof. There was the smell of institutional food, porridge made by the gallon, a sulphurous reek of massed poached eggs that made Bernie think of the prison. But surely prison smelt worse than this: the inmates here were only children.

Further down the corridor a door opened out to the courtyard. There was the jungle-gym that Carl had been so proud of last time, set beside a row of classrooms. A trio of boys were clustered together nearby, in what he thought at first was a sandpit, but as he drew nearer he saw it was a picture of some kind, in relief. One of the bent, grey-jerseyed backs was Carl's — he recognised him by his thick, wiry fair hair; hair that he shared with his dead half-brother, inherited from two different mothers. All the boys were dressed the same, in school uniform. Bernie said nothing, just watched for a moment. It wasn't a picture, but a map of the world, cast in concrete. The boys were exploring with their fingers, feeling along with their feet, which were encased in black regulation shoes. One boy straightened and looked directly at him, his wobbly eyes hugely magnified behind thick glasses. Oblivious, Carl continued feeling and stepping, his face serious, absorbed.

'Hello,' the boy said, one grubby freckly hand extended in a mannish display of courtesy. 'Marcus Martin. Who are you?'

'Bernie Tyler.' He took the hand, shook it, and saw Carl's head snap up at the sound of his voice.

'Dad!' Carl hurried towards him, catching the edge of his shoe on Alaska. 'Dad!'

'Steady on,' said Bernie, reaching out for Carl's shoulder. The boy's voice had sounded tearful. His nerve endings were always too close to the surface. He wished the kid was more like the boy he'd shaken hands with a moment before, who seemed far more mature, with the stance of a miniature farmer on a field day.

Carl had raised his arms for his father to lift him, like a child much younger than his six years. Trying to ignore the withering feeling in his chest, the sensation that was inevitable whenever he saw Carl and so predictable that he should have steeled himself against it but never did — Bernie bent to him and lifted him over the low wall. He would have set him down on the other side but the child clung to his neck, pressing his hot face against his father's skin.

'You're burning up,' said Bernie softly. 'Why've you got your jersey on on such a hot day?'

'Matron made us,' said the boy.

'You talking like a baby again?' The father tried to keep his voice as gentle as before, but failed.

'No,' said Carl, and wriggled against him to be put down.

'Shouldn't you be in class?'

'Me and Ian and Marcus asked to work out the map.'

Marcus was still peering up at him, he realised. The other boy, who must be Ian, was sitting on Australia and carefully negotiating his way around the Japanese coast, seemingly unaware of Bernie's arrival. He was perhaps one of the deaf-blind children. Bernie looked away from him. On the few occasions he'd taken Carl out, he'd hated the way people stared, as if they thought the child was unaffected by it. As if they thought all their staring eyes were as harmless as pebbles dropping to the bottom of a deep pond. The child was aware, of course, his head angled into the sudden silences, his mouth puckered at the acid drip of concerned, sympathetic murmurings.

'Hello? Excuse me?' It was Carl's teacher, standing on the covered verandah above them, outside the classroom, her white hand on the safety rail. 'Mr —?'

'Tyler. Mr Tyler. Carl's father.'

'Did you have an appointment?'

'No. I . . . um . . . Carl rang me and I —'

The woman looked frostily at Carl, then back at Bernie.

'Did you report to the office?'

'No, I just wanted to spend a few minutes with Carl and then I —'

'Quarter of an hour, Carl.' The teacher leaned out of the shadow into the bright sunlight and Bernie saw that she was quite pretty in a horsey kind of way, her hair drawn back into a bun at the back and a long face. She looked like Princess Anne and sounded like her too. Pommy. 'Quarter of an hour. That's all.'

'Come with me, Dad.' Carl's hand in his was hot and sweaty. Bernie would have liked to insist that the jersey came off, but that might get him into trouble with Matron. Or Princess Anne.

Unerringly, the child led him along a narrow path towards the residential part of the school, hesitating only twice at the kerbs of driveways.

'Did you want to show me something?' Bernie asked him after a few minutes. 'Why'd you ring me, son?'

They had come to the hostel. A little girl sat on the step playing with a doll, carefully dividing its hair the way Matron must do hers — or her mother, when she was returned to her. Other children were visible through the window, gathered together in the lounge, one of them playing the piano.

'How's your music coming along?' Bernie remembered to ask. It was as if Nola had years ago given him a list of things to tick off, as if he had to report back to her later. He didn't.

'Fine,' said Carl, noncommittal. 'Down here.'

Their feet squeaked on the shiny cork floors. Nothing but the best in the finishing, thought Bernie, admiring the rimu panelling and furniture in the bedrooms, which opened up on either side. Outside one of the rooms Carl drew up, but he didn't go through the door. It was his room, Bernie was sure. There was a tartan rug on the bed and a crocheted blanket folded at its foot. Askew on the pillow was a ragged, chewed-looking golliwog, probably the one Carl had had as a baby, the toy that had accompanied him on that long-ago visiting day at the prison.

'Do you want to go in?' Bernie asked, but the child shook his head. He was concentrating, his lips moving, making odd little ducking movements with his head.

After a moment he tugged again on his father's hand and they continued on down the corridor, past a bathroom, to a door that led outside again onto a narrow concrete path.

'Can you see the gate?' Carl whispered.

Bernie looked around.

'Over there?' he asked.

'Over where?' Carl responded, his face tipped up to his father, the one remaining eye half obscured by the falling lid.

'Sorry,' Bernie muttered. 'Across a ways from where we are now there's a gate.'

'Up a little hill?'

'That's right.'

'Hurry, then,' said Carl, squeezing his hand.

Across an expanse of lawn they went, up the gentle slope to a gate set into a high wooden fence. It would have been quicker to go around the perimeter of the hostel, thought Bernie, but not saying it. This must be the way Carl knows, the way he must have been taken with the other children.

'What's through here?' he asked instead, while Carl grappled with the catch on the gate.

'The orchard. But that's not what I'm showing you,' he went on, sounding oddly like Nola. It was perhaps the tone she used when she had a surprise for him.

Leaning over him, Bernie helped to open the gate, which knocked at its widest point on a lichen-covered branch of a peach tree. Several wasps rose in a clutch from a rotting gash in a swollen fruit and Carl lifted one arm against the buzz — he must have once been stung, thought Bernie. He's clocked up that experience.

'Close the gate, Dad,' said Carl, businesslike. Bernie did, pushing it against the long grass. It hissed and squeaked and so did Carl, bending forward, pushing air through his teeth.

'Billie Jean?' he called softly. 'Billie Jean — where are you?'

'Who's Billie Jean?' asked Bernie. A thought occurred to him. 'Are you allowed in here, Carl?'

'Shshsh,' said Carl. 'Don't frighten him. Billie Jean —'

There was a grove of apple trees, younger than the peach and more heavily laden with nearly ripe fruit. Further away, at the fenceline, was a blood plum tree, the long grass and paspallum at its foot studded with dropped fruit. An effort had been made to gather some of it: two tin buckets overflowed, a beer crate was mounded with them.

'Do they give you this fruit to eat?' asked Bernie.

'Dunno,' said Carl.

He had stretched his arms out in front of him, low to the ground, and was calling again. 'Billie Jean King, Billie Jean,' when Bernie saw a white shape move quickly through the grass between the apple trees. It came towards them carefully, picking up its little hoofs, its unblinking yellow eyes flickering from man to boy.

'If Billie Jean's a goat she's on her way,' he told Carl.

'He. Billie Jean's a boy,' Carl said, smiling in anticipation of the animal's arrival.

'They must've named her after the real Billie Jean, who's a girl,' said Bernie. 'Tennis player.'

'Shshsh,' said Carl again, and Bernie would have reprimanded him — he'd never told his own father to hush in his whole life — but the goat had reached them and was pushing its hornless head into the soft of Carl's stomach, while the boy rubbed its neck and tangled his fingers in the coarse coat.

'So this is what you wanted to show me?' he asked. 'This old goat?'

'See how brave I am,' said Carl, pushing his forehead into the goat's bony brow. 'Some kids are scared. I'm not. When I grow up I'm going to be a farmer.'

'Are you?' said Bernie, surprised. 'A farmer, eh?' He shook his head.

Suddenly Carl stood up straight, startling the goat, which sprang backwards and Bernie saw that it was indeed a nanny. Had the boy felt the udder and decided it was the goat equivalent of what he had himself? Had nobody explained?

'You don't think I can. You don't believe me. I'm going to. When I leave this place I'm going to take Billie Jean with me and buy a farm —'

'Right.' Bernie laid a heavy hand on the trembling, outraged, narrow shoulder. 'Right you are, my lad. Good as gold.'

It was better perhaps that the boy had ambition, other than the careers blind men usually ended up in, Bernie thought. Piano tuning. Canework.

'Won't be for long, anyway,' Carl continued. He was reaching around for Billie Jean, who'd wandered off a little to gobble up a fallen peach. She lifted her head, chewing, juice glazing her beard, just as Carl gave up feeling for her and dropped down to sit in the grass. Bernie joined him, for a second the probability of grass stains on his new-ish trousers uppermost in his mind.

'What do you mean, won't be for long?' he asked. 'What else are you going to do?'

The answer, he was sure, would be what you'd expect from any little boy: fireman, astronaut, detective. Maybe Nola encouraged him to think of his future just as a sighted boy would.

'Because I'm not going to live long,' said Carl. He held out his hand, palm uppermost. 'See — it's here. Both hands.' The other hand joined the first, grass-smeared, smelling strongly of goat.

'What bloody rubbish is this?' Bernie growled, and the boy recoiled from him, dropping his arms and bringing his knees up under his chin.

'This was your mother who told you this?' He could scarcely choke out the words. 'Did she?'

'No.' Carl was pressing his eyes hard into his knees, wriggling his head to alternate pressure from one eye to the other. It was something he did, press his eyes, and he was always being told not to. 'It feels nice,' Nola had explained to Bernie once. 'It stimulates the part of the brain devoted to sight, that's why he does it. To see the white stars.' But from all the pushing his eyes were retreating into his head. Bernie couldn't stand watching him do it, even in this sneaky way.

'Carl. Lift your head up.'

'No.'

'It isn't true, son. All that nonsense. It's like . . . it's a game your mother plays.'

'Gran believes it.'

'So it was Peg who told you?'

'Yes. But . . .' He lifted his face now, the skin around his eyes rubbed red.

'But what?'

Keep calm, thought Bernie. He'd go round there. Have it

out with the silly old biddy. Fancy telling a child he'd have a short life, let alone a cream-puff like Carl, let alone her own grandson.

'The next morning she said she was sorry, that she shouldn't have said it. She said she'd had too much sherry and that I . . . '

'What?' Gently, gently, thought Bernie. Get the whole story.

'I . . . she asked me not to tell anyone she'd said it. She said little Life Lines don't always mean that. But she . . . '

Bernie waited. The goat was closer again, cropping, in profile, watching them with one steady eye through the long grass, a striated, barred view. What do we look like when we're together? wondered Bernie. Do we look like father and son? He'd had more in common with Brett — common interests, like boats and fishing. And maybe they'd looked more alike, more than he and Carl did. He was different himself, then, that's for sure — wasn't carrying all this extra weight, this big puku. He'd put it on in prison and kept it on since. All the crap food he'd eaten there, and since he'd got out, and too much beer.

'Go on,' he said.

'She was crying.'

'Crying?'

'Yep.' Chest lifting and shuddering, Carl heaved a huge breath. For a moment Bernie wondered if the kid was going to cry himself, at the memory.

'Why?'

'Why was she crying?'

'Yeah. Why do you think she was?'

'Because it's really true. That's why. She didn't want it to be true, but it is. I'll die when I'm about forty.'

Putting his arms around his son, Bernie pulled him onto his lap and held him tight.

'You listen to me. You'll live till you're a little old man. You'll be a little old farmer with nine hundred goats just like Billie Jean. Peg was upset because she was sorry for what she said. Not because it's true . . . Carl? You listening?'

The boy had taken hold of one of his father's hands and spread it flat. Slowly, carefully, he was tracing a trajectory around the base of the thumb.

'You're not going to live long either,' he pronounced. ''Cording to this.'

'When'll I croak, then?'

'When you're forty.'

'Well, guess what? I'm forty-two, so it's wrong already.'

'No, no,' said Carl, in admonishing tones. 'It's not that exact. It means that any minute now you'll —'

He shrieked and the goat skedaddled as far as the fenceline — his father was tickling him, tipping backwards in the long grass, against his big soft tummy, taking him with him. The world flipped over, the smells of the trees and fruit and goat shit, and the little hoofs drumming away and the sound of birds and the cars on the road all rearranging themselves onto different plains. After a moment, when he'd got his bearings, Carl sat up, one knee on either side of his father's big, safe body, and tickled him back.

Merle was asleep in the car and only woke when he turned the engine on. Bernie didn't encourage her to talk, wanting instead to remember the fierce hug his son had given him, after they'd weathered a ticking-off from Princess Anne.

'You've been much longer than a quarter of an hour,' she'd said.

'Come again and see Billie Jean,' Carl had whispered, his face flushed and happy, the weight of his early demise lifted from his skinny shoulders.

And he resolved, Bernie did, as his swanky car sped him home to the Acme Gentlemen's Club, to do just that. When they were rough-housing, as his own mother used to call it, when they were rough-housing in the long grass, he'd felt a click in his head, or his heart: a physical sensation, something he ought to have felt years ago, a feeling he thought he'd never have again after Brett's death. He loved this boy. From now on, he would look out for him.

'And did you? Look out for him?' I ask.

'Yes, I did. Went round to see Peg while you were at work and gave her a blast.'

'She never told me.'

'I asked her not to.'

Sly old Peg, I think, and find myself smiling. As we pull into Claremont Street it begins to rain; heavy sparse drops spread themselves on the windscreen.

'You better wake her up,' he says. 'The girl. I won't come in.'

'Just as well,' I say. 'We're still packing.'

Head back, skinny legs splayed, Tamara is fast asleep. I lean over and gently shake her nearest arm.

'We home?' she asks.

'Have been for ages. Come on.'

As I go to get out of the car Bernie takes my hand.

'One day,' he says, 'I'd like to come over and . . . you see,

I haven't got any pictures of our boy and I wondered if you . . . if you wouldn't mind . . . '

'I'll look some out for you,' I tell him.

'And you'll give me a ring?' He's leaning over towards the open passenger door, looking up at me.

'Yes, okay,' I say. 'You can come for dinner.'

Bernie smiles. 'That'd be nice.'

He pushes the seat up for Tamara to climb out.

'Bon voyage,' he tells her. 'Let us know how you go.'

Righting herself for as long as it takes to climb the fire escape, Tamara immediately assumes the same position on our sofa without uttering a word. I take myself off to her room to finish her packing for her.

I strip the bed, hang the duvet over the door to air, tuck the last of her things into her bags. The room still feels full, crowded even — Carl's stuff. An old amp, a broken microphone stand, an ancient pair of brown headphones big as mouseketeer ears, his shoes, shirts and jackets jamming the wardrobe. Carl never threw anything out. One shirt — purple paisley, a recent favourite — is jammed between the dressing table and the wall. As I pull it free, a waft of him rises to my nostrils: a particular aftershave he liked; the smoke and sweat of late-night jazz; the ti-tree embrocation he used to rub on a troublesome, over-worked knuckle joint — a combination of scents so particular to him; travelling at lightning speed to my heart and head with-out giving me time to prepare, to protect myself. It's too much. The long-overdue, stilted conversation with his father, the awful, gaping loss of Carl. The loss of his body, the boy I raised.

Lord, I hope that girl's still asleep, a small part of my mind thinks while I sob and heave and caterwaul, hunched on the edge of the bed over the bundle of my son's shirt. Lord, I hope Tamara's listening to something loud.

Pull yourself together, the shirt says sternly.

Why should I? Why shouldn't I howl and scream and cry and fling myself out the window?

Because you have to keep going. Carl's shirt has pressed itself to my streaming eyes.

Who for?

Bernie.

Don't be ridiculous.

Tamara, then.

Tamara is leaving, to get on with her life.

And you must get on with yours.

My life?

Your life.

Your life, Mum. You still have one. Stop crying now. Stop crying, old girl . . .

Suddenly I'm calm again, just as suddenly as I was grief-stricken. I'm as calm as death. I feel anaesthetised. And I remember I wished for this, to be able to cry, in the car on the way home from the mall.

From the living room come voices — Sina's breathy laugh, Liu's rapid staccato speech, Tamara's low-voiced responses.

Did they hear me?

From the kitchen comes the sound of water gushing into

a kettle; there's the smell of garlic, hot oil, pastries. They've brought food. I'm starving.

Eventually hunger drives me out, knowing that my eyes are puffy and bloodshot. Sina and Liu make a great fuss of me, gentle and solicitous, sitting me down to a plate of spring rolls and fried rice.

Tamara is even worse company than I am. Maybe she's nervous about the coming journey, still reeling from this morning's meeting, sad about leaving . . . She's taciturn with our visitors, almost rude. Refusing anything to eat, she goes over to Carl's piano and lays her skinny arms along the closed lid. It's become her favourite place to sit.

'Where's Skew?' I ask.

'Hung over,' replies Sina, simply.

'He should start looking after himself,' I say. 'He's no spring chicken.'

'Should've been him that died,' Tamara spits out, venomous. 'If it had to be one of us, it should've been him.'

'No, honey,' murmurs Sina, 'that's not right . . . You sure you're not hungry?'

She's going towards her with a saucer and a single spring roll, a dollop of sweet and sour.

'It's all his fault,' mutters Tamara into her folded arms, tearful.

'It's nobody's fault,' I tell her.

Liu emerges from the kitchen with a pot of tea and I pat the chair beside me for him to sit down. He looks tired too, bags under his young eyes. He sees me scanning his face and gives me a wan smile.

'We've been hitting the piss a bit since . . . you know . . .'

I nod.

'Nola's been telling me stories.' Tamara sits up just as Sina bends over her, knocking the saucer flying. Skidding along the piano top, the spring roll leaps into the air and comes to rest on the floor.

'Haven't you?' Tamara continues. 'Stories about Carl.'

'About when he was little?' Sina asks kindly, scooping sticky red sauce off Tamara's cheek with one finger.

'That. And before then, too. Nola? Are you still here?'

'I am.'

'You want me to tell you about when Carl and I met? About how we fell in love?'

'If you want to.'

'This is it. It's not much. We fell in love the first night we played together.'

'You mean you went to bed the first night you met,' says Sina. 'I know what you're like, Tam.' She picks the dust off the pastry and takes a bite.

'We went to bed and we fell in love all at the same time. It was simple. Simple and true. We could listen to one another thinking. No one believes that, but we could. We'd fit the whorls of our ears together — they fitted perfectly, like they'd been designed to. We'd lie side by side and listen to each other thinking.'

We fall silent then, and it seems to me that we're all of us imagining the same thing: those two heads, one fair, one dark, lying side by side in their bed.

'Nola, you there?' Tamara asks again.

'Yes, love.'

'You know how sometimes I talk about my other men, the ones I had before Carl?'

'Uh-huh.'

'You know what? He never talked about his other women.'

'Didn't he?'

'I want to know. How many? Who were they?'

'I'm not sure that were that many,' I tell her, 'and anyway, he wouldn't have told me if there were.'

There are a couple I could tell her about, from early on, before he went away. More than a couple. But I'm not ready to remember those times, when young girls in love with my son would fly in and out of the house, the secret comings and goings on the fire escape, the occasional girl who would want to rescue him, to discuss with me his future, his blindness, his musical genius, the ones whose hearts he broke, the rare girl who broke his.

Liu has opened his violin case. He plucks its open strings, adjusts the fine-tuners, tightens his bow. The ascending fifths suggest a song to Sina and she hums, begins to sing 'Moon River', and Tamara opens the piano, locates the key Sina's in and begins to play. Liu joins in, his smooth, silvery fiddle slipping around Sina's voice, circling the harmonies of the piano. Tamara is not a patch on Carl but she's not bad and I can tell she's enjoying sitting on his stool, sounding the keys he played so often.

'We never sang that one,' says Sina when they finish. 'We should've. It would've been a crowd-pleaser.'

In response Tamara plays the opening chords of a Tommy Flanagan tune, 'Beyond the Bluebird'. Liu usually played guitar for this one, but because the saxophone languishes still in its case, he takes Tamara's part while she takes Carl's. Tamara gives a shout of laughter and speeds the tempo, as if she wants to trip him up and shake him off. Sina picks up a tambourine, which sheds dust motes with her first blow. She's got her eyes closed, she's humming again, softly, high-pitched, a third above the violin. This is how we'll spend Tamara's last afternoon, drifting from song to song. They might even play some of their own compositions, the music Carl had a hand in making.

This is the last of him. After Tamara goes, Sina and Liu probably won't visit. Skew certainly won't. This is the last time I'll hear the band, the last time I could pretend, if I wanted to, that he was still here.

The minutes slip by, song by song. Sina pulls me to my feet and has me dancing with her during one number, a slow, meditative piece, atonal and almost arrhythmic. After beginning it with confidence, Tamara and Liu trail off. This was the piece Carl called 'Twelve Bars for Tamara'. He wrote it for her. Liu lets the violin swing from one hand, the bow from the other — it can't follow where the sax used to go, and even if he did he could never do the improv Tamara used to do. After the twelve scored bars were over and she and Carl would swing them around for another couple of hundred.

I go to the kitchen, open a couple of bottles of wine, and by the time I get back with the tray Tamara has gone to stand at the open window above the street, her saxophone out of its case and held to her mouth. The first notes, strident but tender, wandering but ineluctable, pure but bending, fill the little flat — all of the contradictions a saxophone is. They say the cello most faithfully mimics the human voice, but surely it is this instrument; how it hectors, sobs and mocks. Watching Tamara now, her slender, urgent body spooned against the fanciful shape of the horn, it is as if each breath carries us further away from everything that is familiar or temporal. It is as if she's willing us all to join Carl, wherever he is, urging us forward, so that each successive note dismisses the last and allows no nostalgia for its passing. It's the opposite of blues; it needs a new name, something grander: a threnody, a brave lament.

Sina's huge eyes have filled with tears and Liu stands with his head bowed as if he's praying. Is Tamara praying too? I wonder, as each soaring phrase grows longer, her elliptical breath smooth, disguised. She shifts keys, swings us down and up again, and my stomach leaps as it does travelling too fast over a dip in a road. The ascending passage she gives us then speaks of hope, of celebration, of how we'll all go on, the four of us, after Tamara lets us down gently. It promises to return us all here, just as purposefully as it speeds Carl on his way. For a moment, only a few beats before she stops, I hear the faint strains of a piano, a farewelling minor chord from far off, from a distant room. Liu hears it too, I swear it: he looks up sharply, catches my eye, and, as if he's embarrassed by this aural hallucination, looks away again just as quickly as the last of the music dies away.

Silence is liquid in the room then, like water in a jug, cool around us, moving in to fill the gaps, washing around Tamara, who hasn't moved from her spot. She cradles the instrument over her shoulder like an infant, her strong, thin arms crossed over the bell of it. Sina goes to her and it is only as her shadow passes over Tamara's face that I see her cheeks are wet. I would go to her too, to dip my finger into those miraculous tears, as if she's a weeping Madonna, but I can't seem to move. The last action I made was to lay the tray on the table, where it still is, condensation beading the glass of the bottles.

Tamara herself is touching her face now, wonderingly, creeping her fingers gently up the route the tears have taken from their origin, before wiping them away. Sina gives her a long hug, neither woman saying anything — but maybe Sina would see nothing unusual in the divinity of Tamara's music, just as she sees nothing strange about her tears. Maybe Sina doesn't know that Tamara has been unable to weep for years, not since she lost her sight.

We drink the wine, none of us talking much. Hasn't Tamara said it all for us? Later in the afternoon Liu gets up and puts a tape in his player, putting his finger to his lips when he sees me start to ask what it is. It's one of Carl's, recorded live in Bernie's club.

'Found it in Skew's van,' he says, resuming his seat, and we listen carefully, even to the rumble of voices between each number. It's not a professional job, and probably twenty years old, recorded when Carl was in his late teens, standards I hadn't heard him play for decades: Dave Brubeck, Nat King Cole, Thelonius Monk. Tamara smiles, and her lips look bruised from the punishing playing earlier.

'The sweetheart,' she says. 'He was only a baby.'

When the tape stops, abruptly, before the end of a tune, Sina goes to look out the window. Late afternoon sun streams around her body as she squeezes between the piano and the end of the sofa.

'He's there,' she announces, 'I can see the van.'

'Who?' I ask. 'A van?' My heart skips a beat. 'What van?'

Sina and Liu are looking at me strangely.

'Skew's,' they say, in unison.

'He's come to take us to the airport,' Sina goes on. 'We can all fit in. Luggage and everything. I told him if he turned up stoned we'd get a taxi and leave him behind. We can all go and say goodbye.'

'Is it that time already?' asks Tamara.

'Yes, love, it is,' I tell her. 'Just give me a moment to fix up my hair.'

In front of the mirror I pull out the hairpins and slides, let the grey-streaked red mass of it fall to my shoulders. After a moment, reluctantly, I meet my own eye and confront my desire for revenge. It's not true what I told Tamara earlier, about it being nobody's fault. I want to punch Skew's lights out. I want to half kill him. When I was younger, I would have been capable of it — physically, at least. Immediately after Carl's death, at the funeral, I felt sorry for him. I thought his conscience would be inhabited by mantras such as 'If only I'd parked the van legally'; 'If only I hadn't got so stoned I couldn't drive'. I imagined the depth of his guilt to be anaerobic, I imagined him gasping for air, even though he gave no indication of this. He was just his usual musty-smelling, slow-talking self, loping around the wake on his spindly legs, lighting spliffs and talking shit.

Avoiding my reflection now, I jam in the last of the pins and go out into the living room where Liu is piling up luggage. The women are in the bedroom: the open door shows them standing by the bed.

'I can still smell him here,' Tamara is saying, bending to pat the mattress. I hear her haul in a lungful of air.

Skew stands by the pile of bags and boxes, steadying it with one hand. He looks different: his face seems collapsed, but younger, more open. His glance, which is rapid — can he read my fury? — is also naked, ashamed, and straight. He knows, all right: he knows what a rat he is. Maybe Tamara said something to him while I was in the bathroom. Certainly, when she emerges with Sina, she doesn't acknowledge him.

As we go out to the van I wonder if I'll have a moment alone with her before she goes. I wonder if there's anything left to say.

I sit up the front by the window, Tamara between Skew and

me, Sina and Liu in the back with the luggage. The van bangs and rattles, the gears screech. If we were to have a conversation we'd have to yell above the racket. Instead, I hold Tamara's hand loosely in mine and sense that she's gone already. She left with her threnody this afternoon; her face is even more impassive than usual, her breathing calm and even. Is this how she was four weeks ago, I wonder, in that other van, when she thought those boys were taking her home? Was she just as trusting and calm?

Over the high, wide sweep of Mangere Bridge we go, the old bridge that *Ngaire* glided under all those years ago slowly sinking into the mud beside it. One day it'll disappear, submerged, to be visible only at low tide, its drowned piles protruding from the silt, another vanishing link to the past. Behind us now is Onehunga and the place where we laid the flowers and planted the cross, and somewhere, walking around, living and breathing, as alive as we are, possibly even behind the wheel of a car, is the person who took my son's life. We'll never know now who it was, or if they drove off afterwards without a backward glance, or if before they raced away they got out to see what they had done. In the end, how inconsequential it all is. All that matters is that he's gone.

As if she senses my sudden rush of grief, Tamara squeezes my fingers, and I feel the city roll out its turbulent, changing streets around us, hoarding up its secrets, old and new and without number.

Skew drops us off at the front of the terminal and goes off to find a park.

'And a smoke, probably,' says Sina as the van lurches off. 'Let's hope he finds us again.'

Ignoring the Passengers Only sign, we all accompany Tamara to the crowded check-in, and then to the gate leading to the departure lounges. She has her beaded cane, her saxophone case and slung over her shoulder, her velvet bag. It's all I can do to stop asking the sort of questions that annoy the hell out of her: Is someone meeting you at O'Hare? Have you got some American dollars? Shall we buy some earplugs? Sleeping pills? Is your Walkman in your velvet bag?

First Liu hugs her goodbye, then Sina, and when it's my turn her arms around me are fierce and brief. Just before she lets go, she lifts her mouth to my ear.

'I'll see you again, Nola Lane,' she whispers. 'One day. And don't you forget — I loved your boy something terrible. He was my soulmate.'

'I know, dear, I know.'

I kiss her cheek and it smells different, the faint salty scent of her dried, eerie tears. Her strong hands slip to my shoulders, squeeze once and release, and she flashes me her beautiful, tough, lopsided smile.

'Goodbye, old girl,' she says, and off she goes, tip-tapping her cane, around the glass wall and out of sight.

ACKNOWLEDGEMENTS

Thanks to Alison McAlpine, Mark Wilson, Mike Hardcastle, Max Cryer, John Yelash, Lindsay, Mary and Pauline at Homai College, Don McKenzie, Bernie Brown, Leonie Wild, Tony and Mal Bouzaid, 'Sylvia' and Roger Linden, and especially to my comrades Beryl Fletcher and Peter Wells, and to my publisher and editors Harriet Allan and Rachel Scott.

Also love and thanks to Mum and Dad for their memories of the sixties, and to Tim, Stan, Maeve and Willa for their pleasure in the journeys the writing takes us on.

'Baby Face'
Composed by Benny Davis and Harry Akst. Published by Memory Lane Music (Australia) Pty Limited and used with kind permission of BMG Publishing Australia Pty Limited.